--- ★ ---

No wonder Carla was upset.

"Let me make sure I've got this right," I said. "The medical examiner isn't sure of the time or the cause of death and the body has already been cremated. Do I understand you, Carla?"

"You understand."

I scratched my head in amazement. "That's just not right. Something is wrong."

"Tell me about it. And that's only part of it, Harry. I still haven't told you about the giant albino that tried to attack me."

--- ★ ---

"...a very good who-done-it...delightful, well-designed and fun to read."
— The Midwest Book Review

ALLAN PEDRAZAS

ANGEL'S COVE

WORLDWIDE.

TORONTO • NEW YORK • LONDON
AMSTERDAM • PARIS • SYDNEY • HAMBURG
STOCKHOLM • ATHENS • TOKYO • MILAN
MADRID • WARSAW • BUDAPEST • AUCKLAND

ANGEL'S COVE

A Worldwide Mystery/March 1999

First published by St. Martin's Press, Incorporated.

ISBN 0-373-26302-3

Printed in U.S.A.

For my brothers Wayne and Bob,
and to the memory of our parents, Pete and Jo

ONE

IT WAS A GOOD DAY to walk the fish. The air was thick with a steambath humidity. Dawn's pewter sky had promised nothing less.

A tropical depression had stalled offshore, pelting the coastline all morning with raindrops the size of gum balls.

The beach was empty. So was the Sand Bar. The tourists had flocked to the malls. The locals with jobs were working. It was Father Shifty's day to do volunteer work as a pink lady at Holy Cross. I sat alone at a window table watching the storm muscle its way across the beach. Palm fronds whipped in the whirlwinds like frenzied tarantulas. Bubbling with whitecaps, the ocean resembled a giant cauldron of boiling shellfish, a feast for the deities. Rings of puddles had begun overlapping on the Broadwalk, constantly changing patterns like bouquets of liquid flowers in a child's kaleidoscope. A streak of lightning flashed miles offshore across plumes of charcoal clouds hovering above the horizon. Thunder clapped repeatedly as if played by a mad cymbalist insistent on a solo.

For all the turbulence outside, I was enjoying an inner sereneness, a liberating peacefulness that had me smiling contentedly for no explicable reason. It was one of those all-too-rare moments that occurs unexpectedly, without invitation, but is always welcome, and makes me feel this is the way life was intended to be. Everything is in harmony. All the ingredients mesh—the sights, the sounds, the smells. Even I'm in sync with it all. I'm in the flow, innocent of malicious thought. It was like recapturing that natural high that was so pervasive back in the Summer of Love when I listened to metaphysical poetry in cellars with a mute fascination, pretending I understood every word in hopes the woman poet would later mete out physical tenderness I easily understood. That was the summer I dined on wild rice and drank Boone's Farm and went skinny-dipping in Silver Lake with all the girls in the play. That summer my cat was born and the air was conditioned with flirtatious dreams and blooming souls and scents of clover. A communal spirit pervaded the campus. We embraced each other's uniqueness and rejoiced in our oneness. It was "Sgt. Pepper's Lonely Hearts Club Band" and "Somebody to Love" and "Strawberry Fields Forever." That summer I misplaced a few of my brain cells. I was oblivious to the fuzzy ethics of politicians and I really believed in a nonviolent revolution. That was before the Chicago Democratic Convention and before Kent State, before my rose-colored lenses were shattered. So much for nonviolent revolutions. The changes would continue. My cat would die and I would come to believe the world is round and finally accept the fact that life isn't as simple as I would like it to be. I could have very easily become a cynic, and perhaps I did. Still, I never forgot that the best highs weren't from pot or wine or other chemicals. They were natural. I just never learned how to obtain them on command or how to make them last.

It would have been so easy at that moment to believe that I, Harry Rice, had at last attained a higher level of enlightenment, which I knew nothing about, a life where people were warm and kind to each other for no particular reason, where I no longer felt like an endangered species or the odd man out, where I practiced patience and forgiveness, a life where I would never have another wasted erection. Of course, that will never happen. But that's all right. I can accept that the good times will always end as long as I believe that they will eventually come back, and usually without warning.

BY LATE AFTERNOON the rains had tapered off to a monotonous drizzle. Business had been sporadic. The highlight had been lunch with Al and Irma from the bike shop next door. Shortly after they left an unpleasant French-Canadian couple breezed in complaining about the universe or when the moon is in the seventh house. That's an illiterate translation. My knowledge of French is limited to a teenage crush on Brigitte Bardot, and French-Canadians refuse to speak English unless they think they can get something free for doing so. They left no tip. No au revoir.

The man who quit the Kiwanis because their breakfast speakers sucked stopped in for a vodka tonic and the prevailing opinion, which I dutifully assured him his was. He left happy.

A morality salesman, without a sample case, ducked in for a quick nip while his wife tried on terry cloth jackets at the Beach Variety. His drink was bourbon and water. His crusade was antiyouth. He criticized the President. He despised animal-rights activists. The American Civil Liberties Union was the only justifiable argument he knew of for abortion. He agreed with the NRA, glory to the gun. He believed that feminists were a whiny group of uglies who couldn't get laid in a men's prison with a handful of pardons. He said homosexuality should be a capital offense and instead of wasting money trying to find a cure for AIDS we should sit back and "let God take out the faggots."

He was the personification of the hate mentality that had made media celebrities out of Ross Perot, David Duke, Rush Limbaugh, and Jerry Falwell.

I leaned over, resting my forearms on the bar. "Indulge me," I said.

He looked questioningly at me.

I said, "Finish your drink and leave. You're not welcome here." So I hadn't attained a higher level of enlightenment where I practiced patience and forgiveness.

He started to object, but he saw something in my eyes that made him reconsider. He gulped down his drink and scurried out. I should have called the police. He had stolen my natural high.

Such is the bar business. If only I had known.

I bought the Sand Bar almost on a whim because a woman tried to hire me to recover the body of the Beach Boys' drummer, supposedly buried at sea. The request wasn't that unusual. Private detectives are routinely asked to solve the impossible. That's how most make their living. Not solving a thing, but trying to, until the client gets tired of writing checks. So a request to find the waterlogged body of a rock star wasn't that strange. What was, though, was I found myself taking copious notes, seriously considering the assignment. I began to suspect it was time for a career change. There had been too many long lonely days and short lonelier nights on the road looking for teenage runaways, too many trips to sleazy motels, catching wayward spouses in acts of infidelity. I didn't want to look for any more child-support dodgers. And to hell with all those inheritance-outraged relatives who wanted someone to dig up dirt on whoever was awarded the largest share of the estate. After years of private detecting, all I had to show for it was an anemic checking account and a scarred body and bruised ego from having been rousted, beaten up, hospitalized, arrested, jailed, threatened with sterilization, knife-cut, and stitched by old-fashioned thugs, kinky wives, marcelled dopers, assorted neighborhood basket cases, hysterical lawyers, and psychotic emergency-room attendants.

I bought the Sand Bar from an ex-stripper. I thought if I owned a bar I would no longer have to deal with the same kind of people who used to hire me to find people very similar to themselves. The very people who frequent bars in droves. Mine is a peculiar logic, full of contradictions.

Though it didn't happen that way, it had been my intention to walk away from private investigations. But shortly after I took over the Sand Bar, a woman I would have done anything for asked me to investigate something for her. She got what she wanted, which, as it turned out, wasn't me.

For the past couple days I had been pinch-hitting behind the bar for Carla Meadows, the regular day bartender. She had been called out of town due to a sudden death in her family. When someone suggested we send flowers, it dawned on me that I had no idea who in her family had died or where. Nor did I know when she would be back. I simply told her to take as long as she needed. The bar is not the same without her. The regulars missed her almost as much as I did.

There is more to tending bar than keeping glasses filled and stocking garnish trays. I can teach anyone how many umbrellas go in a mai tai. When I hired Carla she didn't know a Gibson from a Manhattan, but she did know the name of the Cisco Kid's horse. Carla's still learning the drinks, but she is a good bartender. She ministers to her customers, she doesn't wait on them. She knows more than the insufferable authority, though not as much as the humble dullard. She's a charmer, a peacemaker, a bouncer, an advisor to the lovelorn, and a sincere listener. She knows to avoid hushed conversations. Those are qualities that can't be taught. That's what makes a good bartender. That's what brings in the business. Not some oaf who runs people off because he cannot tolerate intolerance.

I sure missed my Carla.

AT SIX P.M. I was serving wine coolers to a gland-happy couple when my relief trudged in, all gloom and doom. He had been in a grand funk for a couple weeks, ever since his precious Catherine the Widow Woman had dumped him for an HMO doctor who wore Thom McAn wing tips. So much for love. Nick Triandos looked miserable, which was a slight improvement over yesterday. He was primed to work happy hour.

We switched cash register trays and completed the changing of the bar guard routine in silence.

"Hear anything?" Nick mumbled with a trace of hope in

his voice. He missed Carla's motherly counsel, though she was twenty-five years his junior.

"No," I said. "I think the funeral was today. She's probably been busy."

I left the Sand Bar in Nick's care and stopped at Cuban Frankie's for the boliche and a flan. I slumped down in a booth contemplating how quickly I had bottomed out after a halcyon high just hours ago.

The waitress came over, took one look at me, and started singing, "Good-time Harry's got the blues."

I regarded her with a mock frown. "Splendid," I said gruffly. "I'm having dinner with an annoyingly happy waitress hell-bent on cheering me up."

She smiled patiently. "I don't offend easily."

"I know, Connie. I don't understand why I keep coming here."

She reached across the table and warmly clasped my hand. "Because you've got the hots for me, dear."

"Ah, you remembered."

IT WAS A LITTLE before eight when I got home. There was one phone message on the recorder.

"Hi, Harry, it's Carla. It's about six-thirty. Well, seven-thirty your time. I thought you might be home by now. I didn't want to call you at work, just in case you were busy." There was a pause of a few seconds. "Harry, I, uh, I might need some more time off. Something isn't right here. I'm not sure what...Something is wrong. I just don't think I can leave here like this. I know you're probably thinking I'm just upset. And you're right. I am upset. My father is dead. And I don't know why... Wait a second. There's someone outside... What's going on... Anyway, I want you to know I'm not imagining things. There is something wrong. According to the death certificate, the last time I talked to my father on the phone, he was supposed to have already been dead four hours... Wait a sec… Who's out there? Harry, I'll have to call you back. Something's…''

There was another brief silence before I heard her gasp and the machine clicked off.

TWO

CARLA DID NOT call back.

I waited for over seven dog hours for the phone to ring. I would have called her, but I had no idea where she was.

I replayed Carla's message on the answering machine. "It's about six-thirty. Well, seven-thirty your time." That put her somewhere in the central time zone. "My father is dead." I assumed she was calling from where he had lived. "There's someone outside." Someone she knew? Someone unexpected? Did she see the someone or did she hear him? Probably a ground-level residence. Possibly her father's home. I must have listened to the last part of the tape several dozen times. I was able to detect a faint background noise in the space between "Something's…" and the sound of her gasp. As many times as I played it back, I couldn't identify the noise. What was it? Had someone entered uninvited? That was my guess, because her gasp was definitely that of a startled person.

I called the Sand Bar.

"Nick, I'm worried about Carla." I told him about the phone message and my suspicions. "She said she couldn't leave because something wasn't right, something was wrong. She didn't know why her father was dead, I'm not sure what that meant. There was a thing about the death certificate." I told Nick I wasn't going to wait any longer. I was going to look for Carla.

Nick said, "What are you going to do first?"

"Break into her apartment, see if I can find an address for her father."

"I've got her spare key," he said. "Last summer when she went to California with her girlfriends she asked me to water her plants and keep an eye on her place. When she got back she told me to hang on to the key for emergencies."

"I'll swing by and pick it up. One other thing, Nick. I'm going to change the recording on my answering machine, referring calls to the Sand Bar number. Just in case Carla should call when I'm not home. So the problem is—"

"There's no problem," Nick interrupted. "I'll stay here to cover the phone, around the clock if I have to, until we know she's all right."

"Thanks, Nick."

We hung up. I changed the greeting on my answering machine and began the quest for Carla.

SHE LIVED in a two-story stucco building just off the New River. The Mediterranean-style structure was an endangered remnant of an area that once defined Fort Lauderdale in what now seems like another lifetime ago. The charming eclectic neighborhood of old Florida homes with verandas and Spanish tile roofs was rapidly being consumed by the malignant growth of the county courthouse complex and the spread of the parasitic industries of law offices, bail bondsmen, trend-of-the-month cafés, and day-care centers for the tykes of working parents. Live oaks and banyan trees had been razed to make room for asphalt parking lots and uninspired high-rises. Concrete erections had irreparably violated the town I once loved.

I parked between a chinaberry tree and a bicycle rack. The apartment building was surrounded by a dense hibiscus hedge, a fragile bastion against the sprawl of high-tech, lowbrow construction amok. I walked through the hedge's tunnel onto a flagstone courtyard, filled with the sounds of cricket melodies, rippling water from a small mosaic fountain in a pond, and the eleven o'clock forecast of Weaver the Weatherman wafting from a first-floor apartment.

Carla lived on the second floor. I slipped the key in the lock and let myself in. The scent of sandalwood hung in the air with just a hint of what reminded me of baby powder. The apartment was dark except for slices of soft moonlight seeping through the antler-shaped fronds of a staghorn that hung in a bay window. I felt around for a switch and flipped on the light.

Carla's world had more plants than a posy fancier's greenhouse. Ferns, spider plants, philodendrons, a tall rubber plant, and plants that probably had names I wouldn't recognize were scattered throughout the apartment in ceramic and clay floor pots and hung from ceiling hooks in macrame. I could almost hear the distant jungle drums inviting the ghost of Johnny Weismuller to dinner.

The living room was furnished with Pier One wicker and a collection of big cushiony pillows. The only sign of clutter was the wicker etagere stuffed with tapes, books, and magazines. I scanned the titles of several magazines fanned on one of the shelves—*Self, Body, Mind & Spirit, Glamour.* We had different periodical reading tastes. Her books were primarily self-help, travel guides, and several Chinese cookbooks. Our hardback interests were a little closer match. I didn't need self-help, but I liked to travel, and I was always ready to have someone cook good Chinese for me. I picked up a few of her cassettes and a funny thing happened. I began to feel a chivalrous awkwardness, like I was snooping. Over the years I had searched many homes for many reasons without feeling self-conscious about it. I was doing a job. But this was different. This was personal. There was no "official need to know" what Carla read. I wanted to know. I wanted to know more about her. Something about being in her home had drawn me closer to her in a way I couldn't describe because I didn't understand it. I told myself the better I knew Carla, the better the chance of finding her. I also knew I was merely justifying my curiosity about her. I hoped she would understand. Because as inept as my method was, it was well intentioned.

She had a diverse taste in music, probably to fit her moods for when she was melancholy, happy, or just cleaning the kitchen. Bonnie Raitt, Jackson Browne, lots of reggae, and I saw we also shared an interest in classical music, though Carla's preference was more Mozart and mine more Bo Diddley.

Next to the bay window was an oak dinette for two, covered with framing material and a pink-and-gray poster of worn-out ballet shoes on an antique dresser. Its grace was in its simplicity. I imagined Carla just about to put the finishing touches on it when she received word of her father's death. I felt a sharp twinge of pain, her pain. I wanted to hold her tight and absorb her hurt.

Her father's address, I reminded myself.

I figured her address book would be near a phone and phones are usually in kitchens and bedrooms.

The kitchen was Carla's personal statement. An array of mix-and-match yard-sale baskets, pots, and pans dangled overhead from wrought-iron racks. The windowsill above the sink was lined with candles stuck in green wine bottles overlaid with wax stalactites. The walls were a sky blue, the floor an azure-and-white checkerboard tile—a color scheme that carried over from the other room. With a little improvising, she had given the room the seasoned charm of a kitchen right out of a small baroque hotel. It was probably her favorite room.

There was a wall phone, but no directory.

The centerpiece of the bedroom was the big brass-framed bed. The day Carla found it at a garage sale she bought a round of drinks for the bar and proposed a toast to her "pride and joy." Father Shifty told Carla if she bought another round he'd come over to her apartment and bless the bed for her.

Carla laughed. "You'll bless my soul for free or I'll charge you double on your next drink." She added, "I finally have something to put my grandmother's chenille bedspread on. I've had it since I left home. Now if I can just get rid of that tacky Early American dresser and nightstand."

The bedspread was pink and so was the phone on the tacky

nightstand. Beside the phone was a reading lamp, a dog-eared copy of *Dracula*, and a notepad with pen. Again, no address book.

I opened the nightstand drawer and wished I hadn't.

THREE

"MAD MONEY?" Nick said as he hung the closed sign on the Sand Bar door.

I shook my head. "That was more than mad money stuffed in her drawer."

"You count it?"

"No. I leafed though several bundles. It was all old tens, twenties, and fifties wrapped in rubber bands. There had to be thousands of dollars, easily five figures."

Nick's brow wrinkled like that of a confused Senate subcommittee member trying to decide between the egg salad and health-care reform. "Doesn't sound like tip money."

"Hardly."

Nick picked up a toothpick and started to clean his nails. "So where does Carla get that kind of money?"

"That's the second question," I said.

He glanced up at me. "What's the first question?"

"Is it any of our business?"

He regarded me for a moment. "If you hadn't already decided that, you wouldn't sound so worried."

"I am worried. I'm afraid Carla's gotten into something she shouldn't have. I can't help but think she may be in some trouble we don't know about."

"And you're not going to let it go."

"Of course not."

"Which brings us back to my question. Where, or how, did Carla get that kind of money?"

"I don't even know how to begin to answer that," I conceded.

Nick shrugged. "Try thinking like a woman."

"I'm not that smart."

AFTER FINDING THE MONEY, I left it there and closed the drawer. I checked the dresser drawers and came up empty.

I wandered into the bathroom. A garden of little bottles and jars emitted the heart-weakening fragrances of femininity. It was a wistful reminder of the emotions lost and the joys unavailable to a spectator who kept replaying the tape of previous misfortunes.

The search continued.

On a shelf in the closet was a shoe box full of postcards and letters. On the very top was a picture postcard dated three weeks ago. It was signed "Love, Dad." The postmark was Angel's Cove, Florida. It was also the only piece of correspondence in the box from her father.

I went out to the car and got my Florida road atlas. Angel's Cove was in the Panhandle, west of Apalachicola. It was also in the central time zone.

I called long-distance information.

"City?"

"Angel's Cove," I said.

"Name?"

"Meadows. I don't know the first name."

"One moment."

After one moment I was told the number was unlisted. It didn't matter. At least I knew where I was going.

On the way back to the Sand Bar I stopped at Nick's, per his instructions, and picked up his shaving bag and several changes of clothes. He would be camping out at the Sand Bar until further notice.

NICK SAID, "Who are you calling?"

"Big Daddy."

Big Daddy was honorary Kentucky Colonel Ronald G. Harris, who was the spitting image of Burl Ives in *Cat on a Hot*

Tin Roof, down to the goatee on his chin. He detested the comparison, as he rather imagined himself as a white Hakeem Olajuwon playing center in an over-three-hundred-pound basketball league. Big Daddy had the heart of Gandhi, but the late-night disposition of a congenitally irritable man whose aptitude test scores suggested a career in telephone sales. Col. Ronald ''Big Daddy'' Harris was my travel agent.

''Hmmmm,'' answered a groggy voice.

''Hello. Sounds like I woke you.''

''Damn, Rice, nothing slips by you.''

''Sorry, Ron, but I have to get to Angel's Cove as soon as possible.''

''Would you settle for the Angel of Death?'' He groaned loudly, ''Christ! It's one o'clock in the morning.''

''I know.''

''Well, I'm closed.''

''Come on, Ron. This is an emergency.''

''All right.'' He sighed heavily. ''Where do you need to go?''

''Angel's Cove.''

''Never heard of it.''

''It's in the Panhandle, west of Apalachicola.''

''Okay,'' he said. ''Let me think. Well, you'd have to fly into Tallahassee. Or Panama City. Uh, either way you're going to have to rent a car and drive. That's another hour. The earliest you'll get there is noon, eleven o'clock their time.''

''Nothing sooner?''

''Nothing. You're talking about a milk run on a commuter. You won't even get out of here until eight in the morning. You could drive quicker.''

I thought about that. ''I guess that's what I'll do.''

The colonel hung up before I could thank him.

''Well?'' Nick said.

I told him what Ron had said. ''So I guess I'm driving it.''

Nick nodded. He handed me a thermos. ''Hot coffee,'' he said. ''Call me when you get there.''

FOUR

THE RED MORNING SUN could have been the monocled blood-shot eye of a hungover Cyclops as it rose above the white sand dunes that erupted from the Gulf Coast beach.

The beach was an environmental oddity. There were no parking meters, no lifeguard stands, no cabanas, no sun-baked tourists nor their spoor of pop-top cans and cigarette butts. About the only sign of life was an occasional egret. A Sunshine State aberration—a stretch of pristine coastline which had not benefited from man's unrestrained tinkering, which had not been blessed with the marvels that excrete from man's imagination onto blueprints fashioned to correct God's folly—lovely Nature in the raw. One day it would all be concrete. It's only a matter of time in Florida, where the developer's fat wad is king and the politician's asshole is queen.

It was early a.m. central time. I was exhausted and my back was stiff. Driving across flat-chested Florida at night is about as exhilarating as watching an eight-hour black-and-white Andy Warhol film of a Shriner adjusting his fez. I had stopped at a Get & Go convenience store across the highway from the beach. A lukewarm breeze ushered in the sweet smell of salt air from the Gulf. I topped off the gas tank, powdered my nose in the men's room, came out, and bought a cup of coffee.

The store clerk had an expressionless, oily-skinned face unclouded by urban suspicions. She had long stringy hair and was dressed for a Partridge Family reunion—rose-pink stretch pants and a white T-shirt emblazoned with MIRACLES HAPPEN in bright red Gothic letters. Several tangled strands of colorful glass beads hung around her lanky neck.

I paid her for the gas and asked, "Do you know how far it is to Angel's Cove?"

She looked up at me, a crooked little smile scribbled across her face.

"Are you going to see her?" she said almost reverently.

"Her?"

Her head bobbed. She pointed to her shirt. "That's where she is. She's there."

Maybe the coffee had perked, but I hadn't. "Who are we talking about?"

"I have her picture. Would you like to see it? I'll bet you would." She leaned closer. "She signed it."

I was fatigued. I did not want to see any picture, signed or not. I wanted to find Carla. I was in a hurry.

I said, "Sure. Why not."

Even pseudo-Japanese philosopher Harry-san is wise enough to know that sometimes it is best to tend to others' needs before stopping to smell the goat farm. And at that moment I felt the store clerk had need to show me whatever picture it was she was talking about.

The clerk reached into a canvas tote bag and fished out a kraft envelope. She unclasped the envelope and solemnly removed several sheets of tissue paper. Then the picture. It was an eight-by-ten black-and-white studio photo, one of those celebrity publicity stills. The picture was a full-figure shot of a woman standing with legs spread, wearing a neck-to-ankle, long-sleeved white robe. Her head was tilted back. Both her arms were held up, reaching high for heaven's bounty. The words MIRACLES HAPPEN were printed between her outstretched hands. Along the bottom corner was the stamped facsimile signature of a Sister Star.

"Didn't I tell you?" the clerk said, holding the picture carefully at the edges so as not to smear the glossy finish.

"You certainly did," I said. "Are you going to have it framed?" My imitation of sincere interest.

"No," she said matter-of-factly. "I want to be entombed with it."

I glanced up at the ceiling to see if Bela Lugosi was hanging from the rafters.

The clerk was staring at me. Finally she said, "Twenty-two point three miles."

"Angel's Cove?"

She nodded.

"Thank you," I said.

She nodded again.

I turned to leave.

She said, "I'm not crazy, mister."

"That's too bad," I said.

She looked questioningly at me.

I said, "It's crazy not to be crazy in an insane world."

THE DRAWBRIDGE WAS OPEN. A lone shrimp boat glided wearily home to the backwaters after a fortnight on the Gulf. On the other side of the bridge was Angel's Cove.

I imagined Angel's Cove would be like any other rural Florida community that eked its meager living from the rapidly diminishing natural resources. Harvesting a crop of oranges from the rich soils of disappearing groves or harvesting a crop of oysters from the recreationally polluted bay waters, it was all hard, back-breaking, spirit-busting, life-shortening, underpaying, and overromanticized work. There would be good seasons and there would be bad seasons. And each bad season would claim more casualties, while the good seasons spawned no newcomers. It was risky business. With growing government controls and restrictions, investing in small-town America was about as foolish as blaspheming Mouse World in front of the Orlando Chamber of Commerce.

The drawbridge creaked to a close. I started my engine and waited for the gate to lift.

The bridge spilled onto Front Street, a single-block business district mired in a time warp, unaware the Great Depression had ended decades ago. On the corner was a weathered two-story brick building, the ruins of a boarded-up hotel, its sagging veranda shaded by a sprawling live oak festooned with Spanish moss. A sleeping dog did guard duty on one of the porch steps. The rest of the street was equally unimpressive and looked like something the cat had dragged in. There were several stores that were maybe one or two name changes away from their death notices. Stapled to telephone poles were posters for next month's bluegrass festival and last week's fish fry at the American Legion Hall. Displayed in several storefront windows were MIRACLES HAPPEN posters. Angel's Cove had one bank, one IGA grocer, a marine welder, a machine shop, enough Protestant churches for a softball league, and probably a handful of Bubbas.

At that hour of the morning the only two businesses open were those serving the day shift with breakfast dishes I wouldn't have touched with a ten-foot fork. There's a time for Southern cooking, but that time is not breakfast, when recipes usually involve some disgusting concoction of burnt scrapple, ketchup, runny eggs, and leftover grits à la lard. The two open places were aptly named Another Restaurant and The Other Restaurant, one at each end of the block. Parked in front of Another Restaurant were a Florida Highway Patrol car, a power company utility vehicle, and several pickups. Except for a rusted Plymouth, the gravel lot next to The Other Restaurant was empty. That's where I stopped. I wanted information, not company.

A tall, large-framed woman with a cauliflower haircut and Madam Zorita eyeglasses was behind the counter reading a newspaper and humming a ditty from the Dolly Parton songbook. She lowered the paper and greeted me with a genuine smile, the kind of smile I had gone years without seeing until the lady with a deaf cat taught me what to look for.

I sat at the counter. It was just me, an unplugged pinball machine, and Evalinda, according to her plastic name tag.

Evalinda said, "Good morning."

So did I.

She said, "How are you?"

I said, "Hungry and thirsty."

"I can fix that."

"I should have said horny," I murmured louder than I had intended.

"I heard that," she said, her warm smile still intact. "Listen, before this relationship goes any further, I think you should know that I'm not signing any prenuptial agreements."

"Just like that? You're gonna nip the nup before you even know me?"

"What's to know? You're a man."

"Hear me roar."

Evalinda laughed. "Sure, steal the woman's anthem. Is nothing sacred?"

"Gee, I'm glad I stopped here. As if my life didn't have enough guilt."

"Then you should be glad you stopped here. I've just the thing for guilt. How about a fresh novena over easy with a side of home fries?"

I was being waited on by Father Shifty in drag.

I was in more of a hurry than I was hungry. But I was in the South now. In Florida you drive north to reach the South, where the rules are different. The more you try to rush, the slower you'll get there. Take it easy and save a lot of time. Also, I got this thing about going into small businesses and not spending money. I don't know, call it professional courtesy, but I feel compelled to help other small businesses stay in business. Especially used-book stores. I won't walk out empty-handed, even if I can't find anything I want to read. Which explains my copy of *Vanna Speaks*.

If I wanted information, I had to do it the Southern way. Sociable.

"Can you do French toast?" I said.

Evalinda nodded. "Sprinkled with confectionery sugar and cinnamon and then coated with maple syrup."

"Sounds good."

"Bacon and coffee with that?"

"Yeah, but not in the same cup."

She poured me a cup of coffee and handed me the newspaper before dumping a gallon of grease in a skillet. I scanned the local paper. The front-page story was a follow-up on the impact of the recent banning of gill nets in state waters. The gill nets were blamed for destroying Florida's marine life. Both sides of the argument were saying, "See, we told you so." Prior to the vote to ban the nets, the commercial fishing lobby's paid prophet of doom had predicted that if the ban was passed, seafood prices would increase drastically and the state could expect to add thousands more to the welfare roles with the loss of fishing industry–related jobs. The conservationists had said that if the ban was not passed, seafood prices would increase drastically and the state could expect to add thousands more to the welfare roles with the loss of fishing industry–related jobs because there would be no more fish. Both claimed their predictions were right on the money. It was all very clear. Republicans and Democrats, plunderers and environmentalists, alarmists and voices of reason played musical chairs, but in the end it was all just Chicken Little politics.

I turned the page. There was going to be an arts and crafts show in Port St. Joe. A letter to the editor attacked the county commission for not having a strong foreign policy. It was signed by the leader of the pack for the local VFW post.

An old man with pelican jowls and liver-spotted skin entered the restaurant. He wore Sears work clothes and rotting brogans. He surveyed the room, saw me, and hesitated in the doorway. He seemed surprised, not so much that it was me, but that it was anybody. Evalinda looked over her shoulder at him.

She said, "Come on in, Manning." There was a hint of laughter and a dash of daring in her voice.

Manning crossed the room slowly, as if he was dragging the heavy chains of fifty Marley's ghosts. Of all the counter stools in all the diners in all the world, he had to sit on one next to me. He smelled of stale tobacco smoke.

Evalinda delivered my breakfast. I set the paper aside and began to eat. I observed Manning in the mirror behind the counter studying me with a watchdog curiosity, waiting for me to throw him a bone. I took a sip of coffee and turned to him.

"You driving through?" he said.

"No, I'm eating breakfast."

Evalinda said, "Don't be bothering my customer, Manning."

"I'm not bothering nobody," he said. "And when did you reopen?"

"This morning," she said.

"You should have got used to being closed." Manning directed his next comment at me. "There's better places to eat."

"Yeah," I said, "and I've had better company, too."

Evalinda snickered.

Manning said, "What's that supposed to mean?"

"Nothing." I sighed. It's tough being sociable after an all-night drive. "I'm just trying to eat my breakfast. That's all."

"Sounded like you were looking to argue."

I shook my head. "No. I'm only looking for the Meadows place."

Quiet as it was, I still noticed a discernible hush engulf the room when I mentioned the Meadows name. Evalinda was staring at me as though I needed to go back in the darkroom for further development.

"Meadows," the old man said, his tone harsh. "You a friend of his?"

"Never met him," I admitted.

"Then you won't be disappointed."

"How's that?"

"Meadows is dead."

"I know. I'm a friend of his daughter."

"You're not going to impress anyone in this town by being friends with that woman," Manning informed me.

Without an ounce of emotion in my voice I said, "That's fine. I'm not here to impress anyone. And she is my friend. Make no mistake about that."

He leaned toward me. "You want some advice?"

"No. I just want directions."

He grinned. "Not very friendly, are you?"

"No, I'm not," I said in a quiet monotone. "I've been up all night and I'm irritable. Frankly, even if I'd had eight hours' sleep, I still think I'd find your good-ol'-boy etiquette offensive. So it might be best if you sat someplace else before one of us says something we shouldn't. Can you do that? Just leave me alone?"

His face reddened. "Why don't you leave? Why don't you get your friend and take her back where she came from? We don't need her kind here."

On that note he got up and slithered out the door.

I looked at Evalinda. "Is he typical?"

She nodded. Her smile was gone.

I said, "Friendly place."

"They're not bad people, mister," she said, sad-eyed. "They're just afraid. That's all."

"Afraid of what?"

She peered at me for a long time. "Maybe Manning's right. Maybe it would be best if you got Charlie's daughter and took her home."

"If I can find her and if that's what she wants."

Evalinda thought about that for a second. She wrote something on the back of a napkin. "Here," she said. "There's directions to Charlie Meadows's place."

"Thank you."

I had what I wanted. I paid for the relatively uneaten meal. Left a tip. Before leaving I said, "You never said."

"Never said what?"

"What these people are afraid of."

She gazed at nothing, not looking at me. Thinking, carefully choosing her words. Finally she said, "They're afraid Charlie might have been right. They're afraid that's what killed him."

FIVE

MY CHILDHOOD introduction to death was the passing of my first pet, a sickly stray cat. It was a mutual adoption. The cat was ugly, but it was mine. My cat, my friend, for almost a month. And suddenly my cat was dead. I didn't understand. This couldn't be. I wouldn't have it. How could my cat die? I hadn't authorized it. It had to be some horrible foul-up. One of those government things my father was always complaining about. There was only one thing to do. I told God. I didn't like being a snitch, but somebody had screwed up royally. God could fix anything.

My mother wouldn't let me sleep with a dead cat.

I dug a shallow grave in the backyard and buried most of the cat. I left its little head exposed above the ground so the cat could breathe once God realized there had been a mistake.

Two days later I awoke to the sound of my father cranking up the power lawnmower. It was Saturday morning. He was going to cut the grass.

What was wrong with this picture?

I scrambled out of bed, stubbed a toe against the dresser, fell to the floor writhing in agony. I didn't make it outside in time. The head was decapitated before I could warn my father.

Sometimes God can be a little slow on the draw. I suppose that was the child Harry Rice's first hard lesson, his first big disappointment.

What next? No Santa Claus?

That was also my first taste of heartache. Why the gift of love if only to have it snatched away? Sure, the joy was wonderful. But the hurt was nearly lethal. Was that the formula? Four weeks of happiness for four months of pain? It wasn't fair. I was damned if I would give the gods the satisfaction of seeing me cry. I repressed my sadness. My first self-taught skill.

"In this corner weighing infinity, the bully gods. And in the other corner weighing in at sixty-eight pounds, little Muhammad Rice. Only the gods are allowed to hit below the belt. Shake hands and come out fighting."

Years later I hadn't won a single round, yet I was still swinging.

And that was how I felt walking out of The Other Restaurant. Maybe my intuition was out of focus. Perhaps it was exhaustion. Still, there was the real sense that I was taking on windmills. A feeling of futility. Deep down I just knew something bad had happened to Carla, that I would never see her again. The infallible wisdom garnered from years of experience. You look for enough missing people and you learn to recognize the signs. A gut feeling, but it's usually right.

In just two days in Angel's Cove, Carla had made some kind of an impact.

You're not going to impress anyone in this town by being friends with that woman... Why don't you get your friend and take her back where she came from? We don't need her kind here.

Maybe Manning's right. Maybe it would be best if you got Charlie's daughter and took her home.

What was all of that about? What had Charlie's daughter been up to?

IF ROME HAD BEEN BUILT in a day, then most of modern Florida could have been built in less time than it takes to deliver a pizza. Doomed by rampaging mutant developers whose command of the English language was severely limited to "No problem" and who could appear remarkably normal when intoxicated, the state had been pockmarked with gaudy growths from "The Far Side" populated with motivated sellers and strip centers the color of Beanie Wienies. Florida had become infested with imitation rustic, artificially quaint, and horrendously tasteless zoning delights such as Tarpon Springs, Boca Raton, the Magic Kingdom, Kissimmee, South Miami Beach, and Bloomingdale's—some of which had once been idyllic locales. Which is what Angel's Cove still was. There was an authenticity about it. It was picturesque without the pretensions of a Coconut Grove or a Sanibel Island. Driving through Angel's Cove was like driving through a PBS documentary on turn-of-the-century small-town America, narrated by Rod Serling:

"You're traveling into a zone suspended in time and space, a different kind of zone not only of endangered sights and sounds, but of mind-set. Prepare to embark on a wondrous journey to once upon a time, to that remote corner of the imagination that transforms sepia photographs in an old family album into three-dimensional, colorful vestiges of former glories. Your next stop, the Twilight Zipcode." (Spooky-music interlude.) "The time is now. You've just crossed over to a universe of narrow streets lined with laurel oak and blooming magnolia trees; manicured lawns accented with azalea bushes. Listen to nature's lullaby, raindrops harmonizing on the roof at night, perchance to dream. Awake to a morning sky the color of pale wine mixed with a soft blues piano. There are no limits to what can be mixed in the early light. Witness the simple act of children's games in playgrounds, of empty rockers on screen porches, of life moving slowly along the waterfront without a timetable. Beyond there is the brick post office and the piece de resistance—a magnificent Victorian house on the verge of decay, and yet the detailed perfection of its gingerbread is still proudly intact, defying time as if life goes on forever. The place is a small fishing town where the tyranny of money, the tool of conquest, has yet to ravage its innocence and beauty. For the record, it is only a matter of time before the twentieth century intrudes; before the superficiality and the contrived nostalgia of young professionals thoughtlessly turns historic landmarks inside out; before the smell of cash obliterates the last trace of honeysuckle from the air. There is no known cure. And the pity of it is the children will never know the mystic enchantment of traveling without luggage through a sentimental course for which no maps are plotted, only sign posts. There's one up ahead. Submitted for your perusal, a cameo of tranquillity known only as Angel's Cove.''

FOLLOWING EVALINDA'S DIRECTIONS I passed a big billowing tent with the sides rolled up. Several men were inside setting up folding chairs. An immense banner across the front of the tent proclaimed MIRACLES HAPPEN. It had the makings of a spiritual weight-loss theme park that lacked only the Disney bankroll.

A ramshackled oyster bar was the landmark I was looking for. Just beyond it a dirt road was supposed to veer off to the right. And it did. I followed the dirt road through a heavily wooded corridor for almost a half mile. At the end of the road was a clearing.

A small wood frame house in need of paint sat near the water's edge of a backwater bayou. Behind the house a small plank dock jutted out over the water. A sloop was tied to the dock. A pink mist curled over the glazed surface of the still water like swirls of cotton candy. I parked between a redwood picnic table and Carla's old gray Honda Accord. I had found the Meadows place.

I got out of my car and stretched. It was so quiet I could almost hear the mist starting to burn away as the sun began to creep above the cypress trees. The yard had all the messy semblance of a child's coloring book. There was a strange sense of monastic solitude about the place, and yet the yard was a gallery of sociability. Bird feeders hung from branches. There was a carefully tended vegetable garden, horseshoe stakes permanently implanted in dirt pitch holes, a barbecue

pit, a rusted PURE OIL sign nailed to a tree, a hammock strung
between mimosa trees, and the all-too-familiar Sand Bar tank-
tops and stonewashed jeans hanging from a clothesline.

I walked up the stone path to the front of the house and
knocked. Nothing. I called Carla's name. No answer. The door
was unlocked. That didn't mean anything. People don't gen-
erally lock doors in small towns. I opened the door.

I went in.

Death was hanging in the air.

SIX

THE BODY HUNG from a ceiling fan, the chain wrapped tightly around the neck. The eyes were empty and bulging, the tongue protruding and the joints already stiff with rigor mortis.

I've read that when a person is hanged the sphincters will involuntarily contract and relax, releasing fluid and solid body waste. Judging by the mess on the floor, the same was apparently true of kitten hangings. The small animal couldn't have been more than six or eight weeks old.

I did a quick walk-through of the house. There was no other evidence of turmoil, nor signs of struggle. What I did find was not the obvious. It was things that would otherwise be normal, but had suddenly become unusual. If Carla was staying in her father's house alone, why was the toilet seat up? A male visitor or intruder? There was also the half-eaten meal still on the table, as if Carla had been interrupted in the middle of dinner. The most disturbing discovery was finding her purse on the kitchen counter. Her wallet, money, credit cards, and car keys were all there. So where was Carla?

What had she gotten into? I couldn't help but wonder if the money I had found in her apartment had something to do with all of this…this what? Her father's death, her disappearance.

I walked through the house again to see if I had missed anything. I had. The telephone in the kitchen.

I called Nick.

"Sand Bar," he answered.

"Yeah, it's me. I'm in—"

"Carla called," he interrupted.

"When?"

"Less than an hour ago."

"Where is she?"

THE FIRST DATE MOTEL was just west of Angel's Cove, about a mile and a half from the Meadows place. It was one of those run-down stucco motor courts that had been popular back in the fifties. The building was a U-shaped design. In the middle of the U was a swimming pool surrounded by a chain-link fence. The motel was a roadside relic of tourism before traffic was rerouted from the multistoplight two-lane roads to the nonstop six-lane interstate highway systems and before families preferred being bedded in national motel chains endorsed by the-party-is-over celebrities.

I parked in the circular driveway next to a grungy convertible that had hauled its last debutante's derriere twenty years ago. The screen door was unlatched. I walked into a Montgomery Ward scratch-and-dent, neo-Haitian office, tastefully decorated with the discerning bachelor's touch. I rang the bell on the counter twice before I got a response.

He came through a beaded curtain, a spindly man wearing baggy dungarees and a thrift shop shirt. He had skin the color and texture of a cantaloupe. His hair was possum gray, which he cut himself or else he had a barber with a sense of humor.

"I heard you the first time." He spoke slow proper English with the falsetto voice of a eunuch that made him sound like a cartoon mouse reading Shakespeare.

"What room is Carla Meadows in?"

The desk clerk's eyebrows arched. "Are you going to pay her room bill?"

"I'll pay the bill. Where is she?"

"She showed up last night without any money," he continued. "She didn't have bags, no wallet. She didn't have anything but the clothes on her back. She wanted me to just give her a room. 'Trust me,' she said. I trusted her. Now I want to make sure I'm going to get paid."

"You're going to get paid. What room is she in?"

He rubbed his chin. "What about those phone calls? Are you going to pay for her phone calls, too?"

"Mister, I'm going to pay for her room. I'll pay for her phone calls. I'm going to make sure you get everything that's coming to you."

"How is that going to be? Cash or credit card? I don't take checks."

I grew impatient. "You have health insurance?"

He looked puzzled for a second, then caught my gaze. "Room eight."

I knocked on the door to room eight.

First silence, then, "Who is it?" Carla.

"Bachelor number two," I said.

A lock turned, the door opened. Carla stared at me. The confusion in her eyes was obvious. Nick had told her to expect me, still disbelief was apparent in her face. Slowly she absorbed my appearance. Her chest began to rise and fall heavily. Her eyes started to glisten.

"You should see yourself, Harry," she whispered. "You look like you've been up all night."

"Well, my mother told me it wasn't polite to be prettier than the woman. After looking at you, I think I need to stay awake for a couple more days."

She smiled, but her lips quivered. "God, I must look worse than you."

There were dark circles under her eyes. Her hair was matted to the right side of her face.

I nodded. "You have looked better, Carla." Then in a rare moment of unintended sincerity I said, "But never to me."

Carla hurled herself at me. She threw her arms around my neck and squeezed. Her body quaked as I held her.

"I don't believe you," she sobbed in my ear. "I can't believe you're actually here."

"What can I say? I got lost. I was trying to find the Orange Bowl. But you know me. Too proud to ask for directions. Next thing I know I'm at the First Date Motel and some guy tells me if I want a good time go to room eight."

Carla laughed. "Thank you, Harry. Thank you. Thank you."

"No sweat, pal."

She started to cry as we stood there embracing.

Maybe a minute passed. I felt her shudder involuntarily as if she had just awakened from a dreamless sleep. I wanted to offer her assurance, something more profound than a sympathetic smile. Something more insightful than a "There, there" pat on the back and a shoulder to cry on. But Carla's pain was my puzzlement and it bothered me that I didn't know what to do or know what she needed. Which was no startling discovery. My life is something of a well-documented testament to my ignorance of the feminine psyche, though, of all the genders in the world, by far the female is clearly my favorite. I truly like women and more than just as sleeping companions. I love their tenderness and their compassion. I envy their resolve, their strength, their courage. I delight in their secret places and the way that women taste. I am humbled by their unexpected, heart-rushing caresses. Not to mention, their logic confuses me. Perhaps that's why I prefer women. I understand men.

So I stood there and hoped that our prolonged hug was as comforting to Carla as it was to me.

A lazy breeze blew a wisp of her hair in my face. We stepped back from each other at that precise instant as if our movements were being manipulated by some great spiritual choreographer in the sky. Carla looked up at me and sniffled. She leaned forward and wiped her nose on my shoulder before she realized what she was doing. It jolted the pain from her face. She laughed at herself.

"Gee, Harry, does this mean you're not going to ask me to the senior prom?" she cracked.

"Not unless I can rent a snot-resistant tux."

Carla cringed. "Oh, you are so gross."

"One of my more endearing traits. Are you okay?"

She pursed her lips and nodded.

"What happened last night?" I said.

She hesitated. "Were you at my father's?"

"Yeah. Your purse is in the car."

She acknowledged that with a nod. "You saw the…"

"I saw it."

"Let's go back there and I'll tell you about it."

"All right. Let me take of care of the bill." I walked her to the car and asked why she hadn't called back last night.

"When I checked in here last night I didn't have any money, so the desk clerk would only let me make collect long-distance calls, for which he says there's a surcharge. But the operator kept getting your answering machine. So I just waited until this morning when I thought you'd be at the Sand Bar."

"Did you call the police?"

"No." She got in the car. "Harry, I don't know who to trust around here." I started to say something but she cut me off. "I'll tell you at the house." She shut the car door.

The desk clerk was waiting behind the counter.

"I come in peace," I said.

I took care of the bill. "I appreciate what you did last night," I said. "Giving her a room and all."

He grunted.

"Listen," I said. "I want to apologize for that health insurance remark earlier. I was out of line."

The desk clerk looked at me strangely. I suppose in Machoville being a man means never having to say you're sorry.

SEVEN

I BURIED THE KITTEN in the garden next to the house. The burial shroud was a pillowcase.

I slogged back into the house with the energy of an ancient man who has eaten a thousand Chinese fortune cookies to digest but one truth. I was fading quickly.

Carla sat quietly at the kitchen table. She stared at me thoughtfully as I hobbled over to the sink to wash my hands.

"I fixed you a hot bath," she said, her voice mixed with touches of concern and affection.

"What?" I yawned.

She smiled sympathetically. "You awake?"

"Who?"

"Who you, you dope. Go on, relax in the tub while the water is hot."

"Carla, if I stop now, I'll fall asleep."

"Then fall asleep."

"But we need to talk."

"We'll talk later. Now go," she ordered, pointing a finger at the door.

I did as I was told.

The bathroom was engulfed in a sauna heat and filled with a thin fog of steam. The source was a large claw-and-ball bathtub filled with scented water. The cavernous tub couldn't have been more inviting had it been inhabited by a mermaid calling my name. I undressed, slipped into the water, and felt its warmth wrap around me. The soothing sound of water rhythmically slapping against the side of the tub lulled me into an intoxicating tranquillity. I leaned back and closed my eyes. Slowly I sank into the dark pool of dreamland.

CARLA CLEARED HER THROAT. I opened my eyes.

"Feel better?" She was sitting on the edge of the tub observing me. Observing me lying in a tub of cool water. Observing me naked. I jerked upright and brought my knees up under my chin.

"You look like a turtle trying to pull back into his shell," she said with a half-smile.

My eyes darted around the room, looking for I don't know what. A modesty cover of some kind—a washcloth, a brown paper sack, a hot dog bun.

Carla's eyes crinkled as she watched me.

"What…what's so funny?" I stammered.

"You. I can't get over you, Harry. How you came all the way up here to my rescue, just like in a fairy tale. My hero. Of course, the way I remember it, Prince Charming always stood up when a lady entered the room."

"Is that so? Well, why is it I don't remember Prince Charming being bare-assed?"

"He was when he was a frog."

"Carla!" I croaked.

"Oh, be still, Harry. I already looked. I've seen it. So relax."

"Thank heaven for little girls," I moaned.

Carla stared nonchalantly at me. "Don't pretend to be upset. It's no secret that you're an exhibitionist."

"No secret! Thank God. The silent suffering of a dirty young man is finally over. I can take my show on the road. You can sell tickets. See Harry-in-the-tub, more deliciously revealing than Shakespeare-in-the-park." I frowned at her. "Exhibitionist. Next thing I know you'll be telling me the thrill was mine, not yours. That you're the offended party, not me."

"Exactly."

"Meanwhile, back in the bathroom, where I was minding

my own business, you burst in with an uncontrollable urge to inventory my adorable body parts."

"The uncontrollable urge," Carla corrected, "was the pressure on my bladder. I have to use the toilet. Believe me, I have no voyeuristic tendencies. I just have to pee. What's a girl suppose to do?"

"You're amazing, Carla. No matter what you do, it's always me who is in the wrong. It's always me who needs your forgiveness. How thoughtless of me. I was hogging the bathroom."

"Forgiveness granted." She stood up and handed me a towel. "Get out of that cold water so I can have a little privacy."

For the first time I noticed how right she was about the water being cold. How long had I slept?

"Do you think I could have a little privacy while I dry off?" I said.

"Certainly." She took a step toward the door and stopped. She looked back at me. "It's true, you know."

"What's that?"

"About cold water. It really does make some things shrivel." She giggled and made a hasty retreat before I could grab her and drown her.

Carla left me sitting alone, nude in the tub. In pubescent male parlance that is commonly known as a cheap date.

There's no question that I had found it a bit disconcerting to have my body displayed for Carla's continuing physical education. Reports that I moonlight as a stockingfoot flasher have been greatly exaggerated. Yet I suppose whatever twinge of embarrassment I felt, it was worth it to see Carla restored to her typically bemused self. If that was the price of her smile, then modesty be damned. At least I had learned something: the cure for Carla's blues was my emasculation. The curse of friendship.

ALL SHE SAID WAS "Come on. I want to show you something." She had changed into a pair of pink shorts and a blue work shirt tied in a knot just below her ribs. Her hair was pulled back in a ponytail, her purse was in one hand, her car keys in the other. She headed for the door. I tagged along like an obedient seal in an animal act.

It was a warm day. The sun dangled overhead like a garish chandelier casting light through cut glass. The cerulean sky was as pure as a baby's expectation.

Carla drove slowly. The narrow street snaked around a colony of weathered clapboard houses and through a cluster of abandoned cottages that would have been lamentable to demolish and foolish to restore. The road intersected Front Street and continued eastward several more blocks before ending at Water Lou Street, which ran parallel with the river.

Water Lou Street was dominated by Fruit of the Sea, a large seafood-processing plant. There was also a dive shop, an art gallery, a real estate office, some antique stores, a raw bar restaurant, the Fat Otis Bar, and a marina. Carla parked diagonally alongside the public dock. She arched her back and sighed as if this was the last stop on a tour. She hadn't said word one since we left her father's. Neither had I. It was her call and I was content to wait for my cue.

Carla opened the door to the gray Honda and got out. She walked along the wharf to the river bend. She stood there motionless with her hands stuffed in the back pockets of her shorts. I wandered over beside her and followed her distant gaze. About two hundred yards from the bend you could see where the river flowed into the panorama of Mexico Bay.

"Sea haunt," she said. She closed her eyes and breathed deeply. She turned and looked at me with a raised eyebrow. "That's what my father called it. Sea haunt."

I nodded.

We stared at the bay again, at the scattering of boats anchored in the harbor, listening to the drone of a houseboat passing on the river.

"Sea haunt," she repeated. "He said you can't escape the water." She struggled with a tiny smile. "He used to come down here in the evening. Right here. Where we are now. He'd watch the sun set. Sometimes he'd just stand here for as long as an hour after the sun had gone down. All by himself. He once told me he was contemplating his oneness. That's all he said. I don't know if my father was a spiritual man, Harry. I'm not sure if that's what he meant. I always meant to ask him. But it was one of those questions that there would always be time for—so it could wait. Now my father is dead and I haven't been able to sleep through the night. All those unanswered questions that there would always be time for. What was my father like when he was a little boy? What was his biggest joy in life? What were his fears? Did he still miss my mother after all these years? Was I a disappointment to him?"

I placed a hand on her shoulder. She rested her cheek on it.

"I could always call him," she said, "on those horrible nights when I felt like I was all alone in a big adult world and that I was really still the same little girl I've always been, living in a woman's body. I could call him whenever my heart hurt or my stomach ached. If I was troubled, I could always call him." She was quiet for a long time. She lifted her head and looked at me. "Who do I call now?"

I gently squeezed her shoulder, like I understood. And maybe I did. I didn't think Carla was looking for condolences or reassurance. In her own way she was beginning to celebrate her father's life. I was sure she had already cried, and would cry again, for him. She would also replay over and over a lot of memories, dusting off some long-forgotten ones, and if she was lucky, she would find some of her answers, but never all them and never enough. I too had buried my father with oh so many unasked questions.

Carla stepped up and stood on the edge of the seawall. The sun's reflections bouncing off the water caused her to squint as her eyes searched the river for its mysterious secrets. I didn't say anything. I just watched her for several minutes until her whole body just seemed to sag as if she had been double-crossed by the river.

"Water brings life." It sounded like she was quoting someone.

"Your father?" I said to her back.

She turned to me and nodded. She gestured for me to join her in her private space. I stepped up beside her on the seawall. She lowered her eyes to the water. So did I.

At the base of the bulkhead the rippling water was murky enough to have repelled Narcissus. It was shallow along the wall. The river bottom was strewn with barnacled debris, rusted cans, and jagged rocks.

Carla pointed to water directly below us.

"That's where my father's body was found."

EIGHT

"MY PARENTS were hippies," she said. "I was conceived in a sleeping bag at the Monterey Pop Festival and was born in a yellow farmhouse. Daddy rode a Harley and hummed tunes from *Easy Rider.* Mother rolled tea and had an enchanting smile she took everywhere and shared with everyone. I was raised to believe in the magic of a young girl's soul and the magic of rock and roll. They marched in peace parades, demonstrated at end-the-war rallies, and sat in on save-the-planet smokers. They dropped acid, snorted coke, and drank cheap wine. Recreational users, they claimed. They lived the life. So did I. Mom and me wore flowers in our hair. When I was still in diapers I knew more about the Chicago Seven than I did about the Pokey Little Puppy or the Little Engine That Could. Legend had it my parents helped Abbie Hoffman go underground. It was a seductive lifestyle. Not very productive, but seductive. It only cost me my mother. She was twenty-seven years old. She had a seizure. I think that's what they called it. A reaction to a cocaine overdose. I didn't understand it then and I understand it even less now. She died. I know that. Such a tragic waste. I was eight years old. In many ways, so was my father. You know what he did? He traded his Harley for a Day-Glo orange VW minibus. We spent the next six weeks, just me and him, spreading Mom's ashes in the Pacific Ocean, the Grand Canyon, the Atlantic Ocean, and finally the Gulf of Mexico. That was in Panama City Beach. Dad's sister lives there. We stayed at Aunt JoAnn's for about a month. Every day my father would go to the beach and walk for hours. Just walk and look at the water. That's all he did until one morning after breakfast he announced that he was going fishing. I waited for Daddy to come back and get me. And I waited. And waited. Aunt JoAnn raised me. I never knew it took so long to go fishing.''

Carla Meadows was sitting across from me in a booth at Dunn's Raw Bar restaurant. A tray of oysters on the half shell was on the table between us. I refilled our glasses with beer from a pitcher.

"I need to change the subject," Carla said, doctoring an oyster with hot sauce. "Talk to me, Harry, about other things, something, anything."

"Anything?"

"Anything. Just don't burst out into a song."

"You've heard me sing?"

"I've heard what you call singing."

"You're a tough audience, Carla."

"Yeah, well, it's been a tough couple..." She let it trail off.

I nodded. I slopped down a raw one and said, "Did you ever see a snake fight?"

She looked questioningly at me. "You mean two snakes fighting each other?"

"Yeah. It's the strangest thing you'll ever see. What happens is when two snakes start to fight they go after each other's tail. They each grab the other's tail in their mouth and slowly begin to swallow one another until pretty soon they completely disappear." I shoveled down another oyster.

Carla was staring at me.

"What?" I said. "You think I'm making this up?"

She said, "Are you on medication, Harry?"

"No."

Carla nodded knowingly, her diagnosis confirmed.

Our waiter returned.

"Have we pondered yet?" he said, showcasing the personality of a wicked queen recently jilted by seven dwarfs. He was royally attired in regal white painter's coveralls, a pink-

and-black bowling shirt, and an orange-and-black San Francisco Giants baseball cap that he wore, not backwards, but sideways. What at first looked like a dragonfly sucking on his earlobe turned out to be three wire-and-topaz dangling earrings, probably representing an ancient MTV fertility symbol. Fashions from Pee Wee's Playhouse.

I picked up the menu. "I think so."

The waiter rolled his eyes. "So share with me. What's the big decision?"

I looked at Carla. "The grouper sandwich?"

She nodded.

"Two grouper sandwiches," I said.

"Another pitcher of beer," Carla added.

The waiter disappeared.

Carla leaned forward, resting her elbows on the table and cradling her chin on her hands.

"Did you find the money?" she asked.

Whatever expression my face registered, it answered Carla's question.

She laughed. "Were you going to ask me about it?"

"I don't know," I admitted.

"Why not? You think I did something wrong?"

I shrugged.

Her eyes flashed. Stunned, she said, "You do. You think I've done something illegal. You didn't ask me about the money because you thought I'd lie to you."

Of course, that is exactly what I thought. I said, "Why, Carla, whatever do you mean?"

"Tell me what you were thinking."

Buying time, I shook my head slowly and mumbled, "Carla, you're going to drive me into therapy."

"So? You love therapy. Now quit stalling. What's your problem? Why didn't you ask me about the money?"

"Damn, Carla. It's a little awkward to tell someone that you were traipsing through her apartment when she wasn't there and, oh by the way, guess what I found while rummaging through your drawers.''

Carla sat back. ''That's it?'' she said. ''For God's sake, I know you had to go through my apartment so you could track me here. Nick explained that to me. It's not like you were snooping or getting kinky with my diaphragm.'' She sipped her beer and added playfully, ''Is it?''

''Oh. Is that what that was?''

''You're getting strange, Harry.''

On the subject of strange, the waiter approached the table.

''I insist on doing all my own stunts,'' he said, placing a full pitcher of beer on the table.

''Thanks,'' Carla said.

''How sweet,'' the waiter declared. He waved a hand above his head and sang, ''The hills are alive with the sound of gratitude.'' He picked up the tray with empty oyster shells. ''And you wonder why I love this job?'' He whirled and sashayed away like he had just won the Academy Award for best performance by a fascist bowler in a Fellini film.

I topped off our glasses. ''Ready to talk?''

Carla nodded. ''Sure.''

''Tell me about the money.''

She glanced away and then back. ''I'm not sure that I can.''

''Try. How did it get in your drawer?''

''I put it there.''

''And where did you get it?''

''My father. He called me last Thursday night. About nine-thirty. I remember that because *Seinfeld* had just ended. There was nothing out of the ordinary about the call. I'd hear from him every couple months. We talked about typical father-daughter stuff. He asked if I had gotten the brakes fixed on my car, if I had given more thought to going back to school, if I needed anything. That was the gist of the conversation. Except at the end he said, 'I've sent you a package. Call me when you get it.' That's all he said about it, didn't allude to what was in it. We said our good-byes. Saturday evening when I got home from work the package was waiting for me. It was the money. Nothing else. No note, no explanation."

"You called your father?"

Carla stared at me for a long time and slowly nodded. "There was no answer. I kept calling until I went to bed. I never got hold of him. Sunday Aunt JoAnn called and told me he was dead."

"When did he die?"

"Good question." She gazed out the window and watched a pickup truck pulling a trailered motorboat drive by. Carla looked at me. "According to the death certificate, which I have not seen, my father died around five o'clock Thursday afternoon." Speaking each word calmly and deliberately, she said, "In other words, Harry, he had already been dead almost four and a half hours when he called me."

"Who told you that was the time of death?"

"A grief counselor," she said, her voice heavy with sarcasm. "That's what they call themselves these days."

"Who?"

"Salesmen. I don't know. Those people at the funeral home, if that's what it is. Wait till you see this place. You're not going to believe it, Harry. I've never seen anything like it."

"Who had the grouper sandwich?" asked the waiter. He was holding two grouper sandwiches. "Wait. Now I remember." He put the sandwiches down in front of us. "What was I thinking?" He pivoted and was gone.

The bread and the fish were fresh. The sauce tasted like rug shampoo. Whoever said two out of three ain't bad had never tried the grouper sandwich at Dunn's Raw Bar restaurant.

I asked Carla if she had mentioned the time discrepancy to anyone.

She made a face and looked at the sandwich. I don't think she liked the sauce either. "Just to the senile medical examiner and the brain-dead police department. They are 'checking it out.'"

"No doubt." I scraped the rug shampoo off the fish. "What about yesterday? How did you end up at the motel?"

Carla downed a healthy swig of beer. She leaned forward, resting her forearms on the table. "Big picture or little picture?" she asked.

"Big picture."

She hesitated as if she was giving that some thought. She picked a potato chip off the plate and nibbled on it. "I'm trying to figure out where to start."

I suggested she start with her aunt's phone call on Sunday.

She nodded. "Well, after I talked to her, I called you to let you know I needed the time off."

"Back up. Tell me about the phone call with your aunt. What exactly did she say to you?"

Carla shook her head. "Other than 'I have bad news. Your father is dead,' I don't know. I was shocked. I mean it was totally unexpected. I had just spoken to him a couple days ago. I had gotten the package from him the night before."

"She didn't tell you how he died?"

"I don't know. She may have. Harry, all I remember is I kept hearing her words, 'Your father is dead.' Nothing else seemed to matter or register. Like I said, I was in shock. I don't even remember what I said to you. I know I called you, but that's all."

"Okay. What next?"

"I packed some things and drove all day. When I got in Sunday night there was nothing for me to do. It was late. Everything was closed. I drove to my father's. I couldn't sleep. So I just cleaned the place for him."

"Where did you get the key?"

"What key?"

"For your father's place."

"No key. No locks. Ever the hippie, Dad once told me if

there were poor souls so bad off they had to steal, then my father said they were worse off than he and were welcome to anything in his home."

I emptied the second pitcher of beer in our glasses and said, "I think Father Shifty would say your dad was a spiritual man."

Carla smiled. "Thank you," she said softly.

The waiter from *Fantasy Island* landed. "How we doin'?" We said fine.

"I'm so excited I could burst," he squeaked gleefully. He couldn't have been more pleased if we had tipped him with a gift certificate for Victor's Secret. Off he went.

Without prompting, Carla continued, "First thing yesterday morning, the phone rang at my father's. I thought maybe it was my aunt JoAnn calling. No, it was the grief counselor from the funeral home. He asked who I was and I told him. He offered his condolences and then tried to sell me some snake oil," she said cynically. "Almost as bad. He wanted to know if I wanted to select an urn for my father's ashes. He even offered to make a house call, bring a catalog and some samples. I told him that I hadn't really decided on funeral arrangements yet. He said that had already been decided. Then he tells me that my father's body had already been cremated."

I frowned. "Without family authorization?"

"That's exactly what I said. He tells me it was authorized by a Mrs. Cairns. Aunt JoAnn," she explained. "I said, 'This seems awfully quick. What's the rush?' 'No rush,' he said. 'It's all normal.' That's when he tells me my father had died Thursday afternoon at about five o'clock. 'According to who,' I said. 'According to the death certificate,' he says. 'Is that right,' I said, 'and what does the death certificate state the cause of death as?' He mumbled something about natural causes and hung up."

"I'd get a second opinion."

"Yeah, well it did leave me with some natural questions. I

called the police station. Some guy named Wesley. I told Wesley who I was and that my father, Charlie Meadows, had died. Wesley says he knows all about it. I asked him if he knew how Dad had died. Wesley says, 'Who knows, probably a heart attack. Natural causes.' Then I tell Wesley about my problem with the time of death on the death certificate and I tell him why. Wesley says he don't know nothing about that. He didn't sign any death certificate. 'I didn't say you did,' I reassure him. But that there is something wrong with it. 'You're just upset,' he tells me and that it's normal for women to get hysterical when their daddies die. In no uncertain terms I inform him that I'm not hysterical but I am surely getting pissed. 'Take it up with Dr. Galen,' he says, and gives me a phone number.''

"The medical examiner?"

"That's debatable. I called Dr. Galen. I identified myself. I explain to him there was a problem with the time of death. He says, 'Oh.' That's all he says after my long explanation as to why I think he got the time of death wrong. And I said, 'No shit, oh.' He hemmed and hawed and then he says, 'Well, that was just an estimated time of death.' He goes on to tell me that it's hard to set the time of death when the body has been in the water for a period of time. I'm thinking, water? What is he talking about? Dad died of a heart attack. What water? So I asked him, 'Is that how Dad died, from drowning?' 'Well, maybe,' he says.''

I stared at her and blinked. "Maybe?"

She nodded, her eyes shining with anger as she remembered. "Yeah. Get this. He said it was either accidental drowning or a blow to the head from the fall that killed him. 'Don't you know!' I yelled at him. I think I scared him. He said he'd have to call me back and hung up.''

She picked up her grouper sandwich and started to take a bite but stopped. She put the sandwich down and said, "Anyway, after Dr. Galen hung up on me, I called the police station back. I told Wesley that there were more problems. That there seemed to be some question now about how Dad had died. He tells me he doesn't want to hear about it because there is nothing he can do. I said, 'Who should I talk to?' He said, 'Try the chief, he'll be back tomorrow.' Which would be today.''

No wonder Carla was upset.

"Let me make sure I've got this right," I said. "The medical examiner isn't sure of the time or the cause of death and the body has already been cremated. Do I understand you, Carla?"

"You understand."

I scratched my head in amazement. "That's just not right. Something is wrong."

"Tell me about it. And that's only part of it, Harry. I still haven't told you about the giant albino that tried to attack me."

NINE

AFTER TALKING to the police the second time, Carla hung up and stared in disbelief at the phone for the better part of a minute. After four calls—one from the grief counselor, two to the police station, and one to Dr. Galen—she was no closer to knowing how or when her father had died. She shut her eyes and inhaled deeply. She could feel the tightness in her chest weaken as the frustration began to drain. Carla immediately rejected the rush of helplessness that surged through her. She would not wimp out. She clinched her fists as rage began to burn satisfyingly within. She decided she was going to kick ass.

It took Carla twenty minutes to shower, dress, and drive into Angel's Cove.

The old brick building had once been a gymnasium. Panels, drywall, dropped ceilings, and petitions had converted it to a city hall, a library, and a little hole-in-the-wall police station. The police force, all three of them, had to go quietly through the biography stacks of the library to get to their locker room. The holding cell had once been an equipment cage. The entrance to the police station was at the rear of the building.

Officer Wesley Butch was alone, sitting at one of the two desks when Carla walked in. Butch was a burly man with a bloated gut that hung over his leather gun belt like a mutant Peruvian avocado. His sandy hair was thin at the temples and spiffily moussed. He wore aviator's sunglasses and a snug uniform that made him look more like the dictator of a small country than a small-town cop. His official attitude matched the look. Officer Butch glanced up and sucked on his menthol cigarette. He blatantly scanned Carla's body and nodded appreciatively as he flashed his predator's smirk.

Carla had been a barmaid long enough to know the type. Wesley Butch: high school jock; favorite video, *Puke, the Movie;* married his high school honey; divorced twelve years later, ten years after the thrill was gone. Carla imagined that Wesley Butch saw himself as a matinee idol, every woman's Hollywood dream man. Sort of a cross between Clint Eastwood and Hugh Hefner. His routine would include a six-pack of beer at night. Fishing a couple times a month with a cousin. Once a week he would go to nurses' night at the neighborhood bar closest to the hospital. So cocksure was Wesley Butch that each nurses' night would be the night that he bagged a nurse, he never left the house without first showering, shaving, greasing his remaining hairs, and dousing his dick with Old Spice. Carla had him pegged.

Wesley Butch leaned forward and rested hands with long reptilian fingers on the desktop. "What kept you?"

Carla sat on the bench across from Butch's desk. "You know who I am?"

"It's a small town. Sorry about your father."

Carla nodded. "Me too."

"Can I do for you?"

"You can renew my faith in the law by finding out how and when my father died."

Wesley Butch laughed. His teeth were tobacco-brown and ulcerated. "It'll be my priority."

Carla eyed him intently. "You think I'm funny?"

"You guessed it."

Carla stood up. She peered down at Officer Butch and said, "For your sake, I hope it's just incompetence and this isn't a cesspool of corruption. Thank you for your valuable time. I'm leaving now so you can use your considerable talents to investigate the source of the stench in here."

Wesley Butch pointed a serpentine finger at Carla. "Hey!" His face was serious. "Do you live here?"

"You know I don't."

"You're damn right you don't. So why would I give a damn whether or not you have faith in the law?" He pronounced faith as if it was a mental disorder. "Where the hell do you get off prancing in here, criticizing this office, and then start giving me orders? Well, yeah, I think that's funny. I'll also tell you something else."

"No doubt."

"It's not funny when a man dies. That is serious business. We take it serious. Even if it is your old man."

Carla shot him an angry look. "Explain that."

"Officially or unofficially?" Butch said smugly.

"Is there a difference?"

He thought about that for a few seconds. "No. No, there's not. You don't want to hear this, lady. Go back where you came from. Remember your father however it is you knew him. Charlie's dead. Nothing else matters. It's over. Nothing is going to change your daddy being dead."

Carla glared at Butch, but Butch didn't say anything. "Tell me," she said.

Butch shrugged. "Have it your way. Go out on the street and look around. You're not going to find anybody mourning Charlie Meadows. Like it or not, officially or unofficially, your loss is Angel's Cove's gain."

Hearing things she did not want to hear, Carla shook her head as if that would make the words go away. "I don't believe you."

"Don't take my word for it." Wesley Butch folded his arms across his chest, his face impassive.

Carla studied the man's face, the hair growing from his ears, the badge he wore as an accessory to being a bully.

"Anything else you want to know?" Butch said, lifting his sunglasses and perching them on top of his head. "No?" He waved a hand, gesturing her dismissal. "Then have a nice day."

Carla turned to leave, but paused at the door. She turned back and looked into Butch's shallow eyes for a moment. Finally she said, "Where did he die?"

Wesley Butch blew out a long weary breath and nodded. "Come on," he said, rising from the chair. He picked up his hat off the file cabinet. "Just another day of 'Protect and serve,'" he mumbled, intentionally loud enough for Carla to hear.

She said, "I've had better days, too."

Wesley Butch opened the door and was smacked with a bright sunblast.

CARLA SWIRLED the beer in her glass and looked at me. "Wesley's the one who showed me where Dad's body was found."

"Did he tell you when or who found the body?"

"The body," she repeated softly. "Now he's just 'the body.' It's all so cold and clinical."

"I'm sorry, Carla. I—"

She held up a hand. "No, Harry. It's all right. I'm just being maudlin. It's what girls do when their fathers die." She sighed and smiled a little one. "Know how I'm always saying I want to experience it all?"

"Yes."

"I could have passed on this experience." She looked away while she retrieved her thoughts. "Anyway, to answer your question, Wesley didn't tell me anything. He said he didn't know anything. He said he wasn't on duty that night."

"Night?"

Her eyes met mine. "Yes. He did say 'night.'"

"You said you last talked to your father Thursday night about nine-thirty," I said, thinking aloud. "So it could have been later that night."

"Then why wasn't I notified sooner? Why didn't someone call me Friday or Saturday? Why wasn't I told until Sunday?"

The waiter rematerialized next to our booth, almost magically, as if he had been dropped from an off-course intergalactic traveling circus spaceship. "Anything else? A fruit cup? An authentic imitation-crab salad? A cheese sandwich?"

I looked at Carla. She shook her head. I reached for my wallet and asked for the check.

The waiter said, "Dessert?"

"No thanks," I said. "Just the check."

"Key lime pie?" he persisted. "Come, come. Don't deny the urge."

I looked up at him. "I think you are grossly underestimating my urge."

The waiter looked startled. He blinked once, recovered, smiled, and looked up at the ceiling. "God bless him. He's so charming." The waiter left the check and zoomed off to another world.

Carla shifted in her seat. "Something else, Harry. Wesley was right. No one seems to be mourning my father."

"How can you say that?"

SWEATING IN THE SUN next to a depressed woman did not make for a happy Wesley Butch. This was wasted time and in no way moved him closer to achieving his ultimate goal in law enforcement: *The Wesley Butch Show*. One of those truth-enhanced action police shows on television, the ones with real cops. There were more pressing matters that needed to be attended to, though Wesley couldn't think of any at the moment, but he did know that if he was ever going to be on TV, it was going to be from kicking down doors and not playing nurse-maid to some boo-hoo woman whose father had gone to meet his maker. Wesley had fullfilled his obligation, he had done his duty. He had shown the woman where Charlie's body had been discovered. That was as much as he knew and more than he wanted to know. He didn't know who had found it or when it was found. So it was pointless for Wesley Butch to get involved in a round of twenty questions. The woman could wait for the chief to get back. Let the hot-shot chief answer her questions. Wesley Butch left the woman standing alone on the wharf.

Carla hardly noticed she had been abandoned, her mind occupied with an onrush of snapshot images that appeared to flash across the vista of cloud swirls above the open bay. Carla saw her father through the years as he slowly metamorphosed from a young hippie daddy to a young grieving widower to a lost soul to a Hemingwayesque fisherman.

The reverie of the fisherman's daughter was broken by the squawking of a trio of sea gulls gliding over the quay.

Carla emerged from her thoughts hungry. It occurred to her she hadn't eaten anything for almost a day and a half. And even that meal she hadn't finished. She was having breakfast Sunday, reading the morning newspaper when her aunt JoAnn called with the news. Carla threw some things in the car and drove straight through, stopping only for gas. Maybe that explained her light-headedness.

The lunch crowd had thinned out by the time Carla walked into Another Restaurant. The green cinder block walls, the yellowed checkerboard linoleum floor, the long tables with backless benches, the rows of bright overhead fluorescent lights, the aroma of fried fish, even the fat guy wiping gravy off his plate with a slice of bread—it all reminded Carla of her junior high school cafeteria. All of it except the television set perched above the door to the kitchen. Jimmy Swaggart, his face streaked with tears, filled the screen with his annual Forgive-Me-I-Repent Cryathon to raise money for his God-given weaknesses. At least the volume had been turned down. Praise the Lord.

All the locals watched Carla as she scanned the room for a friendly face. She didn't see one. She took a seat at one of the small tables for two along the wall. She perused a menu and felt the eyes of the universe gazing at her. Carla turned and looked right into the eyes of one of the gawkers. He cringed when she caught him staring, almost like she had just screamed "Boo!" In a way it was almost funny how the man flinched, jumped up, and scurried out of the restaurant, as if he was on his way to warn the town marshal that a notorious gunfighter had just gotten off the noon stage from Tombstone. In her peripheral vision Carla could see heads huddling. She heard murmuring whispers. As Wesley Butch had said, it was a small town. A place where nobody knew her name and everyone knew her business.

A waitress wiped down Carla's table and set it up with a paper place mat and utensils. It broke the spell. The local citizenry shifted their attention back to cups of bitter coffee and tales about how the winner of this year's Miss Bayou Mobile Home Beauty Contest had really won. Carla ordered a BLT.

Dressed in grease-smeared khakis, the squinty-eyed old man at the counter glared at Carla as she ate the sandwich. Twice she caught him looking at her. Both times he stared back defiantly until Carla looked away. The third time she stared back, suddenly fascinated by his speckled skin and his wilted, sagging cheeks, which hung like sacks of quivering gelatin. Or else, she thought, jellyfish were sucking on his face; the thought made Carla smile. The man's face puckered with confusion. What was so funny? He broke the stare-down by patting the back of his neck with a napkin while pivoting the stool around.

The first hint that she had company was an odor that smelled like yesterday's ashtray. Carla glanced up. The old man had slid off his stool and was standing next to her table.

"You're Charlie's girl." It wasn't a question. "Been expecting you." He had the raspy voice of someone who had smoked too many cigarettes.

"And you," Carla said, "you must be the welcome wagon."

The sour old man thought about that and shook his head. His jowls flapped back and forth like the flippers of a spastic dolphin. "Don't expect any welcome wagon," he grunted.

Carla smiled. "Anything else I shouldn't be expecting?"

The man hesitated. "Don't expect people to go out of their way for you."

"Really? I always heard Angel's Cove was a friendly place."

"It is." The man forced a smile. "Only you don't have any friends here."

Carla returned the smile. "I'm starting to appreciate that," she said pleasantly.

I SAID, "That sounds like Manning."

Carla tilted her head. "Friend of yours?"

"Well, we're not best friends," I replied. "I met him this morning." I told Carla about my encounter with Manning when I stopped at The Other Restaurant to get directions to her father's home. "Manning cooled considerably when I told him I was your friend. He thought we, me and you, ought to get out of Dodge."

Carla popped a potato chip in her mouth. "I don't get it, Harry. My father lived here for years. He never bothered anyone and as far as I know no one bothered him. Granted, he was something of a loner, but it was always live and let live with him. With the possible exception of Father Shifty, Dad was the least judgmental person I've known. He was trusting to an almost Pollyanna flaw. He wasn't the kind of person to ask for anything. He would loan money, but never borrow it. And even the loans were more gifts. So I don't understand why no one is sorry that he is dead. Why did everyone turn against him?"

"Manning is not everyone, Carla. He's only one man."

"What about Wesley? He's the one who told me that no one was mourning, that Angel's Cove was better off."

"Wesley is not Angel's Cove. He's only one man."

"That's the point. One man plus one man plus another man adds up."

"One man and one man and another equals a whole town? That's some math, Carla."

"A little goes a long way."

"Yeah, well, I think you're stretching it too far."

Carla shrugged. "Maybe."

I paid the tab before the waiter had time for a return engagement. As I started to follow Carla out the door of Dunn's Raw Bar I heard a voice call out, "Toodle-loo!"

WE WALKED ALONG Water Lou Street. Carla stopped in front of an antiques store. She scanned the window and pointed to something. Whatever she said was drowned out by the shrill sound of an emergency vehicle's siren. We turned in time to see a patrol car speed past, its blue lights flashing.

"There goes Wesley," Carla said.

The patrol car made a sharp turn just beyond us. It looped around the boat ramp parking lot and screeched to a tire-smoking stop. The car door flung open. A beefy uniformed officer jumped out. He was holding a shotgun. Immediately he went into a combat crouch and aimed the weapon at nothing threatening that I could see. He held that pose for almost ten seconds before yelling, "Cut!"

Carla looked uncomprehendingly at me. "What is going on?"

That was about the time I noticed a second police officer, eight to ten yards away. He was straddling an empty boat trailer and holding a video camera. He had recorded Wesley's dramatic arrival.

"Over there," I said. I pointed to the other officer. He was much younger than Wesley and not much older than a high school senior. His uniform hung baggy over his lanky frame and his hat was low over white sidewalls.

Carla looked at him and froze. She gripped my arm and squeezed tightly. I searched her face. Something had startled her.

"Carla?" I said.

"That's him. He's the one I saw in the house. The one who hung the cat."

TEN

WE SAT ON A WOODEN BENCH and watched a tug and barge disappear around the river bend.

I said, "Are you sure that police officer was the one you saw in the house?"

She nodded yes, but said, "No."

"That helps."

"I know. It's frustrating for me, too." Carla balanced her feet on the edge of the bench. She hugged her legs and cradled her chin between her knees. She peered across the river and said, "Yesterday was so strange and it kept getting weirder as the day went on. After lunch I thought I'd better see about funeral arrangements. I went back to the house and called Aunt JoAnn, to coordinate with her. She didn't answer and I couldn't remember the name of the gift shop she owns. I also drew a blank on the funeral home. So I got out the phone book, made a couple calls, and found the one that had Dad. They gave me directions. Before I left I decided to rest for a few minutes. It had been a restless night and my eyes were starting to burn. I didn't realize just how tired I was until I sat down. I think I was asleep before I even closed my eyes."

Carla said she woke up about four-thirty, still sitting in the chair. She freshened up before driving to the funeral home.

On the phone Carla had been instructed to head west on the two-lane coastal highway. Following those directions, she spotted a crisscross of steel girders, which she assumed was the embryo for another beachfront condominium until a parked hearse next to the construction site trailer caught her attention. She pumped on the brakes and turned off onto a gravel driveway.

She stopped in front of a large plywood sign that read:

The Lighthouse Mortuary—Future home of the
Lighthouse Mausoleums and Memorial Boardwalk. Honor
thyself and family with the ultimate tribute—an everlasting
memorial—now at preconstruction prices.

The smaller print invited readers to stroll the magnificent memorial boardwalk, upon its completion, through man-made dunes surrounded by sea oats and sea grapes. There was an artist's conception of a Phase I and a Phase II. Phase I was a seven-story mausoleum and Phase II a four-hundred-foot, forty-story mausoleum with two hundred and fifty thousand vaults and a million urn niches. The Lighthouse Mortuary featured its own chapel and on-premises crematorium. Below all the gibberish was a map to the Lighthouse Mortuary, located behind the construction and overlooking the Gulf of Mexico. Prime waterfront real estate was being transformed into eternal vacation shelf spaces for the dead. It had a certain style, even for Florida.

The Lighthouse Mortuary was an old converted seaside Victorian house that would have been a worthy candidate for the National Register of Historic Places. As Carla pulled up, the front door opened and a man walked out as if he could smell a commission with his nose tied behind his back. He had silver hair and wore a tailored gray suit that would have worn well in a Lexus showroom. His shoes shined, his eyes glistened, his face offered professional condolences. He greeted Carla with a friendly handshake. He spoke slowly as he assured her he would do all he could to help her.

Carla introduced herself as Charlie Meadows's daughter.

"Yes. Mr. Meadows is with us. I'm Howard Ashby. Shall we go inside?"

They walked up the small flight of stairs to the entrance. Ashby held the door open for Carla and said, "I empathize with your loss. It was the passing of my father that inspired me to answer the sacred call to serve others in their time of bereavement.''

The front parlor was done in a gold-and-white color scheme with thick wall-to-wall gold carpet. The scent of fresh carnations, commingled with the musty odor of old leather, lingered in the room.

"We'll go to my office," Ashby said, "and complete the vital-statistics form. Then we can visit the selection room, where I think you'll be pleased with our urn display. There's quite a variety of themes to choose from: frontier America, presidential, patriotic, colonial, modern, futuristic, favorite Grecian, and urns shaped like classic cars. Naturally, all urns are designed for eternal preservation of the cremains and come with a warranty. Rest assured, Miss Meadows, our complete service is at your disposal.''

Howard Ashby led Carla to an archway to the business offices. He explained that the "complete service" included all sorts of entitlements like obits and a flag, "if Mr. Meadows was a vet.'' There was something about a slumber room and other benefits Carla didn't hear. It was that word. Cremains. Her father was no more. No more Charlie Meadows. Now he was cremains—ashes, just like Mom. Nothing to kiss goodbye. She stopped under the archway and leaned against it. Her legs were suddenly weak, her stomach queasy, her head fuzzy.

"Mr. Ashby," she said.

Howard Ashby turned to Carla.

"I can't do this now." Her voice cracked.

Ashby looked at his watch and nodded. "It doesn't have to be now."

Carla left the mortuary complex having resolved nothing more than increasing her cargo of obligatory guilt, while simultaneously feeling as if her sense of perspective had finally begun to unravel. The whole experience, ever since she had heard her father had died, had been—not so much unreal as surreal. That was it. Surreal. It was like she was living in a Dali painting.

She had driven about a mile when she spotted a shaded picnic area. She pulled off the highway and parked on a bed of pine needles. Carla sat back in the car and gazed past the trees at the waning late-afternoon sun. A west wind swept fresh air and memories through the open windows. Carla remembered her father's ritual of walking on the beach every day after his wife had died. She got out of the car and walked down to the shoreline. She said softly, "Walk with me, Dad."

A stroll on the beach. It was more than a sentimental tug. It was a good idea.

"I GUESS I walked for about an hour," Carla said. "God, it was so peaceful. I was all alone, like having a piece of the world all to myself. There were no muscle heads in Speedos trying to hit on me, no silicone boobs in bikinis wanting to compete." She paused, then laughed.

"What?" I said.

She held her thumb and finger an inch apart. "I came this close to peeling off all my clothes. The water looked so inviting, I was ready to go skinny-dipping. That's how private my little world seemed. Fortunately, I looked around first and saw someone else walking on the beach a couple hundred yards away. So I thought better of it and decided to get dinner instead."

I glanced at Carla. She was staring at the river, her look distant. I sat quietly beside her though she was faraway. I was all too familiar with the demons Carla would have to grapple with. Pieces of my heart were buried in several graves. Still, despite all my experience, I felt incompetent. I didn't know how to fix Carla. I had never even learned how to fix myself. So I sat there and waited.

"Clam chowder," she said finally. "I stopped at that rundown raw bar on the way to my father's place and picked up some clam chowder to go. Drove home, went in the back door to the kitchen. I sat down and had a bowl. While I was eating I started thinking about everything that Dr. Galen and Officer Butch had said. I knew I was going to need more time off from work. That's when I called you. It was while I was on the phone I started hearing noises, like it was coming from outside. I looked up and saw someone going from the living room into the bedroom.''

''The cop?''

Carla shrugged. ''I think so. I'm not sure. He was a tall skinny man with baggy pants. His hair stood up straight like bristles on a paintbrush. Maybe if I saw that police officer with his hat off. I'm just not sure.''

''All right. What happened after you saw him walk into the bedroom?''

She shuddered. ''I saw the cat hanging from the ceiling fan. I hung up the phone and ran out the back door into the woods. Right away I realized I had left my purse in the kitchen. My car keys were in it. I was stuck. I decided to wait until whoever was in there left. But I didn't see any other car. I'm not sure how he got there. I ended up waiting until dark. I never saw anybody leave, but no lights were turned on in the house either. I assumed he had left. I went back to the house, in the back door, and turned on the kitchen light. Someone else was sitting at the table. He jumped up and I ran.''

''It wasn't the same guy?''

''No. Not even close. This was one about seven feet tall and had long stringy white hair.''

''The giant albino,'' I said.

Carla nodded. ''He was young, Harry. It wasn't an old man.''

''He attacked you?''

''I didn't give him time. I ran back into the woods. I heard him coming after me, but I didn't look back or stop to ask if his intentions were honorable.''

''Don't blame you. Then what?''

"About two hours later I stumbled upon the First Date Motel, you came to my rescue, and the rest is history."

I said, "Let's back up. When you were walking on the beach, you said you saw someone else. What did they look like?"

"I don't know. Too far away."

"Man or woman?"

"I didn't notice. All I could really see was a silhouette against the sky. I wasn't paying that much attention."

"What about when you went back to your car in the picnic area? Was there another car parked there?"

Carla hesitated for a moment. "Yeah. I think there was. Yes. Now that you mention it, there was another car."

"Was it a little blue BMW?"

"I don't know. Why are you asking me all these questions about whether it was a man or a woman on the beach or what kind of car was there? Why are you asking me about little blue BMWs?"

"Well, that's because whoever has been following us all day is driving a little blue BMW."

ELEVEN

NICK ANSWERED on the first ring. "Sand Bar."

I said, "It's me."

"Is Carla all right?"

"She's fine."

"Where are you?"

"Her father's place."

I could hear him breathing into the phone. "There a reason you didn't call sooner?"

"Yeah. I fell asleep soaking in a public bathtub."

Nick didn't say anything. A very loud silence. After a three count I said, "Are you taking notes?"

Nothing.

"Nick, you're right," I said. "I should have called sooner. I'm sorry."

He grunted. "When you coming back?"

"That's the thing. I'm not sure. It could be a day, two or three. I don't know. You might want to check with Stacey Shore, see if she can help out behind the bar in the evenings. She usually closes her bookstore around five, five-thirty. There's also Irma. She can help out during the day. Al's run the bike shop by himself before. If you get in a real bind, ask Father Shifty."

"Yeah, yeah. Don't worry about the Sand Bar. Just tell me what's going on."

I told Nick the money I had found at Carla's apartment had been sent to her by her father without any note or explanation shortly before he died.

"How did her father die?"

I said, "It depends on who you ask. So far the choices have

been natural causes, a heart attack, drowning, or blow to the head from the fall. Her father's body was found along a riverbank, next to a seawall. There also seems to be as much confusion about the time of death as there is the cause. Carla was told the time of death was listed as five p.m. Thursday. Only Carla spoke to her father on the phone Thursday evening around nine-thirty.''

"The autopsy report will clear all that up."

"Ah, there's the rub," I said. "The body has already been cremated."

"Very suspicious."

"You got that right. Let me tell you the rest." I told Nick about the cat hanging from the ceiling fan, which may have been hanged by a local police officer; about the giant albino that scared Carla into the woods; about the little blue BMW that had been following us; about the apparent lack of sympathy in the community for the recently departed Charlie Meadows. "And then," I said, "when we get back here Carla checks her father's mail and finds a statement for estimated charges from the funeral home for nearly ten thousand dollars."

"Ten thousand? For what?"

HOWARD ASHBY theatrically plucked a tissue from the box on his desk as if he was pulling a rabbit from a hat. He wiped his glasses with a slow and efficient circular motion like it was a practiced art. He cleared his throat and put on his bifocals. Squinty-eyed, he perused the statement Carla had received in the mail.

"This would be the estimated charges." Howard Ashby hesitated a moment before adding, "To date."

"To date," Carla repeated. "You mean it could go higher?"

Ashby glanced at me, then Carla. "Yes."

I said, "That's a pretty exorbitant estimate, to date, wouldn't you agree?"

Ashby frowned. "I think not. Actually, it's quite reasonable," he said in a voice that sounded something akin to rehearsed sincerity. "Understand, the Lighthouse is more than just a funeral home. We provide the complete service—which begins with the removal of the decedent to the funeral home and concludes with final interment. The Lighthouse arranges and provides everything. There will be no salesmen from the allied industries bothering the family."

"And tell us," I said, "what would these allied industries be?"

He looked heavenward as if the answer was obvious. "Vault makers, monument manufacturers, crematorium and cemetery sales representatives—all of that is provided at the Lighthouse, including urns and coffins. If Miss Meadows were required to deal with the allied industries separately, she would find her total costs much higher."

I suppressed my gratitude and said, "No matter how you bill it, you still end up burying the wrong person."

Howard Ashby looked startled. "How so?"

"You're burying the living in debt."

"Frankly, Mr. Rice, that is not my concern. I am a registered memorial counselor and a certified grief therapist. My interest is helping the bereaved through their time of crisis; to assist them when they finally confront the moment of truth that the death of a loved one has indeed occurred; to aid them with the healing process, through their mourning and grieving. Some things transcend money, Mr. Rice," he said with all the spontaneity of a recorded message in an airport terminal. "In fact, it is my experience that in times of death, incurring a debt may actually be helpful. Payments often provide comfort by serving as symbolic reminders of the family's everlasting affection for their loved one."

"I see. The more severe the payment, the greater the love?" I said.

"The Lighthouse offers a variety of attractive installment plans."

"You still haven't answered my question," Carla said, her tone impatient. "What am I being charged for, Mr. Ashby?"

Howard Ashby regarded her with an annoyingly solemn expression. "There will be an itemized description on the final statement."

"Will there be an extra charge for that?" I asked.

Carla ignored me and pressed on. "Can you at least give me an idea of what the charges are for? Surely there must be a price list."

Howard Ashby patronizingly shook his head. "It doesn't work that way, Miss Meadows. No two funerals are ever identical. Each service is as unique as the individual it pays homage to. The attendant needs and requirements of a funeral are as different as the family that arranges them. There are no stock funeral services. We would not think of dictating to a family how to memorialize their loved one. It just isn't done. Memorialization is the family's final opportunity to express their love with an enduring tribute, a hallowed testimony to the human spirit. A price list, you ask. No. There is no price list for the rites of transition, for the pageantry of the ceremony. How do you place a price tag on a family's devotion?"

"Some things transcend money, Carla," I added.

Ashby grimaced. His face looked like he was about to lay an egg.

"It seems to me, Mr. Ashby, that the Lighthouse has indeed placed a price tag on my family's devotion," Carla said in a clear and precise delivery. "Now you tell me, just how did they put a ten-thousand-dollar price tag on our devotion? I'll save you some time. I already know it includes your 'complete service.' What I am asking for is some examples of that so-called service."

Howard Ashby tried to soothe Carla with his impersonation of genuine concern. "Of course," he said in a voice lowered to imply confidentiality, "I am not an accountant, so I can't give you a breakdown of the charges for each individual service."

"I understand that. You've already explained I will be receiving an itemized bill. In the meantime, I would appreciate an idea of what the charges cover."

"A myriad of things," he replied. "Basically the charges cover the services of the funeral director and staff. Labor costs, if you will. There's the removal of the deceased to the facilities. The use of the service vehicle and use of the facilities for preparation and embalming. There's the cost of the actual cremation and the cost of the cremation casket. The use of the chapel for the ceremony. The memorial book, prayer cards, guest register, and acknowledgment cards are included. There's the cost of interment, which includes permits, the bronze memorial marker, the urn niche in the mausoleum, the opening and closing of the niche. Then there are the charges that the Lighthouse has already incurred on the family's behalf. Things like long-distance phone calls, newspaper notices, temporary urn for the cremains."

"Wait a minute," I said. "Back up. You said embalming?"

Ashby faced me. "Yes. That's correct."

"Why would the body be embalmed if it was going to be cremated?"

"Embalming is a standard precaution," he explained.

"Precaution from what? Less profits?"

Ashby bristled. "State law, Mr. Rice, prohibits the cremation of a body within forty-eight hours of the time of death. The body will not keep for two days without embalming or refrigeration. It will begin to decompose. We do not have refrigeration facilities here."

"You're saying that state law requires embalming."

"Yes."

"All right. What's this nonsense about a cremation casket?"

"It's required."

"By who?"

"Regulations."

"Is that so? Whose regulations would that be?"

"Mr. Rice, I'm not going to philosophize or argue with you. I do not pass state laws or regulations. Is there anything else?"

Carla answered. "There is something else, Mr. Ashby. It appears to me that the Lighthouse has dictated just how my family would—what was the word you used? Memorialize?—would memorialize my father. I mean, who gave you the authority to make those decisions? Who selected the cremation casket? Who decided on the bronze marker? What chapel ceremony are you talking about?"

"That still needs to be scheduled," Ashby explained. "Much like you still need to select an urn. We have waited for the family to make those decisions," he said as if that would appease her. "Let me say this, too. There is an implied permission that is bestowed upon a funeral home once you have entrusted your care to them. And that, I might add, is a two-way trust. As I said, the Lighthouse has already experienced out-of-pocket expenses on behalf of your family. Most establishments would not even begin to provide care and service without payment in advance."

Carla smiled politely. "And who entrusted the Lighthouse?"

"Your father's sister."

"May I see the contract?"

Howard Ashby tensed, his solemn expression frozen. "Excuse me?"

"May I see the contract?" Carla repeated.

"Well..." He faltered. "I...I don't have the file in front of me."

"You don't say," I said with mock shock.

Ashby's lip twitched.

Carla crossed her arms. "Who does have The File?"

The lines in Ashby's forehead deepened. "Well, the funeral director did make the arrangements."

"With my aunt?" Carla said.

Ashby nodded. "That's correct."

"You didn't talk to her?"

"No."

"Then you don't know for sure that my aunt did tell the funeral director to cremate my father."

Howard Ashby's eyes narrowed. "Your aunt authorized it," he said firmly.

"How do you know that?"

"Because the body has been cremated," he snapped. "That would not have been done without family approval."

Carla stared at Ashby and considered that for a moment. "Fine," she said. "I guess we need to see the funeral director."

"That's not possible." Ashby shifted his weight in the chair. "The director is not here today."

"Frustrated again," I said, "by a nasty old premature evacuation."

Ashby glared at me. "I find your attitude puerile."

"I'll have to work on that."

"Is that all?"

Carla said, "Just one more thing, Mr. Ashby. What are the business hours here?"

"Monday through Friday, nine to five," he answered. "Saturdays nine to noon, unless there is a service scheduled in the afternoon."

Carla nodded. "Closed on Sundays?"

"Always. Without exception."

"Is that just the funeral home that's closed? What about the gift shop and the crematory and the—"

"Everything is closed," Ashby cut in. "Without exception." He leaned back in his chair. "Anything else?"

Carla looked at me. "Harry?"

"No," I said.

We stood up and walked to the office door. I stopped and looked back at Ashby sitting self-assuredly behind his enormous desk.

"Come on, Howard," I coaxed. "Just between us. You really believe all that stuff you threw at us?"

He eyed me with a contempt usually reserved for the hunter that killed Bambi's mother, before he swiveled his chair and peered out the window.

TWELVE

THE OFFICE of Dr. Sabbath Galen was a small clapboard house with a bright blue pancake house roof. It was probably a ten-minute drive from the Lighthouse "more than just a funeral home" Mortuary, though it took us almost an hour to find it. I would have found it sooner if Carla hadn't waited so damn long before she started nagging me to stop for directions.

Located on the fringe of the business district, two blocks off Front Street, the doctor's office sat on a pocket of freshly mowed grass between an abandoned cinder block fish market and a redbrick building crammed with used furniture and country crafts.

We parked along the curb in front of an auto parts store opposite Dr. Galen's and walked across the street. We climbed the stairs of the front porch. There was a screen door, same color as the roof. I knocked, Carla pressed the bell. As we waited I peeked through the screen door. The front area looked like a typical waiting room. There were two matching camel-back floral upholstered couches, two coffee tables with neat stacks of magazines, several overstuffed chairs, and an oval braided rug on a gleaming oak floor coated with polyurethane.

It was quiet inside, except for the sound of a man singing in a back room: "Then Jesus came like an angel in the night, Praaaiisse the Lord, I saw the Light." His voice was scratchy, like an old record, which lent an air of authenticity to the song. He sang as though he was being accompanied by a celestial bluegrass banjo that only he could hear.

"No more darkness..."

I knocked louder on the door and called, "Hello."

"...no more night." The singing stopped midchorus. Unplugged. "Somebody at the door?" he called back.

I said yes.

"You're a day early," the voice responded.

An old man appeared at the door. He was seventyish, maybe five-four with a barrel chest. He had long ears that sprouted tufts of hair, a scraggly salt-and-pepper beard, hazel eyes that twinkled behind lopsided rimless glasses, and as he opened the door a warm smile bubbled his cheeks. His was a joyous face with the contented look of one who didn't worry about such things as the meaning of life. He wore a paper painter's cap, white coveralls with the pants legs rolled up over scruffed tennis shoes, and a white T-shirt speckled with yellow splotches that matched the color on the paintbrush he carried. A diminutive St. Nick laboring in his workshop.

"Come in," he said, stepping back and ushering us inside. "I hadn't expected anyone today. Nolfa said you were coming tomorrow afternoon."

Carla glanced at me and then asked the little painter what he was talking about.

"Nolfa Pearlee," he said. "The real estate agent? At least I think he said tomorrow. Lord knows I'm getting more forgetful by the day. Ever since I lost my Emily...after fifty-three years." He exhibited a sad smile, lost in a moment of reflection. He shook it off and said, "Of course, Nolfa is operating with a slow leak, too... God bless him. Perhaps he got it wrong." He shrugged. "Anyway, it doesn't matter, Doctor. I'd be happy to show you and Mrs. Melancon around. The rooms are small, but sufficient. Please allow for the mess in the examining room." He held up the paintbrush in way of explanation. "What would you like to see first? How about the lab?" He gestured for us to follow him.

"Hold it," I said.

"Yes?"

"We're not here to see the office."

The painter's brow wrinkled. "What do you mean?"

Carla said, "We want to see Dr. Galen. Is he here?"

He hesitated. "Are you Dr. Melancon?" Talking to me.

I said no.

Carla said, "I asked about Dr. Galen."

The old man nodded slowly, letting his mind work on that for a while.

He said, "I remember... Do you have a problem?"

"Yes, I have a problem."

He stared at Carla for a moment as if he was taking stock, said, "Tell me about it."

Carla smiled, just a little. "I'd rather not."

He glanced at me before saying to Carla, "Perhaps if we were alone."

"No," she said, her voice patient. "I don't want to sound rude, but we would like to see Dr. Galen."

"What for?"

"It's a personal matter. This is his office, isn't it?"

"Why, yes."

"Fine. Is he here?"

The old elf gazed at the paintbrush he was holding, looked down at his coveralls, said, "I'm Dr. Galen. I usually look better than this."

Carla's eyes changed. "You're Dr. Galen?"

"Yes."

I said, "We need to talk. Can we sit?"

Carla and I sat on one couch, Dr. Galen across from us on the other, a coffee table between us. I glanced at the magazines on the table. They were several years old. Dr. Galen smiled at us, his face serene.

"I'm retired," he said, sounding apologetic.

"It doesn't matter. Our health is fine."

"What did you want to see me about?"

"A death certificate," Carla answered. "Charlie Meadows was my father."

Dr. Galen's benign expression wilted until his face looked haggard.

"You signed my father's death certificate?" Carla said.

He looked at her, nodded.

"I was told that the time of death on the certificate is five p.m. Thursday," Carla continued. "That's wrong."

Though he didn't say anything, his lips moved. I'm not a lip reader, but it sure looked like he said "I know." Carla didn't see it.

"I talked to my father on the phone Thursday night around nine-thirty," she said.

Dr. Galen looked to me for help, the way a United Nations delegate might look to a translator. His eyes were dull, like balls of clay. He closed them, his head sagged. The small man seemed to be shrinking before us. With his eyes shut he began to cry.

"Damn it." I heard Carla mutter under her breath. She had come in wanting to kick ass, to despise an incompetent medical examiner. Instead she found herself pitying a lonely old widower.

"Dr. Galen," I said. He raised his eyes to me. "Could we see a copy of the death certificate?"

He wiped his eyes and stared at the floor for a moment. He started to speak, stopped, took a deep breath, and let it out. He glanced up at me. "What?"

"The death certificate," I repeated. "Can we get a copy?"

He looked confused. "Charlie's?"

"Yes."

He stood up, looked at Carla, took a step back, turned, and disappeared down a hall.

"He knows, Harry," Carla said.

"Probably."

"No. Not probably. He knows what he wrote down was not the real time of death. He didn't deny it. My God, I mean you saw how he... Oh, shit! It wasn't supposed to be like this. I didn't know he was going to start crying. I don't want to hurt anyone. I just want to find out what happened to my father. That's all."

"I know."

Carla sat back in the couch. "I don't get it. He's retired. How can he still be the medical examiner?"

"Retired from private practice, I would think. And I would suspect he's only an associate medical examiner."

"What's the difference?"

"The governor appoints district medical examiners who are practicing physicians in pathology. The MEs in turn appoint as many associates as needed. I don't think the associates are required to have any expertise in pathology. I'm not sure about that. In a place as small as Angel's Cove, it wouldn't be hard for someone like Dr. Galen to get lost in the cracks of bureaucracy. I don't know. I hate to say it, but I feel kind of sorry for him."

"Yeah, well, I don't have reptile blood flowing through my veins either. The poor little guy could almost be a poster boy for Alzheimer's. So what do we do now?"

"Go easy. Take a look at the death certificate, see where we go from there."

I noticed a gentle breeze moving through the room. A breeze that wasn't there before. I heard a soft tinkling noise coming from the back.

I said, "Do you hear that?"

Carla nodded. "Yeah. Sounds like wind chimes."

"Son of a bitch."

"What?"

"Wait here."

I got up and followed Dr. Galen's path down the hall, which led to a back door that was wide open. The door emptied on to an overhead porch with dangling chimes moving in the breeze that flowed through the building.

Dr. Galen had flown the coop.

THIRTEEN

"REMEMBER WHAT Howard Ashby said about state law prohibiting a body from being cremated sooner than forty-eight hours from the time of death?" Carla said, buckling her seat belt.

I started the car and said yes.

"That's why he did it, Harry. That's why Dr. Galen falsified the time of death. My father hadn't been dead forty-eight hours when they cremated him."

I pulled the car way from the curb. "Maybe."

"Definitely. Don't you see? It's simple math that even I can do. Look, we know that my father was still alive Thursday night at nine-thirty. Forty-eight hours later is Saturday night. Ashby said the business hours were nine to five Monday through Friday and nine to noon on Saturdays. He said they were closed Sundays, without exception. Monday morning when the funeral home called me, my father had already been cremated. So when did they do it? Friday between nine and five or Saturday nine to noon?"

"Hey, I thought I was the detective."

Carla smiled. I could tell from her grin she was pleased with herself. She said, "I never realized how easy you had it."

"Is that a fact, Ms. Detective? And just how do you plan to prove that?"

She gazed out the window as we drove past a cottage with a sign in front shaped like a playing card with a red hand in place of a red heart. Above the palm it said: ACE OF PSYCHICS.

"I have no idea," Carla finally said. "You?"

"Nope. But I do have another question. When did they get your aunt's authorization? Before or after the cremation?"

We were instantly interrupted by the bursting scream of a siren. I glanced at the rearview mirror. It was filled with flashing blue lights. I eased the car onto the shoulder of the road and put it in park.

"Get out of the car!" barked a bullhorn-amplified voice. "Keep your hands where we can see them! Move it!"

I felt like a fugitive blue-light special at the KafkaMart. Let *The Trial* begin.

ACT ONE: The Arrest.

Carla and I got out of the car.

The police car doors swung open. There were two of them. The big one was aiming a gun at Carla and me. The tall, lanky one was pointing a video camera at his partner.

The one with the gun adjusted his aviator sunglasses. He said, "You ready, Jay-Newton?"

Jay-Newton looked up from the viewfinder. "Whenever you are, Wes."

"Roll it," Wes directed.

"Officer Wesley Butch," Carla said to me.

I nodded. "So I gathered."

"Knock it off," Butch warned.

"That must be the condensed version of 'You have the right to remain silent,'" I said.

Wesley Butch put on his mean look and moved toward us with his Marshal Dillonesque strut.

"Assume the position," he commanded.

"What position is that?" I said.

"Turn around and place your hands on top of the car." His voice was strained.

Carla and I turned around and placed our hands on the hood of the car.

"All right," Lawman Wes snarled, "take two steps back,

keeping your hands on the car. Good. Now spread your feet. Farther apart. More. That's good.''

Spread-eagled against the car, my back vulnerable to shameless probes, I silently prayed there was nothing to that sexual myth about cops and their guns. Something round and hard pressed against my spine.

"Tell me you're not glad to see me, Wesley," I said, unhumorously.

"Shut up, scumbag. Don't move an inch. The gun is cocked. I'm going to pat you down."

Much to my relief, I detected not a scintilla of romantic affection or intimate desire in his tone. It really was his gun.

Wesley Butch frisked me. As his hand wandered into the vicinity of my "concealed weapon," I turned my head to the left and coughed.

"You got a problem?" Wesley said.

"No."

"Keep it up and you will."

He grabbed my shirt collar and yanked me into a standing position.

He said, "Put your hands behind your back and lace your fingers."

He slapped handcuffs on my wrists. With me secure, he turned to Carla.

"All right, Miss, you're next. I'm going to pat you down. Don't move."

Carla stood up straight and faced him.

"Don't even think about it," she said sharply.

Butch stared at Carla without betraying any emotion.

Jay-Newton kept them framed in the camera as he zoomed in on the showdown. Just like in the movies.

After a prolonged silence, Wesley Butch slowly holstered his weapon and hooked his thumbs in the gun belt. His signature pose. He stood that way studying Carla while Jay-Newton got it on tape.

Wesley Butch grinned. "Resisting arrest," he said.

"Arrest?" Carla said. "You're arresting us? Is that what you're doing?"

Butch nodded. "That's what I'm doing."

"For what?"

He shrugged. "Resisting arrest."

"No," Carla said. "Before that. Why did you stop us?"

Butch smiled. "Chief wants to see you."

"You pull us over, aim a gun at us, frisk Harry, and handcuff him because the chief wants to see us? Where the hell did you learn your technique? The *TV Guide* police academy?"

His smile vanished. He didn't bother to reply.

Carla glanced at Jay-Newton.

"Is that still on?" she asked.

Jay-Newton said it was.

Carla looked right into the video camera. "Hi there. I'm Carla Meadows. I am being arrested for resisting arrest when I wasn't being arrested until I was arrested for resisting not being arrested. If that doesn't make sense, then you have a good idea of what it is like to be accosted by Pluto and Goofy with guns."

"That's enough," Butch said. "Turn that off, Jay-Newton. The show's over. All right, let's go. Get in the car."

Carla and I rode in the police car with Officer Wesley Butch. Jay-Newton followed us in Carla's car.

ACT TWO: The Police Station.

The police chief was at his desk rummaging through a scattering of papers. His in-basket was stuffed with files. There was no out-basket. He looked up when we walked through the doors with our police escort. He sat back in his chair, took off his steel-rimmed reading glasses, and rubbed the bridge of his nose. He looked more like an unorganized college professor than he did a police chief. I placed him in his late thirties, early forties. He had a full mustache, a three-day-old beard, curly brown hair, a waterman's tan, and a plaid shirt. His eyes were clear and alert.

He watched as we walked over to the wooden bench, his attention fixed on my handcuffs.

Wesley Butch placed a hand on my shoulder and pushed me down onto the bench. Carla sat beside me.

The chief looked curiously at Wesley. "Well?" he said.

Wesley said, "Charlie Meadows's girl and her friend."

The chief's jaw tightened. "Were the cuffs necessary?"

Wesley Butch shrugged. "You said you wanted to talk to them."

"Do I handcuff you when I talk to you?"

Jay-Newton snickered.

Wesley shot his cameraman an ugly look, then said, "Look, Joe, you weren't there. Under the circumstances I thought it was a reasonable precaution."

"He threaten you?"

"I didn't give him the chance."

The chief nodded. He looked at Jay-Newton. "And you. Did you think it was a reasonable precaution?"

Jay-Newton shrugged. "It was a judgment call."

"I see. What about her? Wouldn't it have been a reasonable precaution to handcuff her, too?"

"Yes, sir," Jay-Newton obediently agreed. "But she wouldn't let us."

"She wouldn't let you," the chief repeated. "I imagine that must have presented quite a dilemma. I certainly wouldn't expect you to handcuff someone who didn't want to be handcuffed. If we did that sort of thing, the next you know we'd be arresting people who didn't want to be arrested."

"She resisted arrest," Butch defensively intervened.

The chief held up a hand and looked at me. "Sir, did you want to be handcuffed?"

I said no.

"No?" He turned back to Butch. "Seems like you made a mistake, Wesley. Take the cuffs off the man. He doesn't want to be handcuffed."

Butch answered with a deadly stare.

The chief smiled for the first time. "That wasn't a request." While my hands were being freed, the chief said, "Jay-Newton, tell me everything that happened. Start at the beginning."

"Be easier to show you," Jay-Newton volunteered. "We taped it."

"And Wesley without a haircut. Where's the video camera?"

"In the car."

"Do me a favor."

"Sir?"

"Get it."

"Yes, sir."

Five minutes later Carla, me, the chief, and the two uniforms were next door seated around a long table in the library conference room viewing the tape of The Arrest.

"Amazing," the chief said when the tape ended. "Your camera work is getting better, Jay-Newton. Never hurts to have another marketable skill to fall back on. Never know when you'll need it." The chief stood up and walked over to the steel rack housing the VCR and the monitor. He ejected the tape and slid the cassette across the table to me. He said, "Might want to show that to a lawyer. Possible lawsuit there for civil rights infringements."

Wesley Butch was left with a stunned expression and a gaping mouth. He couldn't believe what he had just seen.

"Th...that's my tape," he stammered.

The chief shook his head. "Not if it was shot on company time. I've warned you about this before. Wesley, you and Jay-Newton are excused."

Without a hint of protest, Jethro and Li'l Abner left, in search of hog heaven.

The chief walked over to me. I handed him the tape. He nodded and put it in his pocket.

"Let's go back to my office," he said.

ACT THREE: The Q&A.

"It's Carla, isn't it?" the chief said, sitting on the front corner of his desk.

Carla nodded. "Yes. This is my friend Harry Rice."

He shook my hand and introduced himself. "I'm Joe Patti." He took Carla's hand, said, "I'm truly sorry about your father. He and I were fishing buddies. He talked about you a lot." Releasing her hand, he added, "He was very proud of you."

"Thank you," she said.

"Howard Ashby called me. You know him?"

Just like that he switched from personal to official. I was surprised at how quick he had shifted into his down-to-business mode. I don't know if it was a typical police tactic or just his innate sense of urgency and importance, but I liked it.

Yes, we knew Howard Ashby.

"The Lighthouse Mortuary is filing a lien against your father's property."

Carla's eyes narrowed. "Is that why you wanted to see me? Are your strings being pulled by the Lighthouse, Mr. Police Chief?"

Joe Patti said nothing for a moment. I couldn't tell what was going through his mind, but on appearance he didn't seem fazed by Carla's comments. When he finally spoke, it was slow and deliberate.

"No," he confessed. "That is not why I wanted to see you. The truth is I'm stalling. It's difficult for me to approach your father's death with a detached objectivity. Losing Charlie is a weak spot for me, too. I've only been back in Angel's Cove

for a few hours and the shock has not completely worn off.
I'm still a little stunned and I feel kind of awkward having to
question you. I'm not sure if I can do it without upsetting you
any more than you already are.'' His eyes crinkled and his
lips carved a little smile under his mustache. ''It sounds like
I'm still stalling, doesn't it? I do that when I'm unsure, not in
control.'' He leaned slightly forward. ''But don't mistake me
for a bought-and-paid-for hick town cop. I'm going to find out
what happened. That's why I wanted to see you, to get
started.'' He spread his hands. ''Look, no strings.''

Carla hesitated, mulling over some lingering suspicions. She
slowly nodded. ''All right. And you needn't worry about me.
You just put me in my place, quite effectively, without upsetting me.''

''Good. I guess I'm back in control.''

''I guess you are.''

They silently regarded each other while Joe Patti zeroed in
on his first question. Eventually he said, ''Why did you cut
down the kitten without calling this office first?''

Carla and I glanced quizzically at each other.

I asked the chief how he knew about the cat if it hadn't
been reported.

He said, ''Jay-Newton told me.''

''I knew it was him,'' Carla said.

''You saw him?''

''Yes. I was in the kitchen, on the phone. I heard something
and looked in the living room. I saw Jay-Newton walking into
the bedroom after he had hung the cat from the ceiling fan.''

''You actually saw him hang the cat?''

''Well, no. It was already hung by the time I heard the noise
and looked to see what it was.''

''Jay-Newton didn't hang the cat.''

''Who did?''

''I don't know yet. Had you not tampered with a crime
scene, we might have found something tangible to go on.''

I squirmed and said, "If Jay-Newton didn't hang the cat, what was he doing inside the house?"

"He told me he had gone to check on Charlie's house, see if any family had arrived. When he got there he saw the cat hanging through a window. He went in to investigate. I believe him. Jay-Newton is not a lot of things, but he is honest."

Carla said, "He could have knocked first."

"He's also a rookie."

"There's an excuse for everything, isn't there?" Carla shot back, surprising even herself from the look of it.

Joe Patti's eyes expressed puzzlement. "For example?" he said. He leaned back and waited for an explanation.

"For example, the time of death," she said. "How do you explain away that?"

"Is there a discrepancy with the time of death?"

"Only if you call talking to someone on the phone four or five hours after the official time of his death a discrepancy, then yes, there is a discrepancy."

Joe Patti didn't respond immediately. "Anything else?"

Yes, there was something else. There was the uncertainty about the cause of death—the choices being natural causes, "who knows, probably a heart attack," drowning, a blow to the head from the fall, none of the above, or all of the above. No, the cause of death would not be determined by an autopsy. Why? Because the body seems to have been prematurely cremated. Yes, that's right cremated. No, that's not all. There was the disappearing medical examiner.

Dr. Galen?

"Yes," Carla said, "Dr. Galen. We went to his office."

Joe Patti sighed heavily. "I wish you hadn't done that. Well, I'm pretty sure I know where he is. Every time he disappears, I always find him at the same spot. His wife's grave."

He walked around and sat behind his desk, picked up a ballpoint, and made a few notes.

"Anything else?"

Just the giant albino.

For the most part the police chief was a good listener, only interrupted to clarify for his benefit. When Carla and I were done he just nodded and said, "I'll be in touch."

We were unarrested and left without having mentioned the blue BMW that had been following us, nor had we mentioned the money that Carla's father had sent her. I had my reasons.

Curtain.

FOURTEEN

IT SMELLED like it was going to rain when we emerged from the police station. A fat menacing cloud from out of town loomed overhead; a serious sky on official business contemplating its next move. Much of the day's heat had been absorbed by the cloud cover. There was no breeze, the air still as if it was holding its breath in anticipation of a storm.

When we reached the car, Carla said, "I can hear you thinking."

I opened her door. "Get in."

She did.

I walked around to the other side and slid in behind the steering wheel.

"Well?" she said.

"You tell me. What did you think?"

"I feel a little better after talking to the police chief. I like him. What did you think?"

I turned to her. "Someone dies in a place the size of Angel's Cove the way your father did, that's big news amidst the small-town boredom. So why wasn't the chief of police notified sooner? It strikes me as strange that he just learned about your father's death a few hours ago, even if he was away for a long weekend. I can't help but wonder why he wasn't called. Where was he?"

Carla looked at me. "You think my father was murdered, don't you?"

There it was. One of us had finally said what I was sure had been baking in the back of both our minds for some time. Handed a free pass, an uneasy silence pushed its way through the turnstile and settled between us for about a half minute.

"Things aren't always what you think, Carla," I said. "We don't want to assume anything at this point. We need to keep open minds, keep looking around, keep asking questions, gathering facts. If you start speculating too early, you tend to overlook information you need in favor of things you think you need. You never know what information is going to be useful until all the data is in. That's the time to weed out the useless from the useful."

After considering that, she said, "What are we looking for?"

"Motive. See if there was a reason why someone would want to kill him."

"The money?"

"Possibly. But let's not jump to conclusions."

She closed her eyes and cradled her head in the seat headrest. She took a deep breath and let it out. Or maybe it was just a sigh. "Were you ever punished for something you didn't do or feel like someone else was being punished for something you did do?"

"Stop it, Carla."

She opened her eyes and rolled her head toward me.

I said, "You're not responsible."

"No?" She sounded skeptical.

"No."

She shrugged. "Let's not talk about it anymore." She turned away and stared out the window. "Stop at the fish market. I'll cook dinner."

The catch of the day at the Fish Milker's Market was some fleshy gray stuff with a ghoulish name. I had dirty socks that looked more appetizing. We bought grouper, a six-pack of cold beer, potatoes, onions, things that Carla said made a sauce.

THE RAIN BEAT US to the house, but had slackened to a drizzle by the time we parked next to the back door. Typical for the season. A late-afternoon downpour, almost a daily ritual. A quick rain burst and see you again tomorrow at rush hour.

The phone was ringing as we walked in. Carla answered while I put the groceries away in the refrigerator.

"Hello. Oh, hi!" Carla said to me, "It's my aunt JoAnn." Into the phone she said, "Where are you? The hospital! What's wrong? Are you sure? No. That's all right. I don't know. We've been out most of the day; we just walked in the door. My friend Harry. No, nothing like that. I work for him. Yes, that one. JoAnn, I need to ask you something. When did you talk to the funeral home? Right before you called me? That was Sunday morning. Is that the only time you talked to them? Was that the first notification you got about Daddy's death? No one else called you? No. Nothing is wrong. You did give them permission to cremate Daddy, didn't you? Oh, I know. I'm sure he would have, too. That's the same thing we did with Mom."

I grabbed a beer and went into the front room. I looked for something to read, found a copy of the local newspaper, a weekly. It was dated nine days ago.

The front page had yet another story about the fish ban. The gist of the article was that when Florida voted to ban the gill net, the effect was save the fish and annihilate the fishermen and their families. Angel's Cove, it read, could not survive alone on the already-plagued oyster industry. With all the bad publicity about oyster-borne bacteria that could produce severe illness and death in persons with liver disease or weak immune systems, the industry was shaky at best. The article recalled the not-long-ago time when the Panhandle was deluged by back-to-back tropical storms, Alberto and Beryl. The torrential rains had flooded the river that flows into Mexico Bay. The sediment from the river and the runoff from overfilled septics contaminated the bay's water and oyster beds. The state shut down oyster harvesting in the bay for three months until the water samples tested acceptable. While the bay was closed

there was an alternative for the watermen. No more. The net
ban took that away. Now there would be more oystermen and
fewer oysters. If the issue was conservation, it wasn't working.
It just reversed the pattern. The results were the same, according to the article. One life would be restored and another
would be wiped out. "I guess I'm entitled to some protection
now that I'm an endangered species," quoted one fisherman.
Where are our priorities? it asked. That's as far as I got.

"What are you reading?"

I lowered the paper. Carla was standing over me.

"What was that about the hospital?" I said.

She sat in the rocker opposite me. "She spilled a cooler she
was packing for the trip over here. She slipped on some ice,
hurt her back. She's been in the hospital for two days trying
to get hold of me. She even called my apartment. This morning she called the Sand Bar. Nick told her I was here and to
keep trying. She wanted to know about the service. I told her
nothing had been arranged yet."

"What about the cremation?"

"They called her Sunday."

"Who called her?"

"The funeral home. They told her it was Charlie's wish to
be cremated, blah blah blah. She said yes. She was sorry she
hadn't coordinated with me. She said she was stunned, wasn't
thinking, she was upset. I know how that is."

"The funeral home notified her Sunday? Your father supposedly died Thursday and no one in the family was contacted
by the police prior to that?"

"No. The funeral home was her first and only call."

"I'm beginning to detect a circus odor."

Carla smiled. "That's a nice way of putting it." She hesitated a moment. "Harry?" she said, her voice hinting there
was something else.

"Yeah?"

"JoAnn wants me to drive over to Panama City tomorrow

morning for a visit. It's about an hour from here. I think I'd like to go. Get away from here for a day.''

"Go."

"You don't mind?"

"No. It'll be good for both of you." I yawned. "And it will give me a chance to snoop around." I shook my head trying to clear the cobwebs. "I'm bushed. And hungry."

"Me too." She yawned—it is contagious. "Why don't you make dinner for us?"

"Come on, Carla," I protested. "You know cooking for me is too much like a science project."

"Science projects are fun."

"I got an F on mine."

"I'll cook."

While Carla conducted her experiments in the kitchen, I took a nap on the couch.

SHORTLY AFTER ten o'clock that night I grabbed a beer from the refrigerator and walked down to the bayou behind the house. Carla had gone to bed about an hour earlier. Since I had napped almost an hour, I had to force myself to stay up awhile. If I went to bed too soon, I would wake up in the middle of the night. It was almost like having jet lag.

I walked out to the end of the plank dock and sat down next to the sloop, dangling my feet off the side.

The faint moonlight was just enough to cast the cathedral-like reflections of the tall trees on the still and shallow water. Since I was a kid I've always been amazed how three feet of water can reflect the image of a twenty-foot tree. Maybe that's what reflections are—one of life's lessons, to remind us that there are things beyond the eye's perception. Reflections suggest that the water has a hidden depth, not unlike people. As they say, there's more than meets the eye. Just look beyond the cosmetics to see it.

It was a very peaceful sensation, sitting there listening to the night sounds, staring at the water. I felt like I was looking into a bowl of Nature's soul.

I was distracted by the distant hum of a car's engine. It was getting closer.

I got up and walked around to the front of the house. The beams from a car's headlights were coming up the drive.

A van eased into the clearing. A lost tour group of neophyte Zen storytellers seeking directions to the last parable? The van stopped several yards away with me caught in its headlights. The driver cut the engine but left the lights on. Sandal-footed tourists curiously examining the rare third-generation Florida native encountered on the muddy road to serenity. An attraction that even Walt World could not compete with.

The lights were turned off. It was as quiet as one hand clapping. The driver's door swung open. Joe Patti, the police chief, got out.

"Do I remember you?" I said.

He grinned. "You should. I'm the man who won't go away." He pointed at my beer. "You got another one of those?"

"Sure. Come on."

We walked around to the back door. I went in and snatched a couple beers. We took them down to the dock.

He said, "Is she asleep?"

I nodded.

He opened his beer, took a sip. He said, "The giant albino's name is Leonitus. He's Dr. Galen's—what is he? His ward? When Leonitus was about four years old he was found at the bottom of a swimming pool. He was revived but not until after there had been sufficient loss of oxygen to the brain to do some damage. I don't know if retarded is the right word or not. Just say that Leonitus is slow. When he was about six, he discovered matches. He's been fascinated by fire ever since. As a teenager he spent time in a detention home for starting fires. Brush fires, that sort of thing. While he was in the detention home, his parents moved away. No forwarding address. The Galens took him in. Leonitus is a six-foot-ten, twenty-three-year-old kid. He is not an albino. He bleaches his hair because he likes Ric Flair.''

Joe Patti glanced at me to see if I understood.

"The wrestler," I said. "I'm a fan too."

He said, "Several weeks ago Leonitus got his first job. At the Lighthouse Mortuary. In the crematorium."

"The pyromaniac's dream job."

Joe Patti nodded. "Yeah. Anyway, for whatever reason—instructions were not followed or were misunderstood—Charlie's body was cremated before it should have been. And you were right. The time of death was falsified to cover up the error. Dr. Galen was trying to protect Leonitus. And to some extent he was probably trying to protect the Lighthouse since they were the only ones to ever give Leonitus a job. Leonitus has a short attention span. There was no way he was going to make a living on the water. Tomorrow I'm going to call the district medical examiner and recommend she remove Dr. Galen from her list. If necessary, I'll pursue it even further. Charge him with falsifying the document. Perjury."

I shook my head. "I'll talk to Carla. I don't think that will be necessary."

"I appreciate that," he said without looking at me. "All right, the other thing is, since there was no autopsy, whether it was or not, I'm going to investigate this as if it was a homicide."

"We appreciate that."

He studied his beer for a moment. "I did some checking on you, Harry Rice, Hollywood, Florida."

"And what did you find?"

"You're a private investigator."

I nodded. "And this is where you tell me to stay out of your way and not interfere with your investigation."

"No. This is where I ask you to help me with the investigation, which shouldn't be too much of an imposition on you since you've already started without me.''

"Why me?"

"I need an objective point of view. I've known these people most of my life. What do you say?''

"I guess I could use your help. When do we start?''

"Now," he said. "First, let me tell you what I have. There are photographs of the death scene.''

"That'll help.''

"Not that much. The body was found lying in water at the edge of the river at night. What we have are pictures of the flashbulb reflecting off the water.''

"I understand why you need help.''

"Jay-Newton did do something right, though. He took pictures of the body after it was taken from the water. There was some kind of laceration on the back of the head. It could have been caused falling off the seawall. Or he could have been hit on the head and then dumped in the river. I'm going to have that picture enlarged, see if we can learn anything from it. Like whether it was a blunt instrument or a jagged rock.''

"How did you find out the time of death was falsified?''

"Dr. Galen. I found him at his wife's grave. Leonitus has disappeared. Carla's sighting of him last night was the first anyone has seen of him since the cremation.''

"Did the good doctor say what the time of death should have been?''

"He didn't know. From what I've gathered, the time of death would have been early Friday morning between one and three. Charlie was last seen at the Fat Otis Bar on Water Lou Street. He left there a little before one. Drunk. The body was found shortly after three a.m. by the barmaid. She was walking to her car after locking up. I thought the Fat Otis would be a good place to start.''

"Now?''

"Why not? It's always locals in there. Probably much of the same group that would have been there Thursday night."

"I was up all night driving," I said. "Can't this wait till tomorrow?"

"No. I want to get the information while it's fresh. Besides, tomorrow night Wesley, Jay-Newton, and I will be busy working crowd control at Sister Star's tent show."

"Miracles Happen?"

"That's the one. So are you going with me to the Fat Otis?"

"You driving?"

FIFTEEN

THE FAT OTIS BAR was in a ramshackle old wooden building that had once been a fish icehouse. It was a place where an out-of-work man could go and not talk about it. He could stand on the sidelines or commiserate about the weather conditions with a meteorologist's aplomb. No one would question his forecast. No poetry readings or blue corn chips dipped in fat-free salsa. A place where men drank beer and whiskey and didn't give a shit about European history. No one ordered fruit-flavored vodkas from Scandinavia. The Fat Otis was a place where a man could find a friend for the price of a drink. It was cheaper than a $3.99-a-minute call to Dial-A-Hard-On. Social skills were checked at the door. Maybe a fishhook had pierced an earlobe or two, but never an earring. If a man lacked the characteristics of a man, how could he be called a man? Men sat at the bar gazing wistfully into beer glasses, like prospectors staring into a gold mine, hoping this would be the one that slipped him into another time, another place. If not, then the next round, the next mine shaft. Or the next. The Fat Otis was an arcade of misplaced manhood.

No one sat at the tables. Everyone was assembled around the bar. One look at the barmaid and I understood. She was a sultry pixyish thing with an enchanting smile. She wore cut-offs that made hot pants look modest and an elastic halter top that snugly engulfed her cupcake breasts. The scenic plane of her tan belly was interrupted by the tiniest rosebud of a button. A seductive nymphet, petite in stature, big in allure. A dream lover who would have top billing in my next fantasy. I resisted an impulse to tip her with my life savings before she had even waited on us.

Joe Patti and I sat at the bar.

The barmaid greeted Joe with an open bottle of beer.

"How's Paulie doing?" she asked him.

He shrugged. "No change."

The barmaid reached across the bar and touched Joe's hand. "I'm sorry. Can I do anything?"

"Pray."

"You already have that."

"I know."

They exchanged little smiles.

"So who is your friend, Mister Police Chief?" she asked Joe, casting her eyes on me.

"Harry," Joe answered.

The barmaid extended her hand to me and said, "Hi, Harry. I'm Babycakes."

"Yes you are," I said, taking her hand.

"What would you like?" she asked with a coquette smile. She gave me a second to think about it, then said, "Besides that, I mean."

"Oh." I was caught savoring her breasts. I've been told I have an obsession with breasts. I don't know that I'd call it an obsession, but if you think of breasts as a gift from God, and I do, then I would consider myself a pretty spiritual fellow. Harry Rice, Breastmaster. I glimpsed at Joe's bottle and said, "Well, in that case, one of those will be fine."

Babycakes smiled. "You should have met me a couple months ago."

"Why a couple months ago?"

"I was single then," she said coyly.

"I know a good divorce lawyer."

She winked and served my beer.

"Joe, you here about Charlie?" she said.

He nodded. "I am."

"Why is that, Joe?" The question came from the other side of the horseshoe-shaped bar. It was barked by a large man sucking on a Groucho cigar. He had feathered sideburns and five pounds of gray country-western-singer hair piled high with a ten-minute lube job sheen.

Joe Patti half-turned and looked across at the man. For an instant they looked like two prize fighters in a stare-down. Finally, Joe simply said, "I want to know what happened."

"Well, hell, I'll tell you what happened," said another man. He had a potbelly cultivated with a lot of time and money. He was dressed in camouflage fatigues, the official uniform of the University of Miami football team. "Charlie Meadows had a big mouth for a small town."

Joe turned toward him. "You had a problem with Charlie?"

The man in the soldier getup squinted, giving him a gassy demeanor. "I'm here to tell you I had a problem with him."

Joe Patti lowered his voice, said, "What did you do about it?"

"What?"

"You heard me. What did you do about it? You're not all talk, are you, Royal? Haven't you always said if you got a problem you deal with it?"

Royal folded his arms on the bar. "Let's get this straight. If I said I take care of my problems, then that's the whole show. I'll tell you something else, Mr. I-Want-to-Know-What-Happened, Charlie Meadows showed up dead the other night before I could take care of my problem with him. The simple fact is I can't take credit for killing him."

"Is that what happened? Someone killed him?"

"You're missing the point. The man is dead. It don't make no difference no more whether God and country killed him or I did, which I didn't."

"It makes a difference to me," Babycakes said.

"Sure, it makes a difference to you," said Royal. "That's because you lost a customer."

A few laughed. Not Babycakes.

"Why, Royal Maddox," she said demurely. "Now I know

why your mama named you like she did. You're a royal ass-hole.''

Most laughed. Not Royal.

Royal snarled, ''You testing me, Babycakes?''

The big man with the big cigar shifted his eyes to Royal Maddox. ''Don't start riding Babycakes, Royal. You don't want to do that.''

The bar fell silent. The tension was thicker than a New Orleans cop's bankroll.

Royal glanced around the bar like a gunfighter looking for someone he could outdraw. He settled on me.

''You got a problem?'' he said.

''Me?'' I smiled. ''No. No problem.''

''You laughing at me? You think there's something funny?''

I shook my head. ''No. I don't think it's funny when a man's backed himself into a corner that he doesn't know how to get out of.''

Royal Maddox evil-eyed me. ''What's that supposed to mean?''

''That means finish your drinks, leave a big tip, and get out of here,'' Babycakes translated for him. ''All of you. The bar is closed.''

A chorus of objections were moaned and groaned, complaints whined. Much ado about something. About being cut off. I understood completely.

''Knock it off,'' boomed the voice of the man with the Jiffy Lube do. ''You heard her. Drink up and get out. We'll see you tomorrow.''

Babycakes sweetened the pot. ''There'll be an extra long happy hour, too,'' she added.

Appeased, drinks were downed, people began making their way to the door. Nothing like the promise of cheap booze to soothe the savage drinker.

Joe Patti and I sat there watching the place empty.

Royal Maddox stopped next to me. He said, "You working for Joe?"

I said no.

He nodded. "You a friend of Charlie's?"

"Friend of the family."

His face scrunched serious. "Well, friend of the family, I don't take to smartasses. You should hope we don't meet again."

I passively ignored the idiocy of the encounter and said, "Nice talking to you."

Royal's mouth tightened. He observed a moment of silence while he memorized my face. Having committed it to memory, he nodded, turned, and left.

And then there were four—me, Joe Patti, Babycakes, and the big-hair man. His name was Ray-Newton, Jay-Newton's father. Ray-Newton was co-owner of the Fat Otis Bar. The other owner was his third wife, Babycakes, who had been in the same high school graduating class as her stepson.

A curl of smoke seeped from Ray-Newton's parted lips, which barely moved when he said, "Explain something to me, Joe, would you? I mean, I understand police work." He sipped from his pewter big-shot mug and glanced at me. "Having been an elected parish sheriff myself in the great state of Louisiana," he said for my benefit. He looked at Joe. "There's going to be times when you got to bother innocent people while they're trying to relax, do a little social drinking. Some things are just so damn important they can't wait. You got to fry the fish while it's fresh. I know that, Joe. You got your job. I got my business to run. Tell me something, though. Who is this? Why is he here?" The cigar was pointed at me.

Joe told him who I was.

Ray-Newton didn't say anything at first. He studied me with a you-got-to-be-kidding look, then rolled his eyes toward Joe. "You asked a private detective to help you investigate an accidental drowning?" His tone was harsh.

Joe said, "I don't know that it was an accidental drowning."

"You got reason to think otherwise?"

"No," Joe admitted, "I don't. No more reason than I have to think that it was an accident."

Ray-Newton ingested that, nodded. "All right. You want to investigate, Joe, that's fine. You do that."

"I'm not here to ask for your permission."

"I know that. I also know that you made a terrible mistake asking a private detective to get involved with a police investigation. That's not right. You need help, you got help. You got my boy. You need help, you use Jay-Newton, not some outsider." It sounded like an order.

Joe shook his head. "He's not ready."

"This could be his lesson. Work with him. Let him see how it's done. Give him a chance. All he needs is experience. We all started that way. Think about it, Joe. Spend some time with the boy. That's all I'm saying. Teach him. That's how you make a good cop—not by threatening to fire him if he makes a mistake." Ray-Newton pontificated like a Sunday-morning TV evangelist.

"Jay-Newton tell you that?"

Ray-Newton glared at Joe. "Never mind who told me. You threaten my boy, you make me look bad. I'm not going to have that. Understand me? I want Jay-Newton working on this investigation."

In a firm voice, with a trace of patience, Joe Patti said, "When he's ready."

Ray-Newton rocked back on his bar stool. "I see. And who decides that? You?"

"No," Joe answered. "He does."

"What does that mean?"

"He'll be ready when and if he decides he wants to be a cop."

"That's already been decided."

"Is that what Jay-Newton told you?"

Ray-Newton took the cigar out of his mouth and aimed it across the bar like it was a pistol. "It's what I told him."

"That's not the way it works."

"The hell it ain't."

"It's not either, sugar," Babycakes said. She had been busy closing out the cash register, listening. "Jay's got to want it for himself. You can't make that decision for him."

Ray-Newton's face twitched like a medical school experiment gone awry. The rhinestone greaser was pissed. He sucked on his cigar, the pacifier of champions. He glared at his wife through squinty eyes and said, "You're talking stupid again, little girl. I've warned you about opening your mouth without thinking. You keep your mouth shut and your legs open." He winked at us. Spare me from good ol' boy bonding.

Babycakes blushed, obviously embarrassed by her husband's tone and put-down. I held my tongue in abeyance.

"You better write this down, missy, because it is the last time I'm going to tell you," Ray-Newton said in a chidingly slow voice, as if he was talking to an idiot. "Words are like tobacco. Chew real good before you spit it out. That too hard for you to understand, Cakes?"

She looked over at Joe and me with a sad smile, her eyes apologetic. A little girl who just wanted everyone to like her.

"Why don't you spare us your cornpone philosophy?" I spat without chewing.

Ray-Newton made eye contact with me. "Cornpone, huh? Well, I tell you something about corn pone. It may be corny to some big-town private detective, but the thing about pone is, it's always true. Like this little bit of corn pone, for example: A police investigation is a lot like walking across a cow pasture." He paused, smiled, finally said, "Watch where you step, city boy."

"That's real nifty. That must take you back to your glory days as an elected sheriff when folks were impressed with your backwoods jawin'. All that's missing is a little jugband music in the background. That's clever, a cow pasture. Is that where you got that piece of shit you've been chewing on?'' I said, pointing at his cigar.

It had been a long day. I was tired.

Ray-Newton's body jerked as though he had been reamed with a jackhammer. People did not talk to Ray-Newton the way Ray-Newton talked to people. It just wasn't done. I suspected it would take more than a monogrammed bowling shirt to cheer him up.

Babycakes started to say something, glanced nervously at Ray-Newton, and reconsidered.

Ray-Newton's eyes were as hard as marbles behind heavy lids. He leaned forward, propping his elbows on the bar and resting his chin on laced fingers. ''There's something you ought to know about 'backwoods' people,'' he said, squeezing the words out like they were swollen with hidden meaning. ''They don't take to being violated by outsiders. Hear what I'm telling you? You don't come into my home, or my bar, and insult me.''

''I like the way you fix your hair.'' Harry Paladin—have tongue, will travel.

He gritted his mottled teeth. ''You going to be around the Cove for a while?''

''It looks that way.''

''We'll talk again.'' He nodded clinically. ''That's for sure.''

''Take a number,'' I said.

First Royal Maddox, then Ray-Newton. Two brand-new adversaries in less than an hour. A new personal best.

He stared at me for a long time. Then he said, ''Cakes, lock up when you leave. I'll see you at home.'' He rose, walked around to where the police chief and I were sitting. His eyes were fixed on me as he said, ''Joe, I got nothing to say to you.''

Joe nodded.

Ray-Newton walked out.

And then there were three.

Babycakes stared at me disbelievingly, her succulent mouth agape in delighted horror. Joe Patti had silently watched the sparring match without expression. He and Babycakes exchanged glances and broke up laughing.

Between peals of laughter Babycakes said, "Mister, that was the most stupid, most chivalrous thing I've ever witnessed. I can't believe you did that. Nobody has ever talked to him like that. God! It was great. Boy! It was dumb."

Joe Patti said, "You got a certain style, Harry. I'll give you that."

"It's a gift," I said. "It's something you're born with. Like talent. Or shame."

"Still," Babycakes said, dabbing her eyes with a tissue, "you shouldn't have done that. Ray-Newton can be trouble."

I shrugged. "Even style has its price."

Eventually the conversation did get around to Thursday night. Joe asked Babycakes if she had worked that night, just to confirm what he had already been told.

She had worked.

"Who else was here that night?" Joe asked.

She thought a second. "Just regulars. Manning was here. Royal. Jack the Brit. Tucker. Evalinda. You're just asking about the time when Charlie came in?"

Joe said yes.

"I think that was it."

"Ray-Newton?"

Babycakes shook her head. "He has dinner with his daddy on Thursdays."

"What time did Charlie come in?"

"It was late. Near eleven."

"Evalinda was here that late?"

"I know. That wasn't like her." Babycakes looked at me.

"She has to get up early to open her restaurant," she explained. "She usually goes home about nine. You know, now that I think about it, Joe, she may have been waiting for Charlie, because as soon as he came in, Evalinda got up and went over to meet him at the door. They talked a little bit. I heard Charlie tell her that he might stop by later and then she left. Charlie sat down and I set him up with a beer."

"Where did he sit?"

"About where you are. Royal and Tucker and Manning were sitting down at the that end. Jack the Brit was across from them rolling dice on the bar."

"Had Charlie been drinking?"

"If you mean was he drunk when he got here, no."

"That's what I meant."

"He may have had a drink or two before he came in, but he was sober."

"Did he seem upset or anything?"

"No. I don't think so. He seemed to be himself. A little more on the quiet side, maybe."

"Did he speak to anyone?"

"Me. Tucker was preoccupied pissing and moaning about getting busted by Marine Patrol for using a gill net. Royal was telling him that that was why Tucker should join up with Royal. Royal said that was the kind of crap he was opposed to and he was going to get the net ban repealed. That's when Jack the Brit said, 'And the South shall rise again.' The way he said it, it was real funny like. Charlie had been minding his own business, ignoring everyone, but that made him laugh. Royal didn't like that. He asked Charlie if he was making fun of him, even though Jack the Brit was the one who said it."

"What did Charlie say?"

"He told Royal he didn't pick on unarmed men."

Joe smiled. "I can hear him saying it," he said. "Did Royal know what that meant?"

Babycakes shook her head. "Not at first. Tucker told him.

Royal went crazy. He started screaming at Charlie. Tucker and Manning had to hold him down. Got so bad they had to drag Royal out of here.''

"What did Royal yell at him?"

"Oh, it was name-calling mostly. He accused Charlie of being against the watermen and how Charlie should be ashamed of himself and how nobody in the Cove liked Charlie." Babycakes thought about something for a second. "Royal said something about money."

"What about the money?" I said.

"As he was being pulled out the door, Royal said, 'I know you stole the money. I know you stole it.' Charlie looked right at Royal and smiled and said he didn't know nothing about that."

"What happened after they left?" Joe asked. "Any of them come back?"

"No. Jack the Brit stayed for another drink. He and Charlie talked for a little bit I think. I was on the phone. After a bit Jack left. Charlie hung around to keep me company."

"For how long?"

"Hour or so."

"Was he drunk when he left?"

Babycakes thought about that. "He was tipsy."

"How long after that did you leave?"

"Couple hours. I caught up on some work around here. I closed out the cash register, swept the floor. Emptied ashtrays, took out the trash. Washed the glasses, that sort of thing. It was close to three. When I left I saw Charlie's truck was still parked on the street. I thought maybe he had passed out somewhere. I started looking for him. I knew he liked to pray on the wharf. So I walked over there." She closed her eyes. After a moment of painful reflection, she sighed heavily. "I found him."

WE LEFT THE FAT OTIS and got back in Joe's car. He slid the key in the ignition and cranked the engine.

"What do you know about the money?" he said.

"Damn," I said. "You're a good cop. You picked up on that?"

He nodded.

I said, "I don't know where the money came from, but I think Charlie stole it."

Joe slipped the car in gear. "Charlie didn't steal it. He confiscated it from me. I'm the one who stole the money."

SIXTEEN

I DIDN'T RESPOND right away. I lowered the car window to let in fresh air. I listened to the whir of tires rolling on macadam, accompanied by a nocturnal orchestra of crickets. I turned back and watched Joe Patti drive. His eyes were fixed on the road ahead, his face serious and tinted by the green glow of the dashboard light. He drove with the single-mindedness of a repo man appropriating the car of a trailer park cutie who had missed too many payments to the loan company.

He waited, not saying anything. It was my turn.

"Whose money is it?" I said.

He glanced at me, then at the road. "You know where the money is?"

"Yes."

He nodded. "I want it."

"Whose money is it?" I repeated.

He smiled. "You don't sound surprised."

"Oh, I'm surprised. Where did the money come from? Whose is it?"

"The fishermen's," he said. "It's the money they got from the net buyback program."

The buyback program was a fund set aside by the governor when Florida voted to ban commercial net fishing in state waters. It was one of the special programs, along with retraining, designed, in theory, to provide relief to the displaced fishermen. The number of nets a fisherman was allowed to sell back to the state was based on the average gross income over a three-year period. The more they earned, the more nets they could sell, up to ten. The buyback paid about seventeen cents on the dollar. A six-thousand-dollar net fetched around a thousand dollars. Of course, the loss could be written off on taxes. The problem was there was no income to apply the loss against.

Joe Patti knew the questions without being asked.

He said, "Remember Royal Maddox?"

"Rhapsody in camouflage."

"Well, I haven't heard him described quite that way, but yeah, he was the one in the M*A*S*H costume. He's the president of the local watermen association and the commander of a newly formed militia."

"That makes a lot of sense. A fish militia. If you can't net the fish, you shoot them with an M-16."

He shook his head slowly. "Don't make fun of these people," he said wearily. "There's a lot of bitterness here. These people are under a lot of pressure. They're out-of-work family men. Some of them come from six generations of fishermen. They don't know any other life, and that's been taken from them. It's been devastating. They're under a lot of stress. They're suffering more than it shows. They're angry, depressed. They're drinking more, families are breaking up. A desperate man will hook on to any ray of hope. Even if it's Royal Maddox."

"What ray of hope is he?"

"None," Joe said. "But that's beside the point. He talks about overturning the net ban, of correcting a 'terrible injustice.' He talks about mobilizing fishermen statewide and enlisting the aid of seafood dealers and restaurants. Royal Maddox spews words of encouragement. Besides Sister Star, he's the only one doing that. He tells the people what they want to hear."

I asked Joe if it was a terrible injustice.

"I don't know," he admitted, his eyes still focused on the road. "That's a tough one to answer. I grew up in a fishing community. It's hard to be objective. I mean, there's no question that the fish population was down. The proponents said it was because of net fishing. And there's some truth to that. But I'm not totally convinced the real culprit was net fishing. The industry was heavily regulated—the size and types of nets, the size and amount of fish, as well as when you could fish for them. Yes, there probably was plundering, illegal catches. But do you pull everyone off the highways because of a few speeders?''

"Marine Patrol wasn't doing their job?''

"It's not that simple. I'm a cop. I know what budget constraints are. I think Marine Patrol had the clout to go after the indiscriminate netters. If they did, I never saw it. Much like I never see them go after the sport fishermen. Now there's something that sticks in my craw. These damn Sunday fishing enthusiasts who don't know the first thing about boating, or if they do, the rules just don't apply to them. Sport fishermen kill about a hundred to one more manatees than commercial fishermen. And yet, the commercial fishermen were the ones portrayed in television ads as the bad guys. You know who paid for those advertisements? Big money. The same big money that has brought coastal development and polluted waters and destroyed mangroves, fish habitat. You think maybe that might have contributed to the dwindling fish population? Look at coastal construction. It's increased the mercury contamination in fish. The problem was not simply the nets. And then the damn politicians. Several years ago Texas banned net fishing. A lot of those netters moved to Florida. The state sold commercial saltwater licenses to out-of-staters. Maybe that's where netting should have been controlled. I'm not sure. You know what it is? A turf war. Well, I guess in this case you would call it a surf war. Between recreational and commercial fishing. Fun versus food. It isn't a question of Save Our Sealife or Save Our Seafood. It's one of allocation. Who gets the fish? The alley cat or the fat cat?''

He tapped repeatedly on the brakes like a cafeteria percussionist. I looked to see what he was slowing for. I saw nothing.

Whatever moonlight there had been earlier was cloaked by clouds. He turned suddenly into a pitch-black opening in the woods that had appeared without warning. We were in a rabbit hole looking for Alice. Or this was the dirt road choked by wooded growth that led to the Meadows place.

Here was the clearing. There was the house. Joe stopped the car by the front door, threw the gear in park, and kept the engine running.

He turned to me and said, "Where is the money?"

I hesitated momentarily, then said, "I'm trying to give you the benefit of the doubt. You admit stealing money. I think maybe you're some kind of Robin Hood on wheels. But if I'm understanding you correctly, you stole from the poor. I don't get it. You seem concerned about these people. What did you do? Go around breaking into their homes after they had cashed their buyback checks? Am I missing something here, Joe?"

Joe Patti looked at me for a long time before answering. "All right," he said. "That's a fair question. After all, I am the one who asked for your help. Yes, I stole from the poor. No, I didn't break into their homes. The money is what Royal Maddox had collected to fund the militia."

I shook my head in disbelief. "Unemployed family men gave their money to that Patton wannabe? That doesn't make a whole hell of a lot of sense."

"Forget common sense. It's not a factor, it's not a part of the equation. We are talking about high-strung emotions. Look, I'll try to explain this the way I see it, though I'm not sure I'm right. The militia is probably viewed as something to do to break the boredom and despair of sitting on a boat all day with no place to go, nothing to do but worry and hope."

"Well, I know nothing makes me feel better than spending all of my money on a Halloween costume and playing soldier."

"Damn it, Harry, listen to me. They are not playing. I wish that's all it was. They are not buying trick-or-treat costumes.

They are buying guns. Desperate men in desperate times. If they don't get some good news soon, there could be violence.''

"Against who? Who is the enemy? Big business? The government?''

"The sport fishermen.'' He let me absorb that for a few seconds before he said, "I'll tell you something else. The sport fishermen are provoking it by their taunting. And in all fairness, the commercial fishermen are not blameless. They've strung nets across the river, entangling the propellers of recreational boaters. I've had to make several arrests. Know what they told me? They said they wanted to do harm to the people who had perpetrated the smear campaign against them. They also told me that it was a sad way to feel.''

I nodded, letting it all sink in. "Okay. I think I understand. You took the money to protect them from themselves. You were holding the money for them until they cooled off and came to their senses.''

"I'd like to say that was true. But, no. I stole the money because I needed it.''

"For what?''

He gazed out the window and shook his head.

Like he said, desperate men do desperate things. Whatever it was, though, he wasn't making any apology for it. What was it? What would make him steal from out-of-work people? Then I remembered something Babycakes had said.

"Who is Paulie?'' I asked.

The surprise was evident on his face. "Damn,'' he said quietly. "You're probably a good detective. Give me this one, Harry. I don't want to go into that. At least not now.''

I shrugged. "One last question, then. What does everybody seem to have against Charlie Meadows?''

"Yeah,'' he said. "We need to talk about that too. But not now. It's late. We'll talk about that later. Where is the money?''

I opened the car door and got out. I shut the door and leaned through the window. ''You're right. It's late. We'll talk about that later.'' I turned away and without looking back I went into the house. A half minute later I heard the car drive away.

Carla had staked out the sole bedroom and was asleep. She had made up a bed for me on the couch. I undressed and laid down. I was asleep before I even had a chance to imagine Babycakes naked.

SEVENTEEN

I WOKE UP feeling like a half-forgotten character in someone else's past. My back felt as if I had slept sitting up in a movie theater with a precious little kid kicking the back of the seat all night. Then again, maybe I should have been grateful. The lumps in the couch were the closest thing I've had to a date since my social life was revoked.

I opened my eyes and winced. A hazy light was creeping through the window above the couch. The sky was the colors of morning. A desperate bladder pulled me into consciousness. I sat up cautiously. Didn't appear to be any permanent damage. I stood up.

The bedroom door was open. The bed was made. Carla was gone. She had left a note, on the toilet seat.

h—i've gone to p.c. to visit aunt joann—didn't want to wake you—heard you come in late last night. where did you disappear to ??? can't wait to hear all about it. back around dinnerish. wait for me—c

I fumbled through a variety of etiquette-endorsed ablutions, mesmerized by the noise emitting from my stomach. It sounded like two stray cats fighting over a last morsel of Tender Vittles.

EVALINDA was behind the cash register making change for a hulking man with a growth on his face that looked more like a roadkill than a beard. From the mess on the counter he had the eating habits of an orangutan. I sat several stools down from the disaster area.

Evalinda set me up with a cup of coffee. "I heard you're a private detective," she said with a glint of interest. The small-town grapevine, spreading news faster than Paul Revere riding Secretariat.

I nodded. "Now maybe you'll quit thinking of me as just another pretty face."

"That's going to be tough."

The day's special was a stack of Aunt Jemima's with a root-hog omelet. I didn't ask.

I ordered a fried-egg sandwich on wheat toast with mayo.

Behind the counter, Evalinda broke an egg over a skillet and dropped two slices of bread into the toaster. She set a place mat and utensils wrapped in a napkin next to my coffee.

"What did you mean yesterday?" I said.

She shrugged. "Mean about what?"

"You said something about people being afraid that Charlie Meadows was right. Right about what?"

Evalinda crossed her arms, her somber eyes staring, as though she were looking through me—her mind elsewhere. The sound of the egg cackling in the skillet returned her to the here and now. She blinked and said, "Are you going to the tent show tonight?"

"Sister Star?"

She nodded.

"I hadn't thought about it. Why?"

She turned her back to me and flipped the egg. "Plan on going. See for yourself."

"Who else would I see for?"

She didn't get a chance to respond. Our conversation was cut short when an adventuring young couple wearing FSU T-shirts walked in. They surveyed the place and nodded to each other as though they had discovered a sub rosa culture that would surely please their anthropology professor. They sat at a table. Evalinda dropped a plate in front of me and carried menus to her new customers.

I had been there long enough to eat half the sandwich when the screen door to The Other Restaurant opened again. Officer Wesley Butch entered looking as though he had just awakened from a horrifying nightmare. He made a beeline for me as if propelled by some chemical stimulant.

"We need to talk," he rasped.

I gestured with my sandwich for him to sit down on the mushroom-shaped swivel stool next to me.

He shook his head. "Not here. At the station." A definite edge to his voice.

I took a small sip of coffee. "I'll stop by after breakfast."

He responded by slapping my arm, pushing the coffee cup to the counter with a jolt. "There's no time for that!" He was hyped.

I grabbed a napkin and wiped spilled coffee from my hand. "What is your problem?"

His eyes narrowed as if the search for an answer required his full attention.

"Come on," he growled like a cop who would be docked a week's pay for acting human. "We are going to the station."

"I don't think so." I turned away from him. "If you have a problem with that, I suggest you take it up with Joe Patti."

He sucked in a deep breath and without exhaling said, "You want me to take it up with the chief?"

I smiled pleasantly. "That's right. Take it up with your boss."

He smiled back. "Well, that's going to be kind of hard to do now."

"Is that so? And why is that?"

"He's dead."

LIMP WAVES OF AIR churned from the small oscillating fan that pinged with each rpm, perched atop the steel gray file cabinet. Caught in the breeze, clumps of cigar smoke sprouted wings and hovered above the room like acrid kites of portent.

Sitting tall behind the deceased police chief's desk was the poor man's Buford T. Justice—former Louisiana parish sheriff Ray-Newton with mythmaking hair and bwana cigar. Jay-Newton sat across from his father on a metal folding chair. The air smelled of lizard boot justice.

It was a toss-up as to whether it was me or Wesley Butch who was the more surprised to find Ray-Newton ensconced in Joe Patti's chair.

Ray-Newton blew a stream of smoke, clasped his hands behind his head, and leaned back in the chair as if the moves had been rehearsed. "Nice going, Wes. I was just about to send Jay-Newton out to bring in Mr. J. Edgar Rice, big-town private detective, for questioning."

Wesley Butch said, "*You* were going to send Jay-Newton?"

Ray-Newton flicked ashes from his cigar. "Right."

"For questioning?"

"Oh yeah."

Wesley appeared genuinely confused.

Ray-Newton waited, didn't comment.

Wesley finally said, "What's going on?"

Ray-Newton, his eyes fastened on Wesley, said without ceremony, "Until further notice, I'm the acting police chief."

Another extended silence.

"Says who?"

"Says the mayor."

Wesley Butch considered that while he wagged his head skeptically. "Nobody told me."

"What does this sound like, Wes?" Ray-Newton said in the tiresome voice of a patronizing don. "I'm telling you."

Genuflect and kiss my ring. He didn't have to say it. And we all heard it.

"I don't believe it," Butch said, shifting his weight from left to right.

"You got reason to believe otherwise?"

Wesley Butch let the question dangle unanswered longer than Ray-Newton cared for.

"There's something else," the acting chief said. "I'm switching you to the night shift effective immediately. Jay-Newton will be working days, assisting me in my investigation."

Wesley Butch protested. Something about nepotism and seniority and by God it just wasn't right.

I kind of felt sorry for Wesley. His day had begun on a positive note—the boss was dead. That was a shame, but the good news outweighed the bad. The top position was vacant. His position. The position he was born for. Wesley Butch was born to star, not to be an extra. With talent so obvious, skills so dominating, Wesley Butch was the logical heir to the vacated throne. Enter Ray-Newton, another dream flushed. Wesley was not a happy man.

"I've been here longer. I belong on the day shift. I've got more experience," Wesley concluded.

Jay-Newton regarded him without expression.

Ray-Newton took it all in quietly like the kingpin of a privately owned and operated police department—where the kingpin's word was law.

Ray-Newton gave an exaggerated sigh. "That is precisely why I want you to work nights. You have more experience. You don't need supervision. Jay-Newton does. He's not ready to handle all the different situations that come up at night."

"Nothing happens at night! This isn't Atlanta. It's Angel's Cove. It closes at night. People sleep at night."

"And they'll sleep better on my watch knowing the police never sleep."

Wesley Butch petulantly volleyed several more objections, which in turn were imperially overruled without even the slightest pretense of consideration.

Suddenly, Papa Doc-Newton held up the judicial hand of a parish dictator. "Wes, we're not voting on this decision, so there's no need to debate it.'' He spoke without a trace of censure, in a quiet and deliberate voice that forced us to keep still to hear him. "The fact is, I'm the boss. We do things my way. When it's your turn to be the boss, things'll get done your way. That's the way of the world. Now, I need to question this man." I was This Man. "You know what your shift is—you can go now."

Unaccustomed to rejection slips, Wesley Butch shifted his weight. He was obviously uncomfortable, uncertain of his next move. He glanced at me. I gestured slightly toward the door, trying to warn him not to push it any further. My eyes fixed on his and I thought, If you don't watch it, Ray-Newton will have you bend over so he can administer his loyalty oath to you.

Floating somewhere in space is that telepathic message I sent to Wesley Butch but was never delivered to the addressee.

Wesley had to shoot off another round in the Great Testosterone War.

"I better get night differential," he warned.

Ray-Newton shrugged. "Whatever you're entitled to, Officer," he said, sounding both gracious and sardonic at the same time. The sign of an undisputed heavyweight orator.

I don't know if the night differential thing was a small victory or not. Maybe it was simply a consolation prize. Whatever it was, Wesley Butch took it and stormed out.

Jay-Newton had sat silently during the whole exchange. He appeared oblivious to everything around him. I think he was truly mourning.

Ray-Newton lung-pulled on his cigar. Ribbons of smoke signals curled almost fiendishly from his nostrils as though he were Satan hailing a cab out of hell. He regarded his sagging son with an animal trainer's stick-to-itiveness.

"Sit up," he commanded.

Jay-Newton straightened his shoulders. Clyde Beatty-

Newton must have been out of Milk Bones. No treats for the obedient that day.

Jay-Newton mumbled something.

"Wes'll get over it," Ray-Newton interrupted with a dismissive wave of his hand to silence any objections Jay-Newton might have voiced. He stared disappointedly at his son a few seconds. I suspected the feeling was mutual. Ray-Newton put on his cop face and looked in my direction.

"All right, J. Edgar, let's have it," he said in an annoyingly official voice. "What's your story?"

"I don't have a story," I said. "I had one, but the dog ate it."

"Is that right?" Ray-Newton turned in his seat and propped his shitkicker boots up on the desk top, hands folded on his bread basket. "Let me see now," he said, gazing at the ceiling as though he were just thinking aloud. "What we have here is one dead police chief—which has everyone upset—and one big-town private detective who wants to play smart mouth with me when I have some serious questions and don't have time for play. The way I see it, we can do this one of two ways. I ask and you answer," he said, staring directly at me. "Or I can have Jay-Newton leave the room and you can find out how I conduct interviews with smart-mouth private detectives when there are no witnesses around. What's going to be? I've got my preference, but it's your call, Mr. J. Edgar."

"Call me Mr. Answer Man."

For the next hour, with no further preliminary, I recounted where I had been and what I had done from the time that Joe Patti had picked me up to the time he dropped me off. Ray-Newton rambled on like a man obsessed with control, a man who liked to hear himself talk, a man full of himself—impressed with his new interim authority. In his mind's eye he seemed to have cast himself in the role of conquering hero, the one chosen to raise the phoenix from its ashes. There was something vaudevillian about his every pose and posture, even in the way he would reload his lungs with cigar smoke and then expel it as though he were deep in professorial thought. He demonstrated a total lack of originality with his questions. There were no surprises. No, I did not speak to Joe again after we said good night. I could only estimate what time that was. No, I didn't know where Joe was going after he left me. There was no mention of him meeting with someone else later in the night. I told Ray-Newton what Joe Patti had said about treating Charlie Meadows's death as a homicide, about the medical examiner falsifying the time of death to cover up the premature cremation. I did not tell Ray-Newton or Jay-Newton or Olivia Newton-John of my conversation with Joe Patti about the stolen money.

It almost took a crowbar to pry the information out of Ray-Newton, but he finally told me that Joe Patti had died under circumstances similar to Charlie Meadows. I asked what similar circumstances meant and was told only that both bodies had been found in the same location at the bottom of the sea-wall in the river. Ray-Newton wouldn't give me any other specifics. If I asked he would reply, "That's police business" and something about my services no longer being needed. "Your work is done here" is the way I think he phrased it. He did say that both deaths would be investigated.

That's when the door to the police station opened and in walked a new player.

She was about my height, tall for a woman but not for a man. God had blessed her. She was achingly attractive. Her auburn hair was cut in a shag and contrasted nicely with her green eyes and creamy skin. She was stylishly dressed in a moss-colored Donna Karan suit and chocolate brown silk blouse. Her outer appearance and her accoutrements—brief-case and bookworm glasses—were strictly professional. And yet, there was an undeniably feminine persuasive quality about her. Outwardly, all business, but underneath I just knew it was

Frederick's of Hollywood. She was not wearing a wedding band.

She gazed at me with a neutral regard and said, "Don't say another word." Not a trace of the South in her speech.

She adjusted her glasses and crossed the room with the regal confidence of a chessboard queen about to checkmate the opposition. She was slender, in her mid-thirties, and moved with the grace of someone who has studied dance. As she walked by I caught a whiff of perfume that was subtle and ambiguous. It seemed to say, Go ahead and try, big boy. What did I know, other than I was enjoying the view of the sculpted contours of her hynotic behind. I'd consider bathing with her.

Both the Hyphen-Newtons were staring at her.

Ray-Newton cleared his throat, but she spoke first.

"What's going on here?" Her words were measured and saturated with authority.

Ray-Newton looked questioningly at her and said, "I'm conducting an investigation and you are interrupting—"

"Good." She cut him off. She placed her briefcase on the edge of the desk and looked at the seated acting police chief. "What do you have to say for yourself?"

Ray-Newton was confused, not used to dealing with women who didn't know their place.

"Why wasn't I called?" she said, staring down at him.

"Who the hell are you? Why would I call you?"

She crossed her arms. "Have you ever heard of Miranda?"

"Of course I've heard of Miranda."

"I see. So you read him his rights and he didn't ask for me?"

"Well, no."

"No, what? No, you didn't read him his rights? No, he didn't ask for me? What?"

Ray-Newton stood up. Cop psychology. Now he was looking down at her. "I didn't read him his rights. There was no requirement to."

"You questioned him."

"That's right. I questioned him. But there are two elements required for Miranda. Questioning and detention. All I did was question."

"I see. So he is not being detained?"

Ray-Newton had to think about that before he nodded. "That's right."

"He's free to leave?"

A reluctant nod.

She picked up her briefcase and walked over to me. "Let's go. We're leaving." She turned to Ray-Newton and said, "Next time, call me first."

We started out the door as Ray-Newton shouted the perennial warning about not leaving town.

"Come on. I'll drive you to your car," she said in the parking lot outside as she unlocked the door to a little blue BMW.

EIGHTEEN

"AM I BEING WOOED?" I said, buckling the seat belt.

She didn't say anything. She regarded me with the amused expression of a fashion model eyeing a man who thinks he looks good in cheap clothes.

Things were looking up.

"I'm not familiar with local custom," I said. "But, in matters of romance, if that's what this is, I'm used to something a tad more old-fashioned. Though I have embraced the cultural trend toward informality. I think there's something else you should also know about me."

She raised an eyebrow.

I said, "I'm wooable."

The laugh lines of her eyes crinkled behind her glasses, but her mouth remained serious.

"Who are you?" she said. "Are you really a private detective?"

"As much a detective as you are a lawyer," I answered, showboating my deductive reasoning skills.

"I'm not a lawyer," she said, sinking my boat.

"You're not? But...I thought...why...who sent you?"

She pulled the car keys from her purse and looked at me over the top of her glasses. "Charlie Meadows," she said.

"Hold it. Back up. Who are you?"

"That was my question."

And a fine question it was. She asked first. She'd tell me who she was if I told her who I was. Pat and Vanna in a Merv Griffin adaptation of my old childhood favorite—*I'll Show You Mine If You Show Me Yours*. I wondered if that's all maturity was—nothing more than adult variations on children's classics. And if it was, did that mean strange encounters with the opposite sex was the norm? Or was it just me?

Who I Am, by the Amazing Harry Rice. I did the resumé bit and told her that in the occupation block, on more than one credit card application, I had written "private investigator" even though I had never played in the NFL and was not an ex-cop fired from the force for being misunderstood. I was a private detective and not a gourmet cook. I told her I abhorred violence, avoided fights, and liked women more than they liked me. I didn't live on a houseboat, I had never been to prison, and I was not a member of any gym or fitness center. I wasn't a war hero and I didn't spend Saturday nights boozing with hookers, only because I didn't know where to find them. And, there was a minuscule possibility that I was not of virgin birth.

She gave me a sidelong glance and started the car. "And you call yourself a private eye."

Her name was Gillian Gable. She was a newspaper reporter from Tallahassee. That's all she volunteered, opting to remain mysterious.

Next time she'd have to show me hers first.

She drove without asking for directions.

"How do you know where my car is?" I was curious to see if she would admit to following me.

"You know damn well I've been following you and your friend. Is she Carla, Charlie's daughter?"

I *saw* what she said, more than I heard what she said. I was fascinated by the sight of her glossy red lips, which were as ripe and succulent as Plant City strawberries, and probably just as sweet. The thought of tasting her, combined with the arousing fragrance that had impregnated the car's womb—Essence of Nasty, or some such perfume—had sparked a pulse in a part of me that had long been dormant. Emotions that I wasn't sure I wanted reawakened were starting to tug at me. I was gun-shy, afraid history would repeat itself. A divorce, an untimely death, and getting dumped for a bigger bank account can have a devastating effect. There was only one thing that troubled me more than the thought of getting involved again with someone and that was the thought of not getting involved again with someone. I know that doesn't make sense, but then that's never been one of my goals. With that kind of thinking it is inevitable that I will spend my senior citizen years alone, teaching logic at Yeehaw Junction Junior College and captaining a shuffleboard team at the home.

"Is she?" she asked a second time.

The lady had caught me staring appreciatively at her.

I told her that it was Carla, Charlie's daughter, she had seen me with.

She nodded, not surprised. "I thought so." Then in her newshound voice, she said, "All right, let's get to the point."

"Wait a minute. I have some questions."

"I know you do. So do I. I'll answer some of yours right now. I saw you leave The Other Restaurant in the police car. I went inside and overheard the waitress telling someone on the phone that the police chief was dead and that you, a private detective, had been taken to the station. The waitress said she didn't think you had been arrested since there were no handcuffs and no video camera—whatever that meant. I went back to my room, changed into my professional clothes, got tired of waiting outside the station, went in, rescued you, and here we are. Now it's your turn. What happened? How did he die?"

Her staccato delivery was as effective as a carny snaring a rube into a shell game. I was suddenly playing by her rules, forgetting my questions and answering hers. I told her what I knew about Joe Patti's death, which wasn't much—hardly enough to read between the lines.

I told her about Joe Patti picking me up and going to the Fat Otis Bar, about him dropping me off and apparently never making it home. Her jade eyes widened behind her glasses when I told her that he had been found in the same spot where the body of Charlie Meadows was discovered. I could hear the reporter's questions buzzing in her mind. I told her I didn't know who found the body or when. I told her that Joe Patti was in good condition when he dropped me off, that we'd only had a couple beers each.

Her gemstone eyes studied my face, looking for something I might be holding back.

"What was Ray-Newton doing in there, sitting at the chief's desk?" she said.

"According to him, he's the acting police chief."

She shook her head in disbelief. "Incredible. What do you know about him?"

"Not much," I said. "He owns a bar. His son is a cop. He's a retired sheriff, Louisiana he said."

"He was a one-term sheriff, not retired. He was never re-elected. It was in a parish where people are baptized Republican at birth. It is rare when anyone runs for political office as a Democrat."

"Meaning most elections are decided in the Republican primary."

"Exactly."

"So Ray-Newton was a Democrat?"

"No. He's Republican."

"He lost in the primary?"

"Sort of. He ran for reelection and was challenged by another candidate. Several days before the primary, Ray-Newton withdrew from the race. There were hints of impropriety."

"In Louisiana? I'm shocked."

"Before Ray-Newton was elected sheriff, he worked as an auto mechanic. He had the good fortune to run for sheriff against a very popular, ten-term sheriff. The sheriff died two days before the election. Ray-Newton became sheriff by default. Anyway, after he withdrew his name for reelection, he moved to Angel's Cove and bought the bar, an eighty-five-thousand-dollar home, and a new Jeep Wrangler. He paid cash for everything.''

''Only a hint of impropriety?''

''One of the rumors had it that the other candidate had the backing of David Duke's people. Supposedly, Ray-Newton was paid off handsomely to drop out of the race.''

''The Klan lives.''

''Only in America, land of opportunity,'' she said. ''But that's another story. I plan to look into that some more when I finish here. At first glance it looks like the Klan is 'buying' political offices in that parish. What next? Another parish? Then Kansas?''

It would make for an interesting news feature, I was sure. But at the moment I was more concerned with why she said Charlie Meadows when I asked who had sent her. How did she know him? Why had she been following us? I wanted to know who killed Carla's father. I was now sure it was no accident. Someone had removed all doubt about that by leaving Joe Patti's body in the same place where Carla's father had been found. Someone was being obvious about it—but why? What was the connection between Joe and Charlie, assuming the motive for killing one was the same for the other? The questions were piling up. The question on the top of the pile was for Gillian Gable.

''How do you know Charlie Meadows?'' I said.

She twirled that question around for a moment before she said, ''Are you going to see Sister Star tonight?''

''Answer my question.''

''I'm trying to. Are you going to see Sister Star?''

''Probably.''

''Go. Then we'll talk about Charlie. And Joe.''

I hesitated.

She said, ''What I have to tell you will make more sense if you see for yourself.''

''Are you going to be there?''

She drummed her fingers impatiently on the steering wheel. "Yes. Now please get out." I looked out the window. We had stopped next to my car in the parking lot of The Other Restaurant. "I'll see you tonight. Right now I have to follow up on Joe Patti."

She was a reporter first.

As I got out of the car she said, "Rice."

I closed the door, leaned over, and looked in through the open window.

She said, "I like the way you were looking at me." My expression made her laugh. "We'll talk about that later, too." Her voice sopping with delightful mischief. She put the car in gear and said, "One other thing. When you are watching Sister Star tonight? I want you to think about something."

I stepped back from the car and said, "What's that?"

As she started to pull away, I swear she said, "Ronald McDonald."

NINETEEN

THE GREEN SEA was streaked with copper reflections, cast from glowing cloud billows in the west that burned a fire orange and red. Across the sand, standing at the shoreline in the foam of the breakers, I saw the silhouette of a solitary heron shimmering against the patina sheen of the ancient and wrinkled Gulf. The sight was spellbinding, the bright fluorescent clouds, the colors of hot coals, melding with the soft pastel blue and pink of the fading evening sky. It was like looking at the cosmic coloring book of an angel—a gift from Nature that tingles the spirit. I guess some days even God works overtime.

I watched a trio of pelicans glide by overhead until they banked right and disappeared behind the tall tops of a palm grove.

I was standing in the crushed oyster shell parking lot of the Sandal Foot See Food & Wet Whistle Place. One of those new tin roof and wood frame places built to look like one of those old tin roof and wood frame buildings that had disappeared several hurricanes ago. It was on the coastal highway a few miles west of Angel's Cove. Carla had called from Panama City and told me to meet her there. For dinner. My treat. Her car was in the lot, surrounded by out-of-state tags. The official "Classic Florida" vacation would not be complete without a visit to an authentic beachfront restaurant serving deep-fried frozen fish and watching the sun set from the motel tiki bar as local talent sings the best of Buffett.

A petite hostess greeted me at the doorway.

We smiled at each other.

"Hi," she said sweetly. "Will you be dining or just having cocktails?"

"I'm meeting someone for dinner. I believe she is already here."

"And your party?"

"Wesson Oil."

She put away her smile momentarily and gave me a peculiar look before she laughed a little the-toilet-trained-customer-is-always-funny laugh. "I meant your party's name."

"Silly me. Carla."

"Ah," she nodded knowingly, as if she had been fore-warned. "You're Harry."

"Yes, I remember."

The hostess motioned for an auxiliary hostess and said, "Misty will show you to your table. Enjoy your dinner."

We smiled at each other again.

I followed Misty. The place was crowded with blue hairs scarfing down half-price meals and two-for-one drinks. It was the tail end of the Early Bird and Happy Hour.

Carla was at a window table overlooking the beach. Her hand was wrapped around a long-neck beer bottle. There were two empties on the table. Her gaze was fixated on the sunset as though she were a backstage intruder to a celestial side-show. I sat across from her. She surfaced from her reverie and looked at me. She looked out the window again. The window was more interesting. God's a tough act to follow.

Misty placed a couple menus on the table. "Tammy will be your waitress," she announced. "Can I get you a cocktail?"

"I'll have what the lady is drinking," I said.

The lady said she'd have another, too.

After Misty went on the beer run, I said, "Are you drunk?"

Carla shook her head, almost disappointedly. "Soon."

Always the optimist.

"One of those days?"

She nodded. "One of those days."

"Me too."

A frown crossed Carla's lips, her eyes shadowed in suspicion as if she thought I was going to try and one-up her when we traded one-of-those-days stories. I don't know what she concluded, but after some time she looked away from me and swallowed more beer.

I waited.

"I want to go first," she finally said with a little pout.

"It's the rule of the sea. Women and children first."

"What a coincidence. It's my rule too."

"In that order?"

She thought about that for a second. "It depends on the child."

Tammy the waitress, who had apparently supplanted Misty the auxiliary hostess as the bearer of cold beer, set two chilled bottles in front of us. Tammy asked if we were ready to order. I asked if there were any specials. Yes, Tammy said the special was something-or-other. I looked at Carla. She nodded. We ordered two something-or-others. And away went Tammy.

From the noise coming from the table behind me, two couples were bickering over the bill. Something about calamari.

"We didn't order any appetizers."

"Well, we didn't either, and even if we did, you ate them."

Carla didn't notice. She had slipped away again, lost twenty thousand leagues beneath the ceiling fan. She sat motionless, almost lifeless, staring at her reflection in the window. She looked lonely.

"Talk to me, Carla."

She blinked. The creature lives.

She turned to me, her brow crinkled. Something was bothering her. That psychology course I took at the junior college years ago had finally paid off.

"Aunt JoAnn likes Neil Diamond," she said in a you-think-you-know-someone voice. Carla finished the beer in her hand and then traded the empty bottle for the full one. "I never knew that."

"Yeah, that would drive me to drink."

"Big deal." She raised her eyes and gave me something that had been in short supply for a while—one of her smiles. "You own a bar. Drinking is your business."

"Coming out of it, are we?"

"I hope not." She took a sip of beer. "I really need to get blitzed, Harry."

"Tell me more," I urged.

"It's this feeling, that nothing is right, everything is wrong, and it's not going to change."

Nothing ever is right when someone you love dies. And never will be. I didn't say that. I just thought it.

"Oh God," Carla said. "You're getting that philosophical look in your eyes."

"Harry Spinoza, philosopher for hire, at your service."

Carla rolled her eyes and shook her head. She began to tell me about her day. She had gone straight to the wrong hospital in Panama City to pick up her aunt. She got directions and eventually found the right hospital. It hadn't mattered that she was late. It would be another two hours before her aunt was released with instructions to do something with a corset, flat on her back, popping pills, with her feet flapping in the air.

"I used to know a girl like that."

Carla ignored me. "I took Aunt JoAnn home and got her settled. Then I ran out to get her prescription filled. I stopped and picked up a bag of hamburgers." She paused like one of Father Shifty's reluctant confessors. "When I got back to the house—" Carla looked away, embarrassed. "Aunt JoAnn was listening to 'Holly Holy.'"

"Could have just been an adverse reaction to her medication."

"We started talking about the bill from the Lighthouse. Aunt JoAnn vaguely remembered the phone call. They told her something about Daddy's wish to be cremated. She admits that she had authorized that. But nothing else, though. Nothing about a crypt or a bronze marker or chapel service. You know,

Harry, as we were talking I remembered a conversation I had with Daddy when I was in high school. We had just come from the funeral of a friend of his. Daddy said he didn't want to be present for his memorial service. He hadn't liked seeing his friend in an open casket. Actually, he didn't like anything about it. He thought the ceremony was lavish, the presentation garish. He hated seeing the body painted with cosmetics so it looked alive. Daddy said it strained decency. His friend never wore makeup in life. It made him feel like a pagan worshiper of the dead. The whole thing made him sad. It did nothing for his grief. He told me if people wanted to have a memorial service for him, then do it in a garden or in a park or at the beach. People can swap memories, he said, but no eulogy. Maybe a united prayer, he said, to make sure he made the transition without any glitches. After that, he said, everybody could go to Morrison's for the blue plate deal.''

Tammy rejoined us. She brought the salads. We waited as she set them in front of us. Tammy seemed to sense she was an intrusion. She made quick with the ground pepper, sprinkling until we each said when. She slunk away quietly.

Carla continued. She told me that she and her aunt had decided that that was what they were going to do. Just scatter Charlie's ashes in the sea, just as he had done with his wife's cremains years ago. Later there would be a memorial service. At the beach.

''There's just one problem,'' Carla said after another pull on the beer.

''What's that?''

''The Lighthouse is holding Dad's ashes hostage.''

On the drive back from Panama City, Carla had stopped at the Lighthouse Mortuary to retrieve her father's ashes. She was met at the door by Howard Ashby. He was wearing his somber undertaker's smile of compassion, which looked about as real as Burt Reynolds's toupee. Ashby was on his way out. A house call. He told Carla he didn't have time for her, come again another day. Carla told him that she just wanted to pick up her dad's ashes and she'd be on her way. Immediately Ashby kicked into autopilot, launching a sales pitch about the latest sports-themed urns, for which you could select the logo of the loved one's favorite team. Carla patiently explained to Ashby that there would be no urn, no crypt, no perpetual care, no bronze marker, no chapel service, no flowers, no extras, no options. Whatever container the ashes were in would be fine. Cardboard box or glass jar, it didn't matter. The ashes were going to be scattered. Hand them over.

Ashby stepped back and glared at Carla as if she were a lower form of humanity with the breath of a dung beetle.

"Miss Meadows, I would strongly advise you to talk to your family about this." His tone openly contemptuous. The effect was magnified by a little horrific shudder as Ashby imagined the devastating consequences to the family's collective psyche and the loss to the Lighthouse profit margin. "Scattering your father's ashes is like saying his death, in fact his very life, was an inconvenience that you don't have the time to be bothered with to decently memorialize, with dignity. Surely, if you didn't care enough for the poor man, there must be someone in the family who loved him and would be better equipped to arrange for the proper care and placement of his cremains."

"Thank you for your concern, Ashby," Carla said, tight-jawed, keeping her rage in check, sort of. "Certified grief counselor? Isn't that what you called yourself, you self-important arrogant celibate. You think you know what grief is? You dare to question my love and my feelings for my father again, or if you try to dictate to my family how we mourn our loss, I'll introduce you to a new definition of grief that will have you walking funny the rest of your miserable life. Now quit jerking me around. I want my father's ashes and I want them now."

Carla speared her salad fork into a cucumber wedge. She

held it up and stared at the seeds as though they were beady little Bette Davis eyes staring back at her. She bit the cuke in half. Had Bette winked?

Carla stirred her salad. She zeroed in on a Spanish olive. "He said I had an attitude."

"Maybe you could trade your attitude for the ashes."

"He wants cash. Said I would have to pay for services already rendered. Plus interest. Plus storage charges."

"How much?"

"He wasn't sure. Five, six thousand. Could be less or more. He'll get back to me." She put down her fork and picked up her beer. "Harry, I wanted to hurt him. It was a terrible feeling. I can't ever remember feeling that way about anyone." She took a swig of beer. "Well, anyone who wasn't in political office," she amended.

Halfway through the salad, "Harry?"

"Yeah."

"There was another one there."

"You lost me, Carla. Another what where?"

"At the funeral home, another man was there. Creepier than Ashby."

Carla said she'd felt someone staring at her as she was talking to Ashby. She glanced over her shoulder and was startled by the bizarre shape of someone's family secret. He looked like something out of a fifties television commercial, like a giant molar ravaged by Mr. Tooth Decay after Bucky Beaver hightailed it with the Ipana. A boxy, bulky torso balanced on spindly legs, he wore a tombstone white-gray suit over a cavity black crewneck shirt. His brush hair was the color of a tequila sunrise. He looked Carla up and down with the elevator eyes of a Calvin Klein pedophile about to receive a preteen goddess, his lips curled in the wicked snarl of a heat-crazed mongrel.

"He had a British accent," Carla said. "It wasn't one of those Masterpiece Theater accents, either. It was sort of an

evil throaty whisper. You know, like an English actor doing
Edgar Allan Poe. Scary. He reached out and touched my arm
with his paw.'' She shuddered at the recollection. ''It was
clammy, like a reptile.'' Another shudder and another hit of
beer. Ninety-nine shudders of beer to go. ''He said he'd walk
me to the car park. That's what he called it, a car park.'' She
paused as if she was going down her checklist of things to tell
me, make sure she hadn't forgotten anything. She said, ''He
smelled like Juicy Fruit.''

With that one clue, Sherlock Holmes could have probably
solved the case. I needed more information.

''Who was he?'' I said.

She shrugged. ''I don't know. We didn't exchange diaries.
I just wanted to get out of there. Ashby wasn't surprised by
him. They seemed to know each other. I guess he worked
there. Oh,'' she said, remembering something. ''Ashby called
him Jack.''

''Dinner is served,'' announced Tammy the waitress.

So it was my turn. Over dinner I told Carla about Joe Patti's
visit the night before.

''You were right,'' I said. ''The body was cremated prematurely. Which is why Dr. Galen falsified the time of death.''

I told Carla about Leonitus, the giant albino who wasn't an
albino. About the brain damage he suffered after nearly
drowning when he was a little boy. I told her what Joe had
said about the Galens taking Leonitus into their home after
the boy was abandoned by his parents. About Leonitus' fascination with fire and how the Lighthouse had given him his
first job—working in the crematory. I told her the early cremation appeared to have been nothing more than human error
compounded by an ill-advised attempt to cover it up by changing the time of death. That's what I told Carla, though I hadn't
completely ruled out the possibility that the body had been
deliberately cremated to prevent an autopsy.

Carla asked where Joe and I had disappeared to.

I told her the police chief had decided, under the circumstances, to investigate her father's death to determine the cause of death. Because Joe had lived most of his life in Angel's Cove and knew everyone, he had asked me to help in the investigation.

"He said he needed an objective perspective when interviewing people. And since your father was last seen at the Fat Otis Bar, that was the best place to start. That's where we went," I said.

I told Carla about Ray-Newton of the heap big hair voicing his displeasure to Joe Patti about my involvement in a police investigation. Yes, Jay-Newton was his son.

I mentioned Royal Maddox, officer in charge of the local militia.

"Royal Maddox didn't like me," I said. I told her Royal thought I was a smartass and said I should hope he and I didn't meet again. And then I told Carla what a nameless barmaid had said about Thursday night in the bar when Royal Maddox had accused Charlie Meadows of stealing some money.

"I don't believe it," Carla said. "My father wouldn't steal to feed himself if he was starving."

"No, he wouldn't. And he didn't. Joe Patti took the money."

"The police chief?"

"The same."

"How do you know that?"

"He told me."

"Why? Why did he steal it? Whose money was it?"

"The fishermen's. It was money they got from the state, part of the net buyback program. Why he stole the money is anyone's guess, and may well stay that way." I looked at Carla. Our eyes met. I said, "Joe Patti is dead."

"Oh shit." She gasped. "How? When? What happened?"

Carla tugged on her beer as I told her what little I knew. I told her about my morning.

"I went to The Other Restaurant for breakfast. I wanted to see the waitress. I was curious about something she had said the day before, about people being afraid your father was right."

"Right about what?"

"She never said. All she said was, go to the tent show and see for myself."

"Tent show?"

"Tent show. Sister Star."

"Who is that?"

"We'll find out tonight. Anyway, before Evalinda, the waitress, could elaborate, more customers came in. While she was waiting on them, Officer Wesley stormed through the door and invited me to the police station. I declined his invitation. He told me that Joe Patti was dead. It was no secret that the police chief and I had been together hours earlier. There were legitimate questions the police would have of me. And frankly, I wanted to know what had happened. So I rode to the station with Officer Wesley, only to be surprised again. Ray-Newton had been appointed acting police chief. I think Wesley was even more shocked."

Carla signaled to Tammy for another round of beers.

I told her that Joe Patti's body had been found in the same location where her father's had been discovered. I didn't have any other details.

"Oh," I said. "Remember the little blue BMW?"

"The one you said was following us?"

I nodded. "Yeah. I met the driver. She's a reporter." I told Carla how Gillian Gable had sprung me from my Q&A session with Newton senior. "She knew your father."

"How did she know him?"

"I don't know."

"You didn't ask?"

"I asked."

"What did she say?"

"She told me to go see Sister Star."

"Again with Sister Star."

"You noticed? She said after we saw Sister Star it would make more sense when she told us how she knew your father. There was something else. She said while you're watching Sister Star, think Ronald McDonald."

"Sister Star giving away Happy Meals?" Carla was getting tipsy.

"Could be."

"Did this reporter say why she had been following us?"

"Not yet."

"What does that mean? You're not going to tell me or she didn't tell you?"

"She didn't tell me."

"Yet."

"Right. She'll be at the tent show tonight."

"Can't wait to meet her."

Tammy was on the scene again with two beers. Her timing was flawless. Carla handed Tammy an empty and the waitress scooted away.

"Is that all you did today?" Carla's tone had an edge to it, like she was challenging me. My day was easy compared to hers. I sensed Carla was on her way to a mean drunk.

There was more, I said. After Gillian Gable had dropped me off at my car I was threatened by Royal Maddox, who aimed a rifle at me. That got Carla's attention. I told her just as I was pulling out of the parking lot of The Other Restaurant, I noticed Royal Maddox and Jay-Newton drive by in a pickup truck. They were both dressed in camouflage fatigues.

Carla asked if I followed them.

"Yes, I did." Even though I knew better. It's hard to be inconspicuous in a town the size of Angel's Cove where everybody knows who drives what. We drove north into the boondocks on a stretch of county road through dense woods. "They made me. The truck stopped right in the middle of the road. Royal Maddox got out and pointed a rifle at my windshield. I stopped close enough to see his toothless smile. Jay-Newton got out and held up his badge. He motioned for me to turn around and go back. I did. As I was driving away I heard a shot. It didn't hit anything. I looked in the rearview mirror and could see Royal laughing. I think he just fired a warning shot in the air.''

Carla slurred an editorial comment about my detective skills, something about me answering one of her questions with ten more questions. I couldn't argue with her. The questions were piling up higher than Ray-Newton's hair, starting with who hung the cat from the ceiling fan? What was Leonitus, a.k.a. the giant albino, doing sitting in the dark of Charlie Meadows's home? What did Joe Patti and Charlie Meadows have in common? What connected their murders—if anything? If they were murdered. Was it this money? Why hadn't Joe Patti been notified sooner of Charlie's death? Was there a common motive and killer? Or was Joe's killer, if he was murdered, trying to tie it to Charlie's killer, if he was murdered? Was the money Carla's father had sent her the motive? Did Royal Maddox or one of his fish militia kill Charlie because they thought he had stolen their money? Did Ray-Newton kill Joe to become police chief or because Joe had threatened his son's job security? Or did Jay-Newton kill Joe Patti for the same reason? What about Wesley Butch? Joe Patti took Wesley's tape and embarrassed him. Did Wesley think he would inherit the chief's job? Then there was Dr. Galen. He seemed harmless enough, but could he have killed Joe Patti because the chief had threatened to go to the medical examiner about Dr. Galen's competence? There were more motives for killing Joe than Charlie. Granted, most of them were pretty lame motives. But coming from south Florida, where people shoot one another over parking spaces, I'd learned not to dismiss anything, no matter how trivial it seemed on the surface. Did the giant albino kill Joe Patti to prevent an investigation

into the early cremation? Was the cremation deliberate to prevent an autopsy? Where had the giant albino disappeared to?
Also, who was Paulie? Did Paulie have something to do with
Joe Patti stealing the money? What else? Was there something
obvious I wasn't seeing? That's usually the case. And why
were Evalinda and Gillian Gable pointing me in the direction
of Sister Star?

TWENTY

THE MOOONLESS NIGHT was fat with atmosphere—the ghostly flicker of headlights vanished in the endless mist, a continuous hissing stream of wind snaked through gnarled and twisted branches of trees older than Count Dracula, and leaves fluttered eerily like batwings. It had it all, everything but the agonizing wail of a dog howling on the moor.

Cars lined both sides of the street for several hundred feet in either direction of the immense tent that rose voluptuously from the earth like a phosphorescent hallucination.

I parked at the end of the line. We had left Carla's car at the restaurant. She was in no condition to drive. I had offered to drive her back to the house. She said, "I think not." And that was the end of that discussion.

We walked toward the tent alongside men dressed for church, men dressed for their night league softball team, men dressed to kill, men dressed for drinking and persuading. There were women, spiffy women in their evening regalia topped with Carmen Miranda fruit salad tiaras. There were other women, women weary from wearing that same old shabby dress. Women dressed like girls on their way to dance class and girls dressed like grown-ups parading proudly toward the tent as though each were the guest of honor. There were blacks and there were whites. But among the unlikely mixture there was a shared sense of excitement as they made their way to the tent.

Vendor tables had metastatically mushroomed around the cavernous entrance. Pitchmen were hawking official Sister Star souvenirs. Accept no imitations. There were T-shirts, Miracles Happen plaques, calendars, tracts, autographed eight-by-ten glossies and Bibles, key chains, cassettes, and caramel apples, "her personal favorite recipe." People queued up to have their picture taken standing next to a lifesize cardboard cutout of the good Sister. It had all the frenzy of a carnival midway.

Carla and I entered the tall, elongated tent. It was larger than it had appeared from the street. It was the size of a school gymnasium and reeked of floral aerosol. The air was tepid and would only get warmer and more offending as it acquired additional body temperatures. Nearly all the seats were taken. We made our way along the dirt and grass floor through neighbors and friends hugging and handshaking to the tune of a hymn seeping from speakers strung along the support beams and poles. We sat a few rows from the back on a rock-hard bench that no amount of shifting and squirming would make comfortable.

At the front of the tent was a makeshift stage, the sides flanked by two giant television screens.

I glanced around the crowd looking for someone I recognized. I didn't see Gillian Gable or the Angel's Cove police force or Babycakes. That's not to say they weren't there. I just didn't see them. I didn't have long to look before the lights began to dim, and with them the volume of conversation seemed to soften to a whisper, as though the lights and people were connected to the same control knob, until it was pitch black and the room was silent, but for the stirring of anticipation.

It was show time.

We sat quietly in the darkness as if waiting for a movie to start. But nothing happened. The blackness and the silence swelled unmercifully as the standing-room crowd was confronted with time to think, a terror few could brave. Taunted by soundless thoughts echoing in the dark, with no place to hide, an uneasiness began to fester under the canvas pyramid. The spooky silence was finally broken when a staccato clapping slowly began to spread as a concession to herd ritual.

Just as the clapping reached a crescendo, a single spotlight directly above the stage came on. The light descended upon a tall Rubenesque woman draped in a loose white neck-to-ankle gown. Her arms were uplifted, her eyes raised to Heaven.

She was greeted by a reverent hush. Her body began to sway rhythmically side to side, almost trancelike, until the house lights came up. She looked out at the gathering and smiled. With arms outstretched, palms up, she approached the edge of the stage. A stagehand emerged from the rear of the stage carrying an armchair, which he placed behind Sister Star. He darted off stage. Without looking back, Sister Star sat down.

"Today Angel's Cove lost one of its brothers." She spoke softly, without a microphone, but her careworn voice could be heard by all.

A murmur rippled through the assembly. Everyone knew she was talking about Joe Patti.

"We are sad because we will miss him. That is selfish, which is not bad. We should, though, be happy for him because he has received God's greatest gift. For surely death is God's great gift. Without death you cannot go to Heaven. Think about that, brothers and sisters. Jesus came to us once. Now we must go to Jesus. Is that something to fear? Are you afraid of Jesus? Death is not something to fear, but we must not take God's gift for granted. We must do it right. And that is why I am here tonight. That is why I have returned with my Save the Dead Crusade to Angel's Cove. To spread the word, the word that death is our reward. It is not the end. If anything, death is when life truly begins, everlasting life."

"Miracles happen, Sister!" exploded a voice from the crowd. "Say it!"

Sister Star smiled evangelically. She stared in the vicinity of where the voice had come from for several seconds. After a few Solomon nods she said, "Yes, miracles happen."

"Shit happens," grunted a brewery-scented Carla.

Her epithet was obscured by a jubilant shriek that erupted from the congregation, though my drunken friend did draw a self-righteous glare of rebuttal from an ample woman sitting in front of us whose face had a sour expression that looked as if it had been there since birth.

Sister Star rose, her hands raised high. She stood that way quietly, surveying the faces in the crowd until they were collectively mute.

"Listen..." Her voice faded to a whisper. "I want you to listen to me." A little louder, still necks were craning to hear. "Right now," she said in a strong voice that resonated throughout the tent, "I want the undivided attention of every God-fearing brother and sister."

"That leaves me out," said Carla. "I was an only child and I don't fear God, I love God."

A tobacco fancier next to me shushed Carla between chaws.

Sister Star had paused, part of her cadence. Carla's commentary hadn't been loud enough to have been heard on stage. Sister Star lowered her arms, her gaze had shifted to a spot on the stage between her feet. She was using the theatrics of silence, effectively working the flock as they sat motionless awaiting her next word.

She looked up and said, "Do we stop caring for our loved ones when they die?"

That summoned a chorus of no's, just the response Sister Star had called for.

"No?" Sister Star repeated. Her eyes scanned the crowd until they eventually landed on a woman in the first row. "Sister dear, is it so? Do we still love our mothers and fathers and daughters and sons and wives and husbands after they die?"

"Yes, Sister," testified the woman in the front row.

Sister Star smiled down on her, like a mother smiling at an innocent baby. "I wish that were so. I used to think it was. Now I wonder." She sat down in the armchair and leaned forward. "Death is nothing more than coming home to roost.

It is our chance to make a last gesture to the Lord, to give our body to the Lord. A time when we can finally have lasting peace in an eternal resting place that is truly eternal. Listen to me, people. I said, truly eternal.'' She studied the crowd for a moment, said, ''Every day I hear of people being evicted from their homes.'' She shook her head sadly. ''Life can be so hard.''

''Come on, Sister!'' crowed a voice from the flock.

Sister Star's eyes shifted to the witness. ''Tell me something, brother. Are you married?''

The brother said yes.

''Do you love your wife?''

The brother said yes.

''Till death do you part?''

The brother said yes.

''That is not God's way!'' Sister Star was standing, so was her voice. She edged toward the front of the stage, her audience paralyzed by her blazing eyes and scolding tone. ''You tell me we continue to love our families even when they die and now you tell me it is till death do you part? Which is it? Do we discard our loved ones when they die? Or do we care for them always so that we can stay together—even in death?''

The brother wasn't sure.

''Are we hypocrites?'' Sister Star held up a hand. ''Don't say anything. Let me show you.''

The lights inside the tent faded to black.

''Where will you spend eternity?'' boomed a deep Darth Vader voice.

The two giant televisions lit up. The screens filled with an aerial shot of a dog sitting on top of what looked like a slab of concrete surrounded by water and floating debris.

''This poor animal, seeking a dry place to rest, is sitting on top of a floating burial vault,'' narrated a five o'clock news voice. ''The vault sprung from the ground when flood waters from the river slashed through a nearby cemetery.''

A wide shot of the flood scene was next. The river was peppered with coffinlike shapes. The stunned audience watched in silence. The next shot was of a man in a raincoat, holding a microphone. "I am standing next to what was once the Riverview Memorial Garden. Yesterday flood waters from the Choctawhatchee River spilled over onto the entire area. At last count, as many as fifty coffins have soared from their crypts. Tragically, many bodies popped out of their coffins before workers could retrieve them."

A still shot showed workers in a row boat towing an open, empty coffin.

The voice-over said, "The remains that have been recovered are being stored at a hardware store until relatives can identify and claim them."

Cut to a sheriff's deputy. He was pointing at a muddy and pitted lot. "This is where most of them coffins come out of. They just floated on out of here, bumping into each other and into trees and fences. Lots of the coffins we got back were empty. Don't have no idea where those dead people are now. First time I ever saw anything like this. Hope it's the last."

The televisions went blank.

The Darth Vader voice penetrated the dark and asked, "Where will you spend eternity?"

The screens lit up with a picture of an old sprawling cemetery filled with elaborate marble headstones, fancy mausoleums with ornate columns and tiled steps. There were shade trees and benches and winding paths. It looked like an upscale neighborhood of dollhouses.

Sister Star said, "This picture was taken the Easter before last at a landmark cemetery over two hundred years old." She paused, let everyone absorb the picture. "The next picture was taken from the same location last Easter."

The screen filled with the after-shot. Headstones had been broken and tipped over. Mausoleums had been destroyed, only their remnants standing. Broken urns were strewn among the rubble. Partial skeletons, grinning skulls, leg and hip bones were scattered amidst the ruins.

"Earthquakes can be devastating," Sister Star continued. "However, this was not an act of God. No, brothers and sisters. This was a crime against Christianity. This horrible, ghoulish scene is the work of twisted, misdirected grave robbers!"

A woman sobbed.

"Yes, sister. It made me cry when I saw this. Hallowed ground desecrated. Jewelry was stolen from corpses—from people's grandmothers and grandfathers. People like you and me. Imagine your loved ones violated. Think of the silk lining being ripped out of their caskets, the brass handles being yanked off, being sold at flea markets. Think how you would feel to know that the eternal homes of your loved ones had been broken into. Weep when you discover their remains *dumped on the ground! Can you see it?* Do you feel it?"

Her chilling words pierced the assemblage like a resounding death knell.

"Oh, sweet Jesus!" a voice cried.

"Be gone, Satan!" another shouted.

"Can you see it?" Sister Star hollered above the clamor.

"I see it!" answered the multitude.

"Do you feel it?"

"We feel it!" they responded.

The crowd was boiling, flamed by hellfire.

She had them.

The television screens went black, and again the interior of the tent was cast in darkness for an uncomfortably long time. People began mumbling and squirming in their seats.

A light from the back of the tent was aimed at the stage. Sister Star was standing behind a simple wooden pulpit, her arms outstretched like a crucified savior. She held that pose until the din of the congregation had dissolved. Looking out at her flock, cloaked in darkness, she smiled serenely.

She nodded, clasped her hands. "Do we really care about our loved ones after they die?" she said matter-of-factly. "Do we? You saw the pictures. Is that how we show our love?"

The house lights came up. Sister Star's eyes scanned the faces looking back at her, one row after another.

"Do you know where your loved ones are?" Sister Star asked, her face serious, her tone conversational. "In California, families who had long ago laid their loved ones to rest are now having to relive their pain and grief. Wives looking for their husbands, sons searching for their fathers, have not been able to find their bodies. They have been 'relocated.' Cemeteries have been lifting bodies from caskets moments after the memorial service and stacking the remains in mass graves. Family plots, grave sites, are being resold, the caskets reused."

She held up a piece of paper. She said, "This is a letter I received from an eighty-eight-year-old widower. He and his wife were married for over sixty-four years. When she died he had her buried in the adjoining plots they had bought so when their time came they could spend eternity side by side. Shortly after his wife's funeral, the old man had a stroke. He was hospitalized. Doctors told him he was not going to survive. Four and a half months later he left the hospital. He went to visit his wife's grave. The headstone he had spent thousands of dollars on was gone. In its place was a marker for someone who had died several weeks earlier. Someone else was buried in his wife's grave. Let me read part of this letter to you. He writes, 'This really hurts, Sister Star. I will never know where my Eufaye is. We spent our lives together and now we will spend eternity apart.'" She held up the letter. "Letters like this really hurt Sister Star. I feel that man's pain. The man died last month. A week ago I learned that police had finally found the wife's headstone...in a Dumpster."

Dozens of people simultaneously wailed and moaned.

"Lawsuits were filed against some of the cemeteries, but

the owners have gone into hiding with all those working folks' money." Sister Star paused for a moment. "Babies," she continued in a caressing voice, "babies. In another state, little stillborn babies were thrown into holes and buried alongside of caskets in a cemetery. Thirty fetuses in fruit jars were found buried under one tomb. The cemetery was littered with amputated body parts—limbs buried in graves on top of caskets and buried in unmarked areas."

Sister Star struck a chord with that one. The gallery bared their fangs. The tent was abuzz with off-key howls of disgust and sanctimonious snorts of indignation. The crowd was madder than hell, as though their world of lollipops and rainbows had been infiltrated by a traveling pack of distempered puppies.

Several rows in front of us, someone dispatched a plaintive "Oh, Lord Jesus."

Sister Star motioned with her hands, like a potentate directing the emotions of her entourage.

She said, "Be still, brothers and sisters. Be still," she kept repeating until she was surrounded by a pin-drop quiet.

"What follows," she began, "is a story that would have been recorded in the Gospels of Matthew, Mark, Luke, and John had it occurred two thousand years ago. For what I am about to tell you is surely nothing less than a Biblical warning. But it is no metaphor. Would that I was never born than to have this story true."

A moment of silence.

"Many of you will remember several years ago when police in Jacksonville, Florida, were investigating complaints against a funeral home." Sister Star's eyes drifted across her audience. "I see some of you nodding. For those of you who aren't familiar with this incident, I will tell you about the police's gruesome discovery. They found, in a shed behind the funeral home, dozens of decomposing bodies piled like cordwood. None had been embalmed. As diabolical as that sounds, what you are about to see and hear is even more horrifying, more shocking.''

The tent was plummeted into blackness. A collage of newspaper headlines flashed on the television screens:

14 BODIES STASHED IN MINI-WAREHOUSE
Unit Leased to Funeral Director

9 MORE CORPSES DISCOVERED IN SECOND STORAGE SHED
Shocking Discoveries Devastate Families

BABY BODY FOUND IN BRIEFCASE
Remains of 3 Infants in Crates

MORE REMAINS FOUND—BODY COUNT AT 43
Police Say There Could Be More
Search Continues

STILL MORE BODIES FOUND
Relatives Needed to Identify Remains

RENOWNED FORENSIC ANTHROPOLOGIST TO AID
Police Investigators Identify Bodies

The headlines sent shock eddies through the big top. Abruptly the televisions were turned off and once again we were cast into a coal mine black. A morgue chill filled the air.

A distant chime rang. That triggered a smattering of whispers and nervous coughs. On stage, a candle was mysteriously lit, illuminating Sister Star's face, mere inches above the flame. Her eyes were shut. A closed-coffin silence gripped the crowd. The chime rang again. Sister Star opened her eyes and stared intently into the blackness before her. In a subdued

voice she began to detail the events that gave rise to the headlines.

The story began one morning when the manager of a mini-
warehouse and storage complex detected the rancid odor of
rotting flesh oozing from an unair-conditioned module leased
to a funeral director. The manager slid open the door to the
unit and found the remains of fourteen bodies scattered on the
floor. One body had been embalmed and was laid out on a
piece of cardboard. Some bodies were badly decomposed and
desiccated, leathery flesh peeling way from arms and legs.
Others were just skeletons. No one was certain how long the
bodies had been there.

The community was offended.

Less than a month later, at a different mini-warehouse, the
owner of the yard caught the whiff of a pungent stench seeping
from a unit rented to the same funeral director. Nine bodies,
in varying stages of decomposition, were found inside the hot
compartment. One body had exploded from the expansion of
internal gases. The floor was infested with crawling bugs. The
owner of the warehouse was forced to hire a firm that spe-
cialized in hazardous and chemical waste to clean the place.
A bottle of bleach wasn't going to cut it.

The search continued.

Days later, at a third location, police found cremains in shoe
boxes and grocery sacks. Three baby skeletons were in an
orange crate. The embalmed body of an infant wearing a bap-
tismal gown was discovered in a briefcase. In time, the briefcase baby was identified. He had died fifteen years ago.

The community didn't like any of this one bit.

Families that had entrusted the funeral director with the care
of their deceased members became concerned. A young
woman decided to open the urn that was supposed to have
contained the ashes of her mother. The urn was filled with
gravel.

More remains were found in a trash bin behind the closed funeral home. More were found here and there. And more.

The candle was magically extinguished. The chime rang.

Darth Vader asked, "Do you know where your loved ones are?"

A stirring in the dark ensued.

The televisions flickered on. A police officer with an authoritative voice was addressing a press conference.

"We have identified some of the remains. Eleven boxes of ashes had names taped to them. Families are still being notified. There was one body still in the closed funeral home. The body had a toe tag. It was found laid out on a gurney with the head propped up on a concrete block. The body was naked, in a clear plastic bag that was tied off at her neck. The family confirmed the ID. It's a tragic shame. The woman's family ought not had to have seen her that way. As for the bodies we have not been able to identify, the University of Georgia is sending a team down to study the corpses. It is my understanding that by examining the shape of certain bones and measuring them, they'll be able to determine the sex. Teeth and bone growth will help them approximate the age. Measuring bones will also give them an idea of the person's height. They'll also look for things they can match against medical and dental records. Things like fractures and maybe old surgery scars. The rest of it is a little too scientific for me. Anyway, that's all I've got for now. As always, as information becomes available, it'll be passed on. We know there are a lot of anxious families out there wondering what has happened to their loved ones. It's got to be a hell of a thing to go through. You think someone is in their final place of rest, and they're not."

TVs off.

Their sensibilities scorched, the gentlefolk were appalled by the wicked deeds of a funeral director more evil than anything conjured on the pages of *The Portable Poe*. Furious whispers rippled between the aisles as though orchestrated by a Simon Says command.

Darth Vader, "Where will you spend eternity?"

House lights up.

Sister Star stood behind the pulpit, her chin propped on praying hands. "These are sad times we live in when people let monetary considerations hinder their moral judgment and their spiritual obligations. I have seen the consequences. I have counseled grief-stricken families suffering guilt for taking shortcuts, for not doing right by their deceased loved ones. I have consoled people suffering the agonies of self-reproach because they did not go that extra mile for their faithfully departed. I have sat up nights comforting remorseful brothers and sisters burdened with shame because they were short-sighted and did not sacrifice a temporary earthly comfort or pleasure to provide their mothers and fathers with eternal shelter. They were all good people, but they did not resist the lure of evil influences, mercenaries who took their money and abused their trust. You have read the headlines. You have heard the stories. You have seen the film. Is that what you want when your time comes? Do you want to be tossed in a hole in a boneyard? Think about that while I tell you this story.

"Remember the flooded cemetery by the river? The day the waters subsided, I stood next to a man beside a muddy hole in the ground where his mother's casket had been for forty years. This lonely man sadly shook his head as he stared at that empty mud pit. He said to me, 'Sister Star, it's not the way.' He said, 'It's not right to throw people into a hole in the ground and cover them with dirt like they was nothing more than compost.' He said, 'If Mr. Jesus had been buried in a hole, He never could have arisen from the dead and mankind would not have been saved.'" Sister Star donned a grim reaper expression, cranked up her volume a notch and bellowed, "If Mr. Jesus had been buried in a hole, He could not have arisen from the dead!"

She paused to let the gravity of her words sink in.

I sneaked a peek at Carla. Her eyes were a half-mast daze, her face a study in shitfaced meditation. Or she had to pee.

"If Mr. Jesus had been buried in the dirt, He could not have arisen from the dead," Sister Star recited as if she was quoting Scripture. "Through the words of that one man I received my message from God. My calling, my divine vision. I knew what I had to do. It was at that moment that I rededicated my life and became a devoted servant caring for those stilled voices that could no longer speak for themselves. I began what was to become my Save the Dead Crusade. The more I thought about what that man had said, the more I realized just how right he was. For truly, if Mr. Jesus had been buried under dirt, there would never have been the miracle of the resurrection. *And we know that—*"

Name that tune.

"Miracles happen!" sang out the congregation.

"Say it again!" Sister Star shouted.

"Miracles happen!"

"Do you believe?"

"We believe!" the impassioned crowd responded.

"Do you believe it is wrong to cheat our parents, our children, our Father who art in heaven?"

"We believe!"

"Do you believe that salvation is in your hands?"

"We believe!"

"Do you believe in miracles?"

"We believe!"

"Do you believe that *you* can make miracles happen?" Sister Star's voice challenged.

"We believe!" The roar was deafening.

"Do you believe that together *we* can make *miracles happen?*"

"We believe!"

Sing along with Sister Star. The pulpiteer had pulled all the right strings. She damn near had them holy-rolling in the aisle.

TWENTY-ONE

THE PULPIT-POUNDING incantations had whipped the acolytes into a demented Old Testament lather. Guttural chants coursed through the tent like spasms of interdenominational contempt. God almighty, the tribe was angry. They were ripe for picking.

Just as the clamor was about to crest, a flash of bright, blinding light from backstage seemed to break the spell. All eyes were transfixed on Sister Star. She raised her hands, commanding silence. She'd had enough. The hubbub gradually faded to a buzz.

"Hush," Sister Star said in the voice of teacher admonishing a classroom of rowdy schoolchildren.

The class hushed.

Sister Star had spoken. She rewarded the single-minded mob with a serene smile.

"Brothers and sisters, the atrocities you have witnessed this evening must never happen again. And happen again, they will not. That became my mission. When I began my Save the Dead Crusade I did not know where to start or what to do. But I took solace in knowing that light always overpowers darkness. I truly believe it is darkest before the dawn. So it was when things were the bleakest, when I thought there could be no salvation for the dead, I saw the light. I had a vision. It was a lighthouse. A lighthouse that would survive the ages. A lighthouse that would beckon God's angels to join the multitude on the shore. And I knew in my heart, that in all the world, there was but one place for this lighthouse, for my tower of angels. Here, in Angel's Cove."

The brothers and sisters applauded and proclaimed their appreciation.

Bored ushers appeared from behind the stage and began to traipse up the aisles distributing free brochures to the obliging congregation while the messianic Miracle Worker never missed a beat, joyously reminding us, should there be any doubters, that life was incurable, we were all doomed, we were all going to die. *Will you be ready to receive God's gift? What about those who have gone before you? Have you forgotten your ancestors? Would they have forgotten you? You say it is too late? I say, miracles happen. It is not too late. It is not too late to save the dead. Miracles happen. Your family can be reunited and you can all join the multitude on the shore. How can this be, Sister Star? By relocating your family before nature loses them in a storm. Remove them from that hole in the ground, bring home your loved ones so they will be waiting for you on your Judgment Day. Do not be alone. Now is the time to make your reservations at the lighthouse.*

I glanced at Carla. Suspicion was churning behind her squinty eyes. She was staring hard at Sister Star.

I am but the gatekeeper who welcomes loved ones.

Here it comes, I thought. The pitch.

My inspiration came from a dovecote I saw in Old San Juan years ago when I was a little girl.

The man with the bulging tobacco-infested cheek handed me a stack of color brochures. Take one, pass the rest.

My father read me Bible stories, not fairy tales. My mother sang hymns, not lullabies.

I flipped through the brochure. There was a rendering of Sister Star's dream for the dead in living color. The tower of angels of the Lighthouse Mortuary of Angel's Cove. It had a blurb about the Sister's vision and how the completed landscape would have on-site lodging available for grieving friends and families who had traveled from afar to visit their loved ones. Turn your tears into a three-day beachside vacation. Each room would have commemorative sheets, pillowcases, and towels that would be available for purchase in the Lighthouse gift shop. The mausoleum was designed to feature twenty-four-hour-a-day taped prayers and messages from the Scripture, as read by Sister Star. Yes, the Lighthouse Mortuary was truly the Forever Gift—the Gift That Gives Forever. There was nothing more important that a Christian could do for another Christian. On the back flap of the brochure was a 1-900 phone number brothers and sisters could call seven days a week to be placed on a mailing list to receive free information about the Lighthouse Mausoleums, gift shop, and motel. Callers would also receive a free copy of Sister Star's newsletter. Cost of the call was $2.99 a minute. Below that was a coupon for one hundred dollars off the purchase of a crypt at the Lighthouse. There was no better investment. Become a partner with Sister Star!

Such a deal.

All partners automatically receive the newsletter and a complete list of the names and addresses of all other partners. Get to know your eternal family before joining them on the shore.

Pen pals beyond the grave.

Sister Star cleared her throat and said, "Listen very carefully. What I am about to tell you is very important. This is probably the most important message of your lifetime."

She bowed her head, seasoning her sales pitch with a dramatic pause for added suspense. The tent was quiet. Not a sound. Ears were straining so that when Sister Star spoke not a word of this important message would be missed.

And from the silence there arose a voice. And the voice sayeth, "What a crock! If it was so damn important, it'd be on Larry King!"

The voice was Carla's.

And the voice was heard by all.

Carla, Carla, Carla. Everybody should have one.

Suddenly we were the main attraction.

Carla had committed a moral faux pas. She had preempted Sister Star's message of apocalyptic importance.

I don't know if it was because Carla and I were the first ones or the last ones to fully grasp the situation. This wasn't a revival. Sister Star wasn't an evangelist saving souls. She was merchandising death. She was a spokeswoman for the Lighthouse Mortuary—the same mortuary that was holding Carla's father's ashes hostage. We were not parishioners. We were customers.

No matter. The crowd responded to Carla's outburst the way a planeload of passengers would have reacted to an exploding firecracker in the lavatory. If looks could kill, we would have been annihilated by a juggernaut of pious sneers. Somehow the crowd had concluded that Carla and I and were a package deal.

People were standing, aiming hate looks in our direction. Lots of gestures.

I searched the crowd for a friendly face. I saw Gillian Gable several rows in front of us. She was laughing. I took that as a good sign.

Sister Star stood speechless, her face screwed in a gargoyle snarl.

A woman in a Ramada Inn housekeeper's uniform stared at me, her expression repelled, like I had raped and pillaged her Barbie collection.

Slowly, as the initial shock of the interruption began to wear off, puckered orifices relaxed and let fly a litany of noises, some not so rhythmical, that soared to the apex of the tent.

"Isn't that the Meadows girl?"

"Just like her father."

"Bad is in the blood."

Carla looked tough.

I looked for the nearest exit only to see the tent flaps fly open and witness the arrival of Royal Maddox and the fish militia. It was as though they had been standing by on pre-arranged alert. As the ranting brothers and sisters heard the cadence of the militia marching up the aisles, the tent grew ominously quiet. There must have been a dozen of them, all dressed up in their Audie Murphy costumes, just looking for an excuse to be a Man. Real men who thought name-calling, cowboy boots, guns, and flaunting their disregard for education made them some tough guys.

Parade halt.

Royal Maddox stopped at the end of our row. He folded his arms across his chest. So did the rest of the fish militia, like it was some kind of present arms drill.

Royal's eyes zeroed in on me and Carla. He said in a loud voice, "Well, if it ain't Mr. and Mrs. Smartass."

Carla shot back in her most ladylike voice, "That's Ms. Smartass to you, pal."

Royal's face went red, his lips stammered.

I hadn't thought it possible but the tent got quieter.

In strutted Ray-Newton in all his glory—freshly pressed acting police chief uniform, has-been country singer hair, and signature stogie.

In so many words we were asked to leave.

THERE WAS a metamorphosis during the ride home. Carla went from belligerent drunk to maudlin drunk. We hadn't said much of anything other than me saying, "Larry King?" She tittered and that was about the extent of the conversation until we were driving up her father's drive. I thought I heard her sniffling.

I asked her if she was crying.

She said, "Harry?"

"What?"

"You know what it's like when someone you love dies."

"Yeah, well, I don't talk about that, Carla."

"Yeah, well, I know you don't, pighead. I just want to know, do you ever get over it?"

I sucked in a deep breath and slowly let it out. "You learn to live with it."

If you're lucky.

When we got back to the cottage we said our good-nights. It had been a long but otherwise uneventful day.

TWENTY-TWO

CARLA HAD THAT bleary-eyed look that my old, long-since-departed cat Pooh-Pooh used to get just before she'd cough up a hairball. Carla was suffering the consequences of an unmerciful hangover.

We were sitting across from one another at a table in The Other Restaurant. Carla was hunched over the table, clutching an empty coffee mug in both hands, looking unusually small, reminding me of the Incredible Shrinking Woman.

A few tables away sat a man with an eggplant physique noisily masticating lumps of southern cooking while his technically female companion was slurping juice and surreptitiously peeking at us with glitterati interest. Undoubtedly she had recognized us as the pagans who had challenged Sister Star's moral authority the night before. I caught the technically female woman's eyes and gave her my showdown stare. She stared back with her best contemptible look of disapproval. It reminded me of that moment when the heel wrestler and the babyface wrestler square off to start the match. I smiled and winked at her. Her face scrunched painfully tight as though she were in dire need of anal lubricant.

Evalinda emerged from a back room carrying a rack of clean glasses. She put the rack down and fiddled behind the counter for a moment until she spotted Carla and me. She grabbed a couple menus and a pot of steamy coffee—elixir for Carla's alcohol-marinated brain.

Evalinda approached our table. She wore clothes of many colors and multiple strands of shiny dime-store beads. She looked like a fortune-teller on a weekend pass from Camp

Tarot. She placed the menus on the table. Carla held out her cup in both hands.

Before a drop had flowed, we heard "Are you going to wait on them?" The Fabulous Moolah objected to the mixed tag team of Mr. and Ms. Smartass being served.

Evalinda looked over her shoulder. "It would appear that way, wouldn't it?"

Moolah hissed some displeasure and made noises to her man about paying up and leaving.

Evalinda poured coffee in our cups. She looked at Carla and smirked. "I heard about last night." She looked back at Eggplant and Moolah as they made good on their threat to leave, then back at us and shook her head. "Haven't heard about anything else for that matter."

Apparently, Carla's impromptu plug for Larry King in the midst of Sister Star's yak-a-thon had already started to mythologize. The town criers had probably been spreading the word all night long about how the sainted Sister had been heckled and jeckled by crazed liberal devil worshipers who could read books.

The special looked like fossilized chicken lips doused in curdled milk of magnesia and sprinkled with old coffee grounds. I offered to trade with Carla. She'd ordered toast and orange juice. She stared at my plate. Her brow crinkled into a fat-chance frown, as if I had insulted her intelligence.

"Come on," I said. "I can't eat this. I don't even know what it is." For good measure I threw on my hangdog look.

"Starve, fool."

Hell hath more sympathy than a woman hung over.

I picked up a fork. The plan was simple. Survive breakfast, then ask Evalinda what she had meant with that cryptic remark about people being afraid that Charlie Meadows was right.

I stirred the slime du jour around on the Styrofoam plate, still not sure it was a risk I wanted to take when I was literally "saved by the bell."

The phone rang behind the breakfast counter.

Evalinda answered it.

It was for me.

Carla glanced at me. Without speaking she asked, Who would call you here?

I shrugged an answer and went over to the counter. Evalinda handed me the receiver.

"Hello," I said.

"Rice?" Female.

"Yes."

"It's Gillian Gable." Earth angel female.

"How…how did you know where I was here?" Where I was here? My Cary Grant has a tendency to come off like Mel Tillis.

"A wild guess. I called Charlie's. There was no answer. The only thing I could think was you might have gone out for breakfast."

I looked back at my plate on the table. "That depends on your definition of breakfast."

"What?"

"Nothing."

"Whatever. I was hoping we were going to have a chance to talk last night."

"We left early," I said. "By popular demand."

"I saw."

"You could have come over. You know where I'm staying."

"I started to but something happened. I'll tell you about it later. We need to talk. Today."

"Sure. Here?"

"No!" she blurted, as if it had been goosed out of her. I heard her take a deep breath. "No." She sighed. "Not there."

"All right. Tell me where."

"Port St. Joe. It's about a half hour from there."

"I know where it is."

She gave me directions to a rental cottage. And then she said, "Rice? Make sure no one is following you."

"Driving a little blue BMW?"

"I'm serious. Someone followed me last night."

"Are you sure?"

"Damn it, Rice! I'm not paranoid. I had to outrace someone all the way to Interstate Ten last night. The only thing that saved me was some advice my first editor gave me when I became an investigative reporter. He told me to always keep a full tank of gas."

I could hear the fear in her voice as she remembered last night.

The only response I could think of was to ask her if she had any idea of who it was.

"Who do you think?" she said. "The killer."

It wasn't so much her answer that surprised as it was the certainty in her voice. Before I could ask she said, "Because if Charlie and Joe were murdered for the reason I think, then I'm next."

TWENTY-THREE

In the mid-1800s the prospering Gulf port community of St. Joseph had the distinction of being one of Florida's fastest-growing boom towns. The growth was spurred by the resources delivered from the neighboring Gulf of Mexico and by the cotton that was railroaded in from Georgia and Alabama. In its heyday, St. Joseph charted on the Florida top-ten hit parade of largest cities, peaking at number six with a bullet.

Among St. Joseph's earliest claims to fame, if not its last claim, was playing host to the state's first constitution convention.

St. Joseph thrived. It looked as if there would be no stopping its growth and development until a devastating one-two knockout punch. Destiny had taken a hand in the name of an unnamed raging hurricane that made previous storms seem like a mere burp in comparison, and a deadly epidemic of yellow fever, known as Yellow Jack. St. Joseph was knocked flat on its tush and would never fully recover. St. Joseph would never again be a bigshot town, never again a contender. And over the years, as the swamp settlement of Fort Dallas indiscriminately deformed into a crime-riddled Miami infested with trend-slaves and imitation thinkers, St. Joseph blossomed into a very small and serene Port St. Joe.

The pillbox cottage looked like it had been built as an afterthought with leftover scrap stolen from a real construction site. The little blue BMW was parked next to the building, cloaked in the shadow of a three-story oak tree. Gillian Gable was sitting on the porch reading a paperback, her succulent bare feet propped titillatingly on the rail. She used the book to shield her eyes from the sun as we pulled to a stop behind her car. She smiled and stood to welcome us. She wore tight red shorts and an oversized T-shirt with big purple flowers. She looked edible.

"Is that her?" Carla said, watching me.

I said it was.

Carla's eyes drifted toward Gillian Gable, then returned to me. "She's quite attractive. Don't you think?"

I faked a think. "I suppose."

She rolled her eyes. "Really?"

"What?"

"Don't *what* me, Harry."

"What?"

"What? What? You should see yourself. You got that goofy I-should-have-stopped-at-the-pharmacist's look plastered all over your face."

On that note, Carla opened the car door and got out. So did I. I introduced the women. They shook hands.

"I'm sorry about your father," Gable said simply, instinctively knowing there were no adequate words.

Carla nodded and Gable led us into the small cottage.

"Furnishings from the showroom of St. Vincent de Paul," Gable said, waving a hand around the cramped room. She was not exaggerating. There was a matching Acapulco gold vinyl couch and chair, a chrome coffee table, a warped Double Bubble pink linoleum floor, and a dinette cluttered with files, loose papers, and a reporter's notebook.

"How do you afford this?" I said.

"An unlimited expense account," Gable deadpanned.

Carla smiled.

The ice was cracked, if not broken.

Caught in a moment of silence, my attention switched to Gillian Gable's juicy toes au naturel. No polish. The ten miniature goddesses of horniness had cast their spell and I was feeling the effect.

I could hear the voice of my junior high school P.E. coach calling from the grave: "Rice, take three laps around Luxembourg." I never had a P.E. coach who didn't think laps could cure everything. Three laps for a periscope up, i.e., a case of the hornies. Two laps for discipline. Ten laps would cure asthma and diabetes. Fifty laps would make you a better outfielder.

"Thanks for coming."

I looked up at Gillian Gable's face and nodded. "Yeah. Sure. What's…what's going on? Who was following you?"

"I don't know."

"You said it was the killer."

"Yes. But I don't know who that is."

Carla said, "Then what makes you think you're next?"

"That." Gillian pointed to the papers spread across the dinette. "Your father was helping me with a story. Actually, it was his story. He's the one who called me."

I said, "And Sister Star is the story?"

"That's how it started, but it's gone way beyond that. This is going to take a while. Let's sit down." We did and Gable continued, "Carla, when your father first called me in Tallahassee, a little over a year ago, he was sure that Angel's Cove was being duped by con artists. It had started with ads appearing in the local weeklies. The ads simply read, 'Miracles Happen.' After running for a couple weeks the ads became billboards and posters and read, 'Miracles Happen—Sister Star is coming to Angel's Cove!' Nothing more. No one knew who or what Sister Star was. Only there was the implied promise of a miracle. Part of Charlie's argument was Angel's Cove was ripe for picking. The net ban was imminent, the oyster industry was hurting, the very economic fiber of Angel's Cove was being threatened, people were concerned about their livelihood and were in urgent need of a miracle. With all the advance hype and promotion for Sister Star, it was like announcing the arrival of the next messiah. Angel's Cove was ready for a miracle to happen. If Sister Star had been a new miracle beer, the people were ready to switch brands.''

"I don't see the miracle," I said. "From what I heard last night, she was selling funerals. Where's the hope in that?"

"When Sister Star arrived, she sold work, or the illusion of jobs, which is how they got Angel's Cove to buy into their plan."

"They?"

"The Lighthouse Mortuary. Angel's Cove has always been against the development of its coastline. Development would bring more cars, more people, more waste polluting the bay waters, contaminating the oyster beds. As far as Angel's Cove was concerned, development for the living would bring death to a way of life. That's how the Lighthouse sold the town council on giving away prime beach real estate, tax free, to build a high-rise condo for the dead. The dead would bring in money without added cars on the street. And the dead don't flush toilets, so the bay waters wouldn't be polluted. Build for the dead and save the living.''

"Sounds too good to be true."

"Of course it is. That was Charlie's point. It's the old adage, If it sounds too good to be true, then it probably is. But that didn't stop the town council from making a deal with the devil.''

"It never does."

"That's why reporters love them so much."

Carla said, "I'm missing something here. How are the dead supposed to bring in money?"

"Construction jobs," I answered, "to build the mausoleum. Of course those would be temporary jobs."

"Which is what the council said," Gable interjected. She turned to Carla. "The money was supposed to come in the form of the relatives that flocked in droves to visit their loved ones stacked on the shores of Angel's Cove. In reality, the Lighthouse had no intention of sharing those dollars with the local merchants. They are building their own beachfront motel on the grounds. Turn your grief into a beach holiday. Granny's ashes would like that. There's already a gift shop there that sells official Sister Star silk memorial flowers. I'm not making that up. The Lighthouse will not allow real flowers because they wilt and have to be cleaned up after. And your construction jobs, Rice? The construction company brought in their own crew.''

"There seems to be a contradiction here," I said. "If these tourists of the dead do materialize, they'll bring cars and flush toilets, won't they?"

"Sounds like Angel rape, doesn't it?" Gable smiled. "You haven't heard the best part. In return the council stood up for the rights of all their soon-to-be-unemployed and made Sister Star promise that every citizen would be guaranteed the opportunity to buy a phantom job with the Lighthouse."

Carla nodded. "I've been wanting to ask you what you meant when you said Sister Star sold work or the illusion of jobs."

Gillian said, "The application fee is seventy-five dollars, nonrefundable. The position is independent sales contractor, or ISC. If an applicant is accepted—"

"What determines that?" I interrupted.

"Satisfying the Lighthouse qualification requirements."

"Which are?"

"Seventy-five dollars."

I nodded. "All right."

"Once the application has been approved, the applicant is entitled to enroll in the Lighthouse Mortuary Independent Sales Contractor Home Study Course. That costs a hundred dollars and is required. Study at your own pace. No time pressure. Once an applicant has completed the course, they are allowed to buy the ISC sales kit from the Lighthouse. The sales kit costs twenty-five dollars and is nothing more than blank sales forms."

"How much do the ISCs have to pay if they sell something?"

"Nothing. In fact, they collect a three percent commission on all sales. But there is one catch."

"Surprise, surprise."

"To qualify for commissions, each ISC must complete one noncommissioned sale. To make it easy, the Lighthouse has agreed to accept a self-sales application from each ISC."

"What does that mean?"

"Just what you think. Each ISC buys a crypt and all the other crap that goes with it for themselves or a family member to qualify for commissions on future sales. But that's not all. To maintain their status as a nonemployee, nonlegal representative of the Lighthouse, each ISC must average at least six sales in any six-month period or have their status terminated. Naturally they can reapply…"

"For seventy-five dollars?"

Gable nodded. "Yes. Also, as an independent sales contractor, each ISC is responsible for all taxes and their own expenses. In return, the Lighthouse Mortuary agrees to encourage all ISCs to promote their independent business and to use official Lighthouse advertising material. Purchasable, of course, from the Lighthouse."

"Any takers?"

"You'd be surprised."

"Who do they sell to? Each other?"

"Their families. As you heard last night, the Lighthouse isn't going after just the future dead. They're going full force after the past dead. That's what all the videotape was about. Re-interment. It's the wave of the future. Don't your ancestors deserve better than earth worms? Dig them up. Re-inter them at the Lighthouse on the Gulf, where they'll have beautiful sunsets throughout eternity." She sat back and didn't say anything for a moment. "Here's the real kicker. ISCs don't receive one dime of commission until the bill is paid in full.

Most people buy on the installment plan. Thus, the Lighthouse collects interest on the principle, but pays no interest on the delayed commissions.''

"What if there is a default?"

"No commission. Lighthouse keeps what's already been collected.''

"And if the crypt is occupied? Do they evict?"

"No. They go after the collateral. It's always property."

"How do you know all this?"

"I'm an ISC. Don't look so shocked. The newspaper paid for it.''

The three of us sat silently for a moment like a tobacco industry triad of Fifth Amendment devotees practicing their right to refrain from telling the truth.

Carla rocked back on the couch. She looked at Gillian Gable strangely and said, "All that construction, the funeral home—all that money and expense—I don't know, it seems to be an awful elaborate front for a con.''

"Oh, it's no con," Gillian Gable said. "It's much worse than that. It's legitimate, all somewhat legal.''

"Somewhat legal?" I said.

"Nothing that can be proved illegal. Even though everything I've turned up is either fishy, immoral, unethical, unscrupulous, borderline fraud, or misrepresentation at best. Just legal enough. What laws you might argue are being violated are toothless consumer protection rights that no one seems to have an interest in enforcing.''

"Even Joe Patti?"

"Outside his jurisdiction.''

"He was working with you and Carla's father?"

Gillian nodded.

"Working what?" Carla said. "You said my father thought Sister Star was a con artist. Next you say there's no con. So what were you working? What story?''

"When I first heard about the scheme to build a forty-story

mausoleum with a million niches, I was positive it was con. Why Angel's Cove of all places? Your father and I didn't think it would ever be built. Even when they first broke ground, we were sure they were just salting the mine. But we were wrong. We had no idea how lucrative the funeral business was. It's a nine-billion-dollar-a-year industry and growing. The sums of money to be made are staggering. The profits are so outrageous it has become an absurdly overcrowded field. Which is why the Lighthouse is making such a big push on the re-interment market. They want to recycle the dead because there are simply too many undertakers and not enough stiffs to go around, combined with the funeral director's 'gravest' distress—the fact that people are simply living way too long.''

The funeral world according to Gable was not only after past and recent dead, but was placing a priority emphasis on future dead. Preneed selling, locking up future business before the competition did, a variation on the old Buy Now, Go Later plan. The idea was to pay in advance as a hedge against inflation. Preplanning was practical and made sense. Prepaying was not smart business. The risk was having money tied up in a funeral home that may or may not be in business at the time of death and need. There was little or nothing to prevent the funeral director from absconding with the funds.

''One of the prepayment sales pitches to the elderly is that they can use prepaid funeral arrangements as a way to not only shelter their money, but to actually make money. The way it is supposed to work is you can prepay whatever amount of money you want for a funeral. The law can't limit the amount you spend. People are told to put aside whatever they have, say twenty-five thousand dollars, for a funeral so they will be poor enough to qualify for free Medicaid care. Let the taxpayers pay for their nursing home while the benevolent funeral director protects their life savings. Here's the clincher. When the relative dies, you go back to the funeral home and instead of the prepaid twenty-five-thousand-dollar funeral, you're told you can pick out a twelve-, fifteen-thousand-dollar funeral. The funeral director kicks back the extra thirteen thousand or whatever dollars to the beneficiary and Medicaid can't touch it.''

"What a scam," I said.

"Big time. Not only is the taxpayer being bilked, but the funeral home ends up selling an excessively inflated funeral because the beneficiary has been an accomplice to fraud and isn't going to squawk about being charged two or three times the cost of a typical funeral, especially when they are getting money back.''

Gillian Gable told us that the real money was in at-need sales, when survivors were most vulnerable and easily manipulated, when memorial counselors could prey on sorrow and exploit grief, when merchandise like eternal-comfort posture-pedic coffin mattresses and arch-cushioned slumber footwear and ultralight postmortem restoration bras for eternal support could be peddled as guilt balm. Survivors were discouraged from seeking help from neighbors or friends or ministers in making final arrangements.

Carla asked why.

"The party line is it's part of the healing process," Gillian said. "Making arrangements and throwing away money is good grief therapy. The more you spend on a funeral, the better you'll feel.''

The better the undertaker will feel too, I thought.

I remembered Father Shifty once telling me a story about when he was still in the priesthood. A funeral director actually refused to let the priest into the office with the grieving family.

The funeral director told the young priest, "There is no reason for you to be here. Priests do not help their parishioners buy new furniture or pick out their next vacation. I don't tell people where or how to worship and you don't tell people how to express their sorrow. Good day, Father.''

I heard Carla say, "I've got a question. If it's such an over-crowded field, how can they get away with charging so much? I should think it would be a buyer's market. Why doesn't the competition keep the prices down?"

"Price fixing," Gable said, matter-of-factly. She looked at me and then at Carla again. "It's a strange business. Funeral directors aren't so much competitors as they are allies. They share a mutual interest to extract the maximum payment for a dearly departed's ticket to eternity. Think about it. How often do you see funeral prices advertised in the newspaper or on television?"

Carla and I drew a blank.

"You don't," Gillian answered for us. "Theirs is a very secretive society when it comes to their costs and their charges. Advertising would only undermine the profit structure of the cabal. It's the unwritten commandment: Thou shall not upset the applecart."

"Still," I said, "it would take a helluva lot of apples to construct a forty-story mausoleum on beachfront property. Where does a funeral home get that kind of money?"

"Good question, Rice," she said.

"Glad you liked it, Gable. So what's the good answer? Where do they come up with that kind of money?"

"The stock market."

"The stock market?"

"Yep. The Grim Reaper has gone Wall Street and is yield-ing some nifty returns."

I shook my head. "Hold it. Shares of funeral homes are being publicly traded on the exchange?"

"Not individual funeral homes. Chains."

"Chains?" I repeated. "Chain funeral homes, like in res-taurants?"

She nodded.

"Great. Let's go off to the nearest Funeral King and get a McCasket to go."

"Actually, that's about how it started. Years ago casket manufacturers started taking over funeral homes to keep out other coffin builders. The funeral home became the manufacturer's outlet for their caskets. The more funeral homes the casket company bought, the more caskets they obviously sold and the fewer outlets the competition had for their coffins. The company also was saving on commission by selling its own caskets. Soon they found other ways to cut overhead without passing the savings on to the consumer."

"Like what?"

"Well, they could use a centralized motor pool for hearses. Then they started building funeral homes at cemeteries. That's one of the things that makes the death industry so highly profitable. Cemeteries are established as nonprofit corporations and don't have to pay income tax on grave sites. Another way the company found to save money was to cut out duplicate services. One sales staff could market all the funeral homes in the chain. They could also centralize embalming facilities and use the same crematorium."

"Which the family-owned funeral home couldn't compete with, so the independents are squeezed out of business."

"Or forced to sell to the chain. Which is usually what happens. The corporations know the 'warm' appeal a family name brings to a funeral home. They don't want to lose the appearance of personal attention. So they buy the funeral home with the name and keep the family staff on as hired help. You think you're dealing with a caring trustworthy neighbor and all the time it's the profit-oriented Death Mart."

Carla frowned. "Warm?" she scoffed. "Have you met Howard Ashby? If that man's got a family it's cold-blooded and sheds its skin."

"Ah, yes. Mr. Empathy," Gillian Gable said, mocking Ashby's solemn tone. "His is a touching story. Inspired to answer the sacred call to serve the bereaved when his sister and brother and mother and father and beloved Kerry blue terrier all succumbed to the toxic fumes of a jasmine-scented air freshener gone foul.''

She dabbed her eyes with a make-believe Kleenex.

Carla shook her head and smiled in spite of herself. "Gee, what numbskull would buy a story like that.''

"Don't feel so bad. It comes at a time when people are most vulnerable and have a real need and desire to trust others. They just assume the funeral director would not take advantage of them. They are not in the mood for comparison shopping, so they trust the funeral director to make the right choices for them.''

"What gets me is they get away with it. We might as well trust the used-car salesman to protect our interest.''

"It's not quite the same thing, Carla.''

"No?''

"No.''

"Sleaze is sleaze.''

"That's true, but we are talking about image, and that is something the funeral director really cultivates. Self-image is very important to funeral directors. Even their trade association calls them professionals. It sets them above other businessmen, puts them in a category with doctors and clergy, although the technical education requirement is minimal, only a notch above high school and a mile below a college degree. They even try to link themselves to other professions, like psychologists, with titles such as grief therapists. You'd be surprised at how much time and energy goes into fostering their image. You'll always find the local funeral director active in a church and community organizations. I suppose the idea is if you can't trust a fellow Rotarian and Shaker, who can you trust?''

"A sanctimonious celibate,'' I said. "While undertakers strive for that image, others have it thrust upon us.''

The women looked at me as if I had just intruded on some juicy locker-room gossip.

I shrugged. "It seemed like a good time for a strange interlude."

No reply.

Sensing the interlude had run its course, I said, "Who owns the Lighthouse?"

Gillian Gable said, "The Thames Group, a London-based corporation. Thames owns cemeteries and funeral homes throughout Europe, Australia, Canada, and South America. Last year their revenues topped a quarter billion dollars. And they are not even one of the major players. The biggies are Service Corp International and Loewen. Service Corp took in over a billion dollars last year and Loewen came in at about a half billion. It's truly a global business. They are all over the place. The Lighthouse is Thames' first venture into the U.S. market."

"But why Angel's Cove?" Carla asked.

"Demographics. You go where people are dying. Florida has a high percentage of retirees."

"Still," Carla persisted.

Gillian Gable nodded. "I know. They could have built anywhere in the state, so why here of all places. Your father had an interesting theory about that. Remember I said that the Lighthouse always wanted land as collateral? Land is cheap in the Panhandle. A lot of the property the Lighthouse was accepting for collateral was valued at less than the cost of the funeral being bought. Charlie figured that the corporation was looking long-term. As the state continued to overbuild and overpopulate in central and southern Florida, it would only be a matter of time before people began looking to north Florida, to the Panhandle, to get away from the crowds and the crime, without giving up Florida's generous bankruptcy loopholes and no state income tax benefits. It makes sense. The Lighthouse has not evicted anyone who has defaulted. Let the tenant keep paying the property tax, but as soon as they die, the Lighthouse lawyers close in on the land. Gather enough land

and in the future Thames will be able to diversify and build housing."

"Theory," I said.

"Yes. Just theory. Nothing I can substantiate. Yet."

Carla said, "You said if you were right and my father and the police chief were murdered for the reason you thought, then you were next. Are you saying my father was killed because of his theory?"

"I can't say that for sure."

"I'm not asking for sure."

"I know that." Gillian Gable hesitated a moment, said, "I don't want to reopen any wounds."

"The wounds are already open," Carla said. "They never healed."

Gable's eyes studied Carla for a long time. "All right," she said. "There's a lot of money at stake. The Lighthouse is spending millions to erect that grotesque mausoleum. Your father was making waves. He was doing what he thought was best for his friends. He was trying to protect them."

"How? What was he doing?"

"Last night, after you two left early, Sister Star began to denounce a cancer that is spreading through the nation. Namely, low-cost burial and cremation societies, like Neptune. She called the societies anti-Christian, contrary to every principle dear to the American way of life. She said those who seek to destroy the Christian funeral customs were atheists and did not share the God-fearing reverence for the dead and didn't understand the healing power of a decent memorialization. To hear her talk, the American funeral is the last bastion against the spread of communism. The message being, The more you spend on a funeral, the more American you are.

"Your father called me because of a series of newspaper articles I had written on the low-cost societies and how much money they were saving people. I mean, it's gotten to the point that after a home and an automobile, the biggest expense people are facing is funerals. Your father wanted more information. The more he and I talked, the more I began to sense there was a story. I mean, a forty-story mausoleum in Angel's Cove? Miracles Happen? And who was this Sister Star character?''

Gillian Gable turned to me. ''Remember the last thing I said to you after I dropped you off yesterday?''

I thought about it a second. ''Yeah. Something about Ronald McDonald.''

''Do you think that there is only one Ronald McDonald who travels all around the country?''

''Of course not. There's a bunch of hired clowns,'' I said.

''And?'' she prompted.

Sister Star—Ronald McDonald, I thought. ''Sister Star is a hired clown?''

''Exactly. There's an equivalent Sister Star in England, in Spain, in Italy, in Portugal, several throughout Australia and South America. They are nothing more than scripted corporate spokeswomen. Once Charlie found that out he started spreading the word.''

''And came off as the bad guy in all of this.''

''Yes. The Lighthouse billed itself as the shining savior of Angel's Cove, selling pretend jobs and nonexistent miracles. Charlie told people they were being bilked, spending more money than they should on the dead, especially when there were living who were having trouble making their next mortgage payment. Charlie began telling everyone about the low-cost alternatives. The Lighthouse found out about it and let it be known that if people wanted to side with Charlie Meadows, then the Lighthouse would take their jobs elsewhere to a more deserving and appreciative community. The thing is, it wasn't like the Lighthouse was offering anything of substance, but what little they were offering, Charlie's so-called friends didn't want to lose. I guess in the end, the Lighthouse was offering them hope, meaningless as it was.''

"But at a price."

"No shit."

"People are afraid Charlie was right."

"What?"

"Nothing," I said. "It was something I heard. What about Joe Patti? What was his involvement?"

"Joe didn't like what he was seeing either. He started asking questions, said bad words like consumer protection agency. He was like Charlie. He thought a disproportionate amount of money was being spent on the dead and not enough on the living. There are kids here going to school with holes in the soles of their shoes and people are spending a hundred dollars for a pair of burial footwear."

TWENTY-FOUR

THE BIG MYSTERY was how the Lighthouse planned to fill a million urn niches and two hundred fifty thousand vaults in a little coastal town with a population slightly larger than the Garden of Eden had in the days before Adam petitioned for more babes.

Gillian Gable had the answer.

"Infomercials," she said, wiggling a chorus line of nude toes. "Do you ever watch television after midnight?"

"Rarely," I said. If I am up after the witching hour, I'm usually not shopping for the revolutionary new Weed Whacker home hair-cutting system or for a psychic singer who knows the way to San Jose. I'd rather listen to China Valles do his jazz thing on the graveyard shift of a Miami radio station.

Gable asked if we had access to a VCR.

I looked at Carla. I didn't even remember seeing a TV at her father's place.

Carla shook her head.

I asked Gable why.

She said she had a videotape of Sister Star's infomercial back in her motel room in Angel's Cove, along with her clothes and toiletries. She had not gone back to the motel last night after being followed, afraid Rosemary's grown-up baby would be waiting for her at the room.

She tugged on her T-shirt and said, "This morning I went into Port St. Joe and bought these clothes, some toothpaste and a brush."

I glanced at the papers scattered on the dinette. "You always take your notes with you?"

"Always," she said.

"What about last night?" Carla said. "What happened?"

Gable pursed her lips as if she was wondering where to begin, so I started the story for her.

"It was a dark and stormy night," I said, coaxing her to pick up the narrative.

She feigned indignation, said, "Reporters do not embellish their stories."

"That's not embellishing," I corrected. "That's setting the tone. A perfectly acceptable journalistic technique."

"That was not setting the tone. That was embellishing." A slow smile spread on her lips. "I know the difference."

The way she said it. *I know the difference.* The pain gripped me like barbed wire being yanked tight around my heart. *I know the difference.* The exact words, the same tone. The familiar look, a smile from a recurring dream. Someone dead, many tears ago.

IT WAS MORNING. We were still in bed, just back from a romp through Wonderland. She said she knew she had me when I had forgone watching professional wrestling on television to make love.

"Make love?" I said nervously. "What are you talking about? That was sex."

"*That* was love," she said. The little smile. "I know the difference."

"There's a difference?" I had said then, and heard myself repeating aloud.

"The difference is," Gillian Gable said, "embellishment is something you can prove isn't true. Check last night's weather report."

"The night was clear and the moon was yellow?"

"Just like the night Stagger Lee pulled his forty-four and shot Billy. No. It was a ghost story night, dark and eerie."

The tent show let out around ten o'clock. By the time the reporter had driven to Highway 98 most of the parade of pickups and cars had veered off in various directions. She headed west on the two-lane highway lined with sand dunes. She glanced in the rearview mirror. One set of headlights, the luminous eyes of a metallic swamp creature stalking its prey. Her stomach began to contort like a spastic yogi doing warm-ups.

She checked the rearview mirror again. The headlights were still there, the same distance as before, keeping pace. She was starting to get mad. At herself. Damn it, Gillian, she thought. It's a public highway. It's probably nothing more than tourists heading for the redneck riviera or Leonard Nimoy in search of mumbo jumbo. Jesus, she thought, you're getting to be like John. That thought made her shudder. John was the new reporter who had recently moved to Tallahassee from Atlanta. On his best day he was an obnoxious paranoiac blowhard that she avoided like she avoided children's birthday parties. John's paranoia was textbook material. She had even told him that he was the most paranoid person she had ever met. In all seriousness he shot back, "You would be too if everyone was out to get you."

The irony of the statement was lost on him.

No. That wasn't for her. Still, just to prove to herself how silly she was, she pressed down on the accelerator, putting some distance between her and the swamp monster.

In that instant the headlights inexplicably disappeared as though suddenly cloaked in the nocturnal embrace of an ancient insanity. She would have noticed if the lights had turned off the highway, but she had passed no roads to turn on. The lights were there one second and gone the next. It was like a medieval wizard had blown out the eternal flames on his birthday cake candles. The narrow road had become dark and desolate and seemingly endless. Alone with just her thoughts and the hum of tires on asphalt.

"It was spooky," Gable said. "The lights just vanished as if it had been a figment of my imagination."

A few miles later the illusion was exposed. Caught in the beam of an oncoming car, Gable saw the flickering glint of her nightmare on wheels in the rearview mirror. With headlights off, it was directly behind her. Like a persistent little dog, it was close enough to sniff the tail of her blue BMW.

The race was on.

"Which I obviously won or I wouldn't be sitting here telling you about it," Gillian Gable said. "I tried to outrun him, but he stayed right behind me for over an hour before he finally coasted to a stop. I assumed he ran out of gas. I didn't go back to ask and I had no intention of going back to the same motel, or anywhere near it, where he could find me."

I said, "Could you tell what kind of car it was?"

She shook her head. "The only thing I could see was my name in headlines and I don't mean the byline."

Carla said, "So you don't know who it was or even if it was the same person who killed my father."

Gable hesitated. "No, not for sure. But who else could it have been? We were working on exposing a multimillion-dollar business that's taking advantage of people."

"The Lighthouse?" I said.

"Yes."

"You think the Lighthouse is behind the murders?"

"Yes. Don't you?"

"Not necessarily. Just because the hooker was strangled by a man wearing gloves, don't automatically assume it was the glove salesman," I quoted from Pudd'nhead Rice's calendar.

"Give me a break. I'm not stretching it that far. What other connection could there be between Joe Patti and Charlie?"

"The money," I said.

Gillian Gable frowned. "What money?"

"The money Charlie stole from the police chief."

She studied me with reporter eyes. "What money did he steal from Joe?"

"The money Joe stole from the fish militia."

She gave me an annoyed, get-to-the-point look. I told her what Joe had told me about the fishermen pooling the money they had gotten from selling their nets to buy guns.

"Guns?" Gable said. "What were they going to do, shoot the fish since they can't net them?"

"No. I think they were planning to scare off the sport fishermen."

"That stupid militia. It's nothing more than a bunch of cowardly kooks playing frontier days. Bullies, that's what they are."

"That may be, but don't underestimate them. It's not easy to defend against minds dulled by the ravages of fear and hate."

"Brain dead, in other words. No wonder Joe took the money. He was baby-sitting. He didn't steal their money. He confiscated it for their own protection."

"No. He said he stole it."

Her eyes grew big with surprise as if she was mentally undressing me. "He told you that?"

"Yes."

"Did he say why?"

"He said he'd tell me later, only—"

"Later never came. Now we'll never know."

"Maybe not. There's something I want to follow up on. It may explain why Joe took the money."

Carla said, "What is it?"

"It's just a hunch. I'll tell you about it after I've checked it out."

"When are you planning to do that?"

I shrugged. "I guess now is as good a time as any."

Gillian Gable said, "I need a favor."

The favor was to go to the motel in Angel's Cove, pick up her things, and bring them back to her. She gave me the key to the motel room and a company credit card to settle the bill.

I looked at Carla. "Whenever you're ready."

Carla glanced at me and then Gable. She said, "I think I'd rather stay here and talk to Gillian about my father, if that's all right."

Gable nodded. "Of course."

I said, "Good. I'll see you ladies sometime this afternoon."

"Take your time," Gable said. "Carla and I have a lot to talk about."

I stood up to leave with the motel key in hand. "Anything else you need while I'm out?"

Carla said no.

Gillian Gable said, "Just my belongings."

I said okay and started out the door.

"And Rice?" Gable called after me. "One other thing. Don't be trying on my undies."

The best-laid schemes o' Rice and men.

TWENTY-FIVE

THE WOMAN behind the checkout desk had a pedigree haircut and looked like an aging queen of the hop who apparently spent much of her time reliving scenes from *American Bandstand*. The motel office was a testament to the early years of Dick Clark's televised diaper service. The walls were cluttered with framed magazine covers and pictures of pompadoured Bobbys, beehived girl groups, smiling Frankies, fabulous Fabians, and a special section for the angels of rock 'n' roll heaven.

I set Gillian Gable's garment bag and cosmetic case on the floor and placed her credit card and room key on the counter.

I said, "Awopbopalubop."

THE FAT OTIS BAR was my next stop.

Babycakes was on duty. The uniform of the day was a nipple-pink halter and tight little butt-sucking shorts.

Babycakes welcomed me with one of those take-me-you-savage smiles that can curl the toes. She plucked a bottle of beer from the cooler and put it in front of me. It was the same brand I had had the night before last with Joe Patti.

She said, "I never forget a man or his drink."

She remembered me. It wasn't much, but it was the closest thing to a poignant encounter with the opposite sex I'd had since the man with the big wallet and the well-hung portfolio had outbid me for a woman in love's auction. Money was more enticing than romance. Love does have its price. Heartache is even more expensive. Only dreams are free. At least Babycakes remembered me and I was grateful.

I said, "You've just earned a place in my memoirs."

"Cool," she chirped. "These memoirs have a title?"

"Guzzler's Travels."

She laughed. "You're pretty swift."

I blinked and stared at her the way Hugh Hefner stared at his first bunny. I was definitely surprised she had made the literary connection and by her quick rejoinder. Babycakes read my expression perfectly.

"How about that," she said. "I can read."

I cringed as if I had just been flushed with a toxic enema. Which I would have deserved. There are some lessons that I need to learn over and over again.

"Sorry," I said. "Didn't mean to shortchange you."

"I'm used to it," she said without a trace of self-pity.

"You shouldn't have to be."

She shrugged. "Just don't shortchange the tip," she said with a sly grin.

Moving right along, I changed the subject.

"The other night," I said, "when I was in here with Joe Patti? You asked him how Paulie was. Who is Paulie?"

She regarded me skeptically for a moment. "You were working with Joe, weren't you?"

"Yes."

She leaned forward against the bar. "Paulie is Pauline, Joe's little sister. She's a student over in Gainesville, at the university. She has an inoperable brain tumor. I don't know, maybe a week ago, she went into a coma. She's been sick longer than that. I know for the last couple months Joe was driving over to Gainesville every Friday after work and spending the weekend in the hospital holding Paulie's hand. He'd drive back here late Sunday night in time for work Monday morning. Sometimes he'd stay over Monday and get back Tuesday morning. The way he looked, I don't think he was getting any sleep from the time he'd wake up on Friday mornings until he went to bed Monday nights or whenever he got back."

There it was, a motive to steal—medical expenses.

The men's room door popped open and out walked the son
of Blob. He had a butcher-block torso, no neck, spindly legs,
reddish hair, and boa arms. He stopped when he saw me sitting
at the bar. His eyes flicked between me and Babycakes.

"Jack the Brit," Babycakes said by way of introduction,
"just back from doing manly things."

Jack the Brit smirked, unfazed. "Quite right," he said.
"Back from ye olde crap shoot." He had a Benny Hill accent.

He walked to the opposite end of the bar where a half-filled
mug was waiting. He climbed on the stool. He studied me
intently for a moment and then snapped his fingers.

"Last night," he said. "You're the chap who had the mis-
fortune of being with that dreadfully rude woman at the tent
show."

"Tongue, much like Polaroid film, exposes fool in sixty
seconds," I uttered in a tone of spiritual tranquillity, which I
had mastered from watching a sleepy-eyed David Carradine
in *Kung Fu.*

Jack the Brit frowned, not sure if I was talking about his
tongue or Carla's tongue or the great universal tongue.

The front door opened and in walked his hairness, Ray-
Newton. The acting police chief swaggered through the door
like he was the best man at Buford Pusser's wedding. His
uniform was starched, his leather shined, his badge sparkled,
and his tidal-wave coif was glossy. He was a sure bet to be
the next inductee into the Brylcreem Hall of Fame.

Ray-Newton eyed me with The Cop Look, taught in most
accredited police academies.

Babycakes said, "Hi, hon."

Hon nodded, still looking at me. He hooked his thumbs in
his gun belt. Intimidating Cop Pose. Second-semester stuff.

Ray-Newton's eyes narrowed. "You're still here," he said.

"That's amazing," I said. "You figured that out all by
yourself."

The acting police chief squared his feet with his shoulders.

The Get Ready To Duel Position. I think he got that one from *Robocop*.

I held up my hands. "I'm unarmed, Slick."

Jack the Brit chuckled.

Ray-Newton's face scrunched as if he was trying to pass yesterday's burrito. He was pissed. I may have unwittingly contributed to that.

He said, "I should have arrested you last night."

"For what?"

"Disturbing the peace. I just figured you'd be smart enough to haul butt out of here. You're not welcome in Angel's Cove."

"I'll make you a deal," I said. "When you can tell me who killed Charlie Meadows and Joe Patti, I'll pack my bags and catch the next stage out of Dodge."

"I can tell you right now." Ray-Newton smirked. He walked over and parked on the bar stool next to me. He looked to see if Babycakes and Jack the Brit were listening. When he was sure he had an audience, he said, "It was Leonitus. Start packing."

Leonitus, Carla's giant albino. Leonitus, who worked in the crematorium at the Lighthouse Mortuary. Leonitus, the ward Dr. Galen the medical examiner had taken into his home after the boy had served time in a juvenile home for starting fires. Leonitus, brain-damaged as a child after nearly drowning in a swimming pool.

I was skeptical. Apparently I wasn't the only one.

"I don't believe it," I heard Babycakes whisper.

Jack the Brit nodded sagely, as though he had known it all along.

I said, "Have you arrested him?"

Ray-Newton said, "Not yet. Still looking for him."

"What makes you think he did it?"

"Evidence. We found strands of his bleached hair on Joe's body. After that I went through the clothing Charlie was wearing when his body was discovered. Found bleached hair in them.''

''How convenient.''

''Yeah. Well, sometimes that's the way it is in police work.''

''Did you find any motive in the clothing?''

Ray-Newton shrugged. ''We will. Right now the way I'm figuring it is Charlie may have been an accident. He had been drinking. Maybe he was drunk and insulted Leonitus. That wouldn't be hard to do. Maybe Charlie and Leonitus got into a fight. Charlie fell in the water, hit his head, and drowned. Leonitus may have panicked and cremated the body before there was an autopsy. His simple mind probably thought that's all there was to it. Except when Joe gets back, he starts to ask questions about the circumstances surrounding the death and the cremation. Leonitus gets scared, afraid of being arrested and sent to prison, so he kills Joe. That's my theory. Course, we'll know for sure after we get him.''

''You're sure about the hair?''

''Being Leonitus'? Yeah, I'm sure. But I did send it to the lab for confirmation. I'm not going to lose a case to some smartass lawyer on any technicality.''

''That's all you've got? Just the hair?''

''No, that's not all I've got. I've got two bodies dumped in the exact same location. Only a damn fool would be stupid enough to do something like that.''

I shook my head slowly.

Ray-Newton said, ''What?''

''I don't know. It's too simple.''

''Like I said, we're dealing with a simple mind.''

Yeah, I thought. I know the feeling.

TWENTY-SIX

As far as the goat cheese between Ray-Newton's ears was concerned there was nothing more to say, the case was solved. No room in there for further discussion or thought. He might as well have pasted a DO NOT DISTURB sign on his forehead.

I took care of my tab and Babycakes and left. I walked out onto the streets of Angel's Cove, where anything was possible and everyone with bleached hair was a suspect.

I started toward the wharf, probably taking the same path Charlie Meadows had walked the night he died. The air was warm and smelled of saltwater. The sidewalk was staffed with characters out of a lost Lewis Carroll or H. G. Wells manuscript. There was the frumpy wench with the demeanor of a woman who didn't enjoy sex anymore and her husband with the faraway gaze of a space ranger just back from a strange galaxy. There was a four-hundred-pound man with the itchy groin. An apprentice bank clerk with acne. I saw the waiter from Dunn's Raw Bar restaurant. He was dressed like Liberace's pool boy. He walked by fast, as if he was late for a very important date. Everyone I passed had one thing in common. Hostility oozed from their pores, the standard response from a small-town populace that's afraid you are trying to force your way into their most guarded secrets.

At the wharf, I sat on a bench and stared across the water. I wondered about Leonitus. I wondered if he could be that calculating to destroy the body and deliberately prevent an autopsy. I wondered if that was the working of a simple mind. I wondered about the strands of hair that Ray-Newton had found. I wondered if Gillian Gable was right, if the Lighthouse was behind the killings. Leonitus worked for the Lighthouse,

but then so did most of Angel's Cove as independent sales
contractors. I wondered about the fish militia. I wondered if
having their money stolen was enough to push one of their
loose cannons over the edge. I wondered who, who wrote the
book of love.

THE DAY'S luncheon special was hand printed on a chalkboard
outside The Other Restaurant:

JAMBALAYA W/BREAD & ICED TEA
$4.50

There was one customer. She sat at a table next to the window overlooking the street. She looked worn out. She had on
an olive-colored fedora with a popped-up crown over her
stringy gray hair. The rough terrain of her face was parched
from sixty to seventy years of exposure to the sun, wind, and
rain. Her hands were gnarled and red. Hers had not been a
pampered life. She wore a flannel shirt with rolled-up sleeves,
work pants cut off at the knees, and aged laceless brogans that
might have been World War II surplus.

I looked at her. She looked at me. I nodded. She nodded.

I walked over to the counter and sat on one of the aluminum
toadstools. I could feel the old woman's wise eyes following
me.

Evalinda had her back to me. She was filling salt and pepper
shakers, stuffing napkins into black and chrome dispensers.
She looked over her shoulder casually when she heard me sit
down.

"Well, look who is here," Evalinda said. "Did you come
back to moon over me or do you think you're man enough to
survive my cooking twice in one day?"

Actually, I hadn't planned on eating, but the jambalaya
smelled lusty enough to play the French Quarter. And as the
wise Asian detective Harry-san once said: Rice cannot cook

words. Which translated means, spend money free the tongue. If I wanted information I was going to have to eat.

Evalinda set a menu on the counter. I pushed it back without opening it.

I ordered the special.

"Sweet or unsweet tea?" she said.

"Un."

She poured from a sweaty plastic pitcher.

I said, "Let me ask you something. The other day, when I was in here for the first time, you said something about people being afraid Charlie was right. Remember that?"

She nodded, not taking her eyes off the pitcher and glass.

"Right about what?" I asked.

Evalinda glanced over my shoulder at the old woman sitting at the table. It was almost as if Evalinda was seeking permission to talk to me. Apparently it was granted.

Basically, Evalinda told me the same thing Gillian Gable had. Charlie Meadows was skeptical about the Lighthouse Mortuary. He did not trust them. He did not see them as the savior of Angel's Cove.

"If anything, Charlie thought they were ripping off people. I mean, whoever heard of paying somebody else so you could work for them? Charlie tried to talk sense at people, but they didn't want to know from it, even if they knew it was true they were being suckered. I told that man more than once that people were going to believe whatever they wanted and no amount of facts was going to change their minds. Then when Charlie started trying to get one those cheap burial societies to come into Angel's Cove, people were afraid he was going to run off the Lighthouse, run off those make-believe jobs of theirs."

She put a bowl of jambalaya in front of me.

I tasted it. "Mm-mm. This is terrific. I don't understand why you don't do a better business here."

"I'm being boycotted," she said pleasantly as if it was a time-honored custom.

I stared at her.

"I was friends with Charlie," she explained. "I refused to jump on the anti-Charlie bandwagon, so that made me a traitor. People seemed to think if nobody talked to Charlie he'd leave town. I wouldn't play along. Either would Joe Patti and a few others." Evalinda motioned with her head toward the old woman. "She's sitting by the window to help me out, so people can see her eating here, so they know it's all right for them to eat here."

"She has that kind of influence?"

"Oh yes. Joe Patti calls her…called her the matriarch of Angel's Cove."

I swiveled on the stool and looked at the old woman. She wagged a spoon at me.

Evalinda said, "She's inviting you to join her."

HER NAME was Captain Della. She knew about Carla. She had heard about me.

Captain Della said, "Harry, isn't it?"

I was sitting across the table from her. I nodded.

"I hear you're a detective of some kind," she said.

"That's right."

"But you're not a cop."

"I'm not a cop."

"Well, Harry," she said slowly, letting my name linger in the air like a clay pigeon, "in the short time you've been here, you seemed to have made yourself about as popular as a disordered colon."

"Is that what you wanted to tell me?"

Captain Della smiled. "No." She picked at a tooth with a fingernail, and said, "Welcome to Angel's Cove."

"Given a choice, there's other places I'd rather be."

"I'm sure. We don't always get to choose when and where we're going to be."

"What about you, Captain Della? Where would you like to be?"

She didn't even have to think about it. "I'd like to be out on my boat hauling in a netload of fish," she said more with resignation than bitterness. "Are you going to be asking detective questions about Joe and Charlie?"

"What about Joe and Charlie?" I wanted to hear her say it.

"They were murdered," Captain Della said. Her eyes also had a lot to say. "You want to know what I think, just ask. You don't need to test me."

"Somehow, Captain Della, I suspect I won't even have to ask."

"What about Joe and Charlie?" Her voice weary from having to give birth to the same question twice.

"Ray-Newton says he's already figured out who killed them."

"Ray-Newton would have trouble figuring out which end of a filtered cigarette to light."

"He's got evidence. He's says it's Leonitus."

"Leonitus! I don't give a damn if Ray-Newton has a confession. That boy didn't kill anyone."

I shrugged. "Ray-Newton's wearing the badge and he says otherwise."

Captain Della squinted at me as if she was looking through salt spray. "I'd appreciate it if you'd keep foraging around. That's the only way we'll ever know what happened."

"I would need help."

"What kind of help?"

"Answers. To questions. I need people to talk to me."

Captain Della nodded. "I'll take care of that."

"That includes you, Captain."

"It'd better. What do you want to know?"

"I need a motive."

"Motive? Like what reason would there be to kill both Charlie and Joe? A link?"

"That's right, a link. Can you think of one?"

She stared at me for a long time without saying anything.

"What about the net ban?" I suggested.

It took her a moment to catch the implication. Her jaw tightened when she did. "One of the fishermen? Is that what you think?"

"That's what I'm asking."

She considered it, said, "All right. I'll take that from an outsider. You don't know any better, so I'll explain it to you. Yes, the net ban has brought a lot of ugliness with it. People are volatile. No doubt about it, it's an emotional time for them. Sometimes I think it will take a generation to ease their pain. I'm seeing people do things I never thought I'd see."

"For example."

"For example, every morning I bait and put out about fifty crab traps. It's dirty, backbreaking work. But it's honest work. When I go back to pull the traps about half of them are empty. You know what it means when a crab trap pulls up without crabs or bait? It means poachers got there before me. Mister, I started fishing on my daddy's boat when I was still in diapers. Never had problems with poachers until now. Another thing. Used to be a time when pleasure boaters broke down, commercial fishermen would always stop to tow them. Now the fishermen don't even slow down unless they see children on board."

Captain Della paused and took a sip of tea while she searched for her next thought.

I said, "I've heard Charlie Meadows wasn't well liked around here."

"We don't kill people just 'cause we don't like them."

"What about Joe Patti? Was he disliked?"

"Joe always had the best interests of everyone at heart. So

did Charlie for that matter. Problem is if you're not telling folks what they want to hear, they'll assume you're against them. I'll tell you something else, too. There's outlaw netters. It's no secret. They paint their boats black so it's hard to see them at night. They use spotters to look out for the marine patrol. They stash their nets on small islands."

"I thought the netters sold their nets to the state in the net-buyback program."

Captain Della's eyes sparkled. "They did. All of them sold their nets. Then the state turned around and gave three million pounds of net to an environmental company to recycle. Have you guessed yet?"

"The company sold the nets back to the netters?"

Captain Della nodded. "For pennies on the dollar. Is this a great state or what?" She chuckled. "Anyway, my point is, everyone knows there's outlaw netting going on. I don't approve of it. I've always played by the rules. I think if everyone had played by the rules we'd still be netting. Netters are just like anyone else. They're their own worst enemies. I can't pretend there weren't abuses. You're always gonna have a greedy few who don't abide by the rules and end up ruining it for everybody. But that's my sob story. You were asking about Joe. He knew about the outlawing. He even caught some. All he did, though, was chew them out, confiscate their nets and catch, and let them go. Joe didn't want to contribute criminal records to the fishermen's woes. The fish he confiscated was distributed for free to families in need. Joe Patti was not an enemy to these people."

"Would the fish militia agree with that?"

Captain Della's expression was quizzical. "Are you talking about Royal Maddox and company?"

I nodded.

She said, "What are you getting at?"

I told her what I knew about the net-buyback money being stolen from the militia by Joe Patti, about the same money being taken away from Joe by Charlie Meadows. I told her it sounded like a motive for murder to me.

Captain Della absorbed it all quietly. When I was finished she nodded and said, "Do you have a car?"

"Yeah. Why?"

"A picture is worth a thousand words."

TWENTY-SEVEN

CAPTAIN DELLA SAID, "Turn here."

I taxied off the main highway onto a back road and followed it through a corridor of images and scenes from a Florida I thought could only be found encapsulated in my childhood memories. We drove through trailer park communities with ramshackle juke joints that were last year's oyster bars and next year's poolrooms. I smelled barbecue smoke and heard the croaking of frogs coming from a duck pond next to a neglected cemetery of families and friends wiped out a century ago by the yellow fever epidemic. In front of a cinder block coin-operated laundry I saw a washerwoman deep in meditation. She was sitting in a cane chair holding a cold bottle of Nehi against her face. We passed the ruins of an antebellum plantation house partially hidden from the road by willow trees and scrub oak. There was a white clapboard church with little black children laughing and playing in a garden sanctuary, which for the briefest of time would protect their innocence until it was betrayed by the harsh realities of human misery. I wanted to stop the car and apologize to the children for what they would be exposed to in the years ahead. I didn't. I drove on.

Ten minutes later Captain Della said, "Turn here."

Here was a dirt road that corkscrewed through a pasture.

"Much farther?" I said.

She pointed to a clump of cypress trees two hundred yards ahead.

I angled the car between two trees and parked in their shade. Nearby was a pickup truck plastered with the mandatory bumper stickers so essential for Rambohood. One of the stick-

ers, BULLETS ARE OUR BALLOTS, read like the title for the ral-
lying theme song from an NRA political fund-raiser. Most
bumper stickers were nothing more than flags of hate and ignorance. Even the Scripture wasn't sacred. "And he that hath
no sword, let him sell his garment and buy one" had been
changed to AND HE THAT HATH NO GUN, LET HIM SELL HIS NET
AND BUY ONE. Captain Della told me that.

Father Shifty once told me that all zealots, including the
sermonizing most holy reverends of the One True Official
Ministry of God who sold genuine Bible interpretation tapes
on Sunday-morning television, the vicious radio talk-show lu-
natics who championed intolerance, the race supremacist dis-
guised in the camouflage fatigues of a self-proclaimed pa-
triot—all of them were campaigning in the name of Jesus,
while their rhetoric was at best an abuse, a distortion of Christian philosophy.

"Their actions are contradictory and conflicting with all
Christian precepts. Christianity," Father Shifty concluded, "is
one thing and those who hawk the word of God in the name
of special interests and profit is quite another thing."

Captain Della and I got out of the car. I followed her along
a mossy path through a cypress alley swarming with dragon-
flies—mosquito hawks, she called them. Small lizards scurried
across our path. I could hear rippling water.

The path ended at a clearing on the edge of a large creek.
A skiff was tied to a cypress knee.

Captain Della told me to get in the skiff. I did and she
nudged the boat, easing it into the water. She hoisted herself
in the boat and began to paddle.

"Turn back, my captain. The Dramamine!" My voice was
chock full of eighteenth-century twang. I was born to play
Fletcher Christian.

There was a long dramatic pause. The casting director was
torn, trying to decide between Clark Gable, Marlon Brando,

Mel Gibson, or me. Call it intuition, but I could hear Hollywood beckoning.

"I was kidding," I said. "Don't take me too seriously."

A lopsided grin gradually chiseled its way through Captain
Della's wrinkles. She said, "I doubt it's possible to ever take
you serious."

We had each other figured.

After less than a minute on the creek, Captain Della pulled
the oar out of the brown water and let the boat drift onto the
sandbank of a small oblong island thick with foliage.

Captain Della climbed out of the boat and wrapped a moor-
ing line around a bush. She ushered me through an overgrown
path no wider than a bowling alley gutter. I didn't ask where
we were going. Captain Della would have said had she wanted
me to know. I think she wanted the element of surprise on her
side.

She walked fast, I kept pace. Maybe thirty steps, could have
been less, Captain Della grabbed my arm and pulled me down
behind some shrub. We were on the other side of the island.
She pointed through the growth to the opposite shore of the
creek. I hunkered there and stared at the scene before me.

Royal Maddox was leaning against what was left of a gun-
wale on the beached remains of a charred hull. He was fueling
his bloated beer belly with a can of Busch. He was watching
a small group of militia guys standing around a horseshoe peg.
The game was already in progress. This was the campsite for
today's army. Fort Campo DeLuxe it was not. I felt like I was
watching a repertory theater-of-the-absurd group playing a
third world police force guarding its territorial waters. Or a
Monty Python skit about a hole-in-the-wall bar mitzvah, the
ceremony reduced to swilling a six-pack. Now I am a man.

I glanced at Captain Della. "Did they burn that boat?"

She nodded.

"Whose boat was it?"

She shook her head. "No one's. It was an abandoned wreck,

half-submerged in mud. They pulled it out, towed it here, and practiced on it. Royal called their maneuvers.''

''Practiced what?''

''Setting it on fire. That was their plan. They were going to burn sport fishermen boats.''

''Did they?''

''No. They tried once. They can thank God Joe Patti caught them before they could start the fire. They'd've killed a young family sleeping on board. I think that experience scared some sense into—''

''Who's there?'' Royal Maddox yelled. He and his goons were standing on the bank staring at the island. ''Who's over there?''

Captain Della stood up. ''Pipe down, Royal. It's only me.''

''Captain? What are you doing…who are you talking to?''

The look on Royal Maddox's face was disturbing. If he was going to go crazy I didn't want him taking it out on Captain Della. I wanted him taking it out on me even less, but that didn't stop me.

I stood up and flashed my goon-pacifying smile.

Royal Maddox looked at his gang and then stared at me with the intense eyes of a deranged trainer for the Olympic belly-flop team.

''What are you doing here?'' His voice shook like tassels on a Bourbon Street dancer.

''Looking for Havana. I think we're lost.''

Royal Maddox's face burned red. He had no sense of humor, a Riceproof personality. He sucked air noisily and said, ''You shouldn't have brought him here, Captain Della. Can't have him spying on us.''

''Nobody is spying on you,'' Captain Della said. ''I'm helping him work out this murder thing. I wanted to show him that you're no killers.''

''Is that a fact? Is that what you wanted to show him?'' Maddox turned to me, and said, ''You're in the wrong place.

I told you before you didn't want to meet with me again. You messed with the wrong man. You're in a lot of trouble.''

I said, "Am I?"

Captain Della jerked my arm. "Don't argue with him."

"Get him the hell out of here, Captain," Royal barked.

The Captain said, "You're being rude."

"You want me to say it again?"

We left.

THE GUN was pointed at my chest. He had materialized from behind the bumper stickeradorned pickup truck. He had a GI haircut, a big head, a bigger neck, and big tattooed arms. He wore scruffy combat boots, fatigue pants, and a shirt with torn-off sleeves. His eyes were like coffin nails and full with disappointment.

I sensed trouble.

TWENTY-EIGHT

CAPTAIN DELLA SAID a bad word.

I stood frozen like a silhouette target.

The man with the rifle said, "Fraternizing with the enemy. Not a good idea, Mom."

Mom?

Captain Della said, "He's not your enemy, Terry."

"He's not my friend."

Mom? I could marry Captain Della and be his stepfather if I couldn't be his friend.

Captain Della walked over to the man who called her Mom. She put a hand on the muzzle of the rifle and pushed down till it was pointed at the ground. She patiently explained who I was, why she had brought me here, and what I was trying to find out.

"Give me the gun," she ordered. He did. She said, "Now tell the man what you're doing."

Terry said, "We didn't kill Joe or Charlie. We're not killers. That's not what this is about."

"What is it about?"

"It's about the haves and the have-nots. It's about the big fish wanting to keep the small fish out of the pond. It's about the small fish fighting back."

It was stock rhetoric I had heard or read before in all the propaganda releases issued by both sides during the great To Ban or Not to Ban debate. Terry said the voters had been duped by invective advertisements bought and paid for by the wealthy elite to smear the meek who were supposed to have inherited the sea. The purpose of the militia was to stop further erosion of liberty and the pursuit of same. They weren't out to harm anyone.

"Why the guns?" I said.

He said it was a show of force, but only a show. There were other ways than bodily force to retaliate.

I asked what those were.

He explained that one of the purposes of the militia was to seek reprisal against marinas that rented dock space to sport fishing vessels, that harbored the enemy. What type of reprisal, I asked. He said economic sanctions, boycotts, that sort of thing.

I said, "Destruction of property?"

"If it comes to that," he admitted candidly.

No one, he assured me, had been or would be physically hurt. Their battle cry was: Take our nets, take their boats.

It would have been easy to discount the fish militia as another F Troop. Their encampment looked more like a fat farm for retired revolutionaries than a guerrilla boot camp. But it would have been a mistake to underestimate them. I listened carefully to what Terry said and how he said it. He believed the words he spoke. He was sincere, more hurt than angry. The opposite of the militia leader. The leader's fuse was short and burning. Like all violent people, Royal Maddox was a know-it-all, beyond enlightenment. He would rather shout than listen. He would rather beat up than shut up. There was no room for reason and understanding in his dim little mind. And that was what was scary. Not the Terrys, but the sunbaked commanders. For in the militia, the real game is not liberty and justice for all, it is follow the leader.

Captain Della stayed behind, said her son could drive her home, which was fine with me. Had we ridden back to town together, I'm sure she would have quizzed me, wanting to know what I thought—did I still think the fish militia was directly or indirectly responsible for the killings? Frankly, I didn't know what I thought. I just wasn't as sure as Captain

Della was that the militia had nothing to do with the murders. Maybe they didn't. The picture she showed me was not worth a thousand words. It wasn't that clear for me. Obviously one of us was seeing something the other wasn't. And it wasn't my view that was blinded by motherly love.

THE ANGEL'S COVE Library was crammed in the restored gymnasium between the police station and city hall. Two bicycles were parked, unlocked, out front. The library was air-conditioned. There was enough wax on the hardwood floor to keep Ray-Newton's hair in place till Valentine's Day. The walls smelled of fresh paint.

A man with an armadillo complexion, perhaps sixty, sat behind the circulation desk reading a magazine. He wore a stained white shirt and tie. If Mad Dog 20/20 made an after-shave, it was his brand.

"Does the library have a VCR?" I said.

"Couple of 'em," he said without looking up from the magazine.

"Can I use one?"

He looked up and squinted at me. "Know how?"

"Yes."

He stood up slowly as if he were weighted down by a backpack full of rejected disability applications.

He said, "Come on."

I followed the scent of eau de Mad Dog to the rear of the library. He unhooked a key ring from his belt loop and opened what looked like a closet door.

"Lock up when you're done," he said and went back to his post of duty.

It was a small room the size of one of those X-rated store private viewing booths that I've read about.

I loaded the VCR with a cassette labeled SISTER STAR IN-FOMERCIAL. It was part of the belongings I had picked up for Gillian Gable at the motel. I grabbed the remote control off the top of the TV, aimed, and pressed the play button. The screen filled with electronic snow for several seconds before being replaced with a shot of the Great Pyramid of Egypt.

Thirty minutes later the videotape ended with Brother Johnnie inviting viewers to become eternal partners on the shore with the beloved Sister Star.

I rewound the tape, impressed with what I had seen. Not so much with the content, much of which was a rehash of the tent show song and dance. No, what caught my attention was the big-budget production value. The infomercial was done with state-of-the-art technology and graphics. It was professional broadcast quality, nothing remotely amateur or chintzy about the production.

The program began like a documentary on the history of funerals, interwoven with religious traditions and ethnic customs of the times. All very calculating—opening with the ancient pyramid and concluding with the modern pyramid being constructed on the shore of Angel's Cove. What goes around, comes around, always stressing that funeral rites were rooted in religion. The Sister Star tie-in.

After that was sampler snippets of overflowing riverbanks, flooded cemeteries, floating coffins, open and empty. An announcer who possessed the vocal skills of an Alistair Cooke told the viewers how they could purchase, for only twenty-nine ninety-five plus shipping and handling, the complete uncut director's version of the preceding footage that also included vandalized graveyards and desecrated remains. There was also a most important message from Sister Star on the videotape. Special operators were standing by at the number superimposed on the screen. Have your credit cards ready. Call within one hour of the end of the program and also receive with your purchase a special collector's edition of the Miracles Happen Bible, inscribed and personally autographed by Sister Star.

At the end of the commercial Brother Johnnie had the privilege of introducing Sister Star after a sappy two-minute bio.

Sister Star chaired a panel discussion with a moral majority preacher, an anthropologist from Bob Jones University, and a former wife of a former governor of Kentucky. The panel concluded that funerals had come full cycle. God never intended for His children to be buried beneath the ground, closer to Hell.

There were celebrity tributes. A soap opera star cried when she confessed she had given her deceased daughter everything but a proper, above-the-ground entombment. She was so grateful for this second chance that Sister Star had provided. Miracles Happen.

The Alistair Cooke guy came back. Call now for more information. Funerals have never been this affordable. Plan ahead. Easy payment plans. Nothing more important a Christian can do for his family—present, past, and future. What would you do if you saw your mother's empty coffin floating down a flooded street? Don't wait, it could rain tomorrow. Act now. Call the toll-free Love Line on your screen. Brother Johnnie concluded with a call to join Sister Star in eternity.

The tape stopped rewinding and I hit the eject button.

TWENTY-NINE

LATE AFTERNOON I drove back to Port St. Joe thinking about Babycakes' outfit, among other things. Mostly I thought about the Sister Star infomercial, the Miracles Happen tent show, the related merchandise, the Lighthouse Mortuary with motel and gift shop, and the international corporation that was spending millions of dollars on most of the above. Enough money to buy celebrity endorsements and television time on stations across the country. Enough money to purchase prime waterfront real estate and construct a forty-story mausoleum. But enough money that a harmless little murder or two could be written off as a cost of doing business and an acceptable risk to insure construction and sales moved along without obstruction? That was Gillian Gable's theory, if I understood her. I struggled with that idea. What could Charlie Meadows and Joe Patti have possibly known or been doing that could scare the Lighthouse people into contracting for a hired gunslinger? Even if Charlie and Joe had been marketing do-it-yourself burial kits, they would have been no competition or economic threat to the big-money boys. Like a lot of other things in the life of a lone wolf detective, I just didn't see it.

"SEEN THE LATEST?" Gillian Gable said, greeting me with the current edition of the local weekly gazette.

The latest was Sister Star's plans to open a funeral museum on the Lighthouse grounds. A can't-miss tourist attraction, a death theme park. Only in Florida. And why not? Orlando had Disney World, and soon Angel's Cove would have FUNeral World.

I scanned the news article. The goal of the museum was to

offer a "panorama" of artifacts and memorabilia related to
death and mourning over the last one hundred fifty years.
Through purchases, loans, and donations the museum had assembled a collection of hearses, horse-drawn funeral coaches,
Civil War embalming apparatus, and assorted funerary bric-a-
brac, such as mourning pins used to pin back a widow's hair.
There would be a display of unusual caskets, including a
wicker-woven coffin and an ice casket with a glass panel in
the lid. According to the article, ice caskets were used for
children's funerals to save embalming costs. The bottom of
the casket was filled with ice, the body put on top. The ice
preserved the body long enough for viewing. The reporter concluded that while transportation and technology had changed,
a funeral was still a funeral.

"Hi."

Carla had joined us on the porch.

"Did you read this?" I asked her.

She nodded. "So what were you up to all afternoon?"

I told the ladies about my day. About stopping at the motel
to get Gillian's stuff. About my visit to the Fat Otis Bar and
how acting police chief Ray-Newton had fingered Leonitus for
the killings.

"Based on what?" Carla said.

"Strands of bleached hair."

I rocked back in the porch chair and described the trail of
incriminating hairs, as sniffed out by Ray-the-bloodhound-
Newton.

Gillian Gable sat on the steps. "Has there been an arrest?"
she said.

I shook my head. "They're looking for him."

"What do you think?"

"I think Ray-Newton needs to reshuffle his deck and deal
another hand."

Carla said, "Why? Maybe the giant albino did do it. He's

got a cruel streak. Don't forget the kitten I found hanging from the ceiling fan.''

''We don't know that he did that.''

''My God, Harry. We know that he was there. We know that he was sitting in the kitchen, in the dark, waiting for me. We know that he chased me into the woods.''

I looked at Carla. Carla looked back at me. She wanted to believe her father's killer would be caught. She needed desperately to believe in something.

I said, ''Carla, I want to be sure. I want to be sure he did do it, if he did. I want to be sure someone else doesn't get away with something.''

''Who else?'' her voice pleaded.

I shrugged. ''There are other possibilities besides the giant albino. We can't discount anyone.'' I told Carla and Gillian about Captain Della and my visit to the fish militia military academy of arts and sciences, about Royal Maddox threatening me, and about having a gun pointed at me.

''After that,'' I said, ''I stopped by the library and borrowed a VCR to watch the tape of the Sister Star show.''

''Did you hear that?'' Gillian Gable interrupted.

I sat upright. ''Hear what?''

Gable crossed her arms. ''My stomach. Carla and I are hungry, Rice. We haven't eaten. We waited for you to get back so you could take us to dinner.''

Carla said, ''Are you hungry, Harry?''

From the famished looks on Carla and Gillian Gable, I thought it best not to mention the delicious jambalaya I'd had for lunch.

I said, ''I can always eat.''

Gable grabbed her things. ''Give me five minutes to change,'' she said before disappearing into the cottage.

I looked at Carla leaning against an overhanging post. ''So how was your day?''

''Good,'' she said.

"Yeah?"

"Yeah, it was. Gillian and I had a nice long talk. She's an interesting lady."

Dinner was hot dogs, cole slaw, and Dr Pepper. We ate at a roadside stand on the beach. We talked a little bit about the infomercial and the mega bucks behind the Lighthouse project. Gable repeated her suspicions about their involvement in the murders. I disagreed with her. I said that kind of money can afford good help. The murders weren't the work of a pro.

"Bringing us back to the giant albino," Carla said.

"No," I said. "It brings us back to the beginning. And that is, who had the most to gain. Find that out and chances are you found the killer."

AFTER WATCHING the horizon suck the sun out of the sky, we left the roadside eatery and dropped Gable off at her rental cottage. Twenty-five minutes later Carla and I were back at Casa de Meadows.

Carla opened the door and knew something wasn't right.

"Somebody has been here," she said.

I didn't see anything out of the ordinary. "How do you know?"

"I just know." She was adamant.

"All right. Wait outside."

I did a quick walk-through of the house. Even though I didn't find any sinister Catholic girls hiding in the shadows, it did begin to seem as if Charlie Meadows's karma had been rearranged while we were gone. I really don't know what it was Carla had felt, but a peculiar feeling came over me. Nothing supernatural, just one of those things that's hard to explain. Like "In a Gadda Da Vida." Then again, it might have just been the power of suggestion.

I walked outside and told Carla to come in.

"Did you find anything?" she said.

"No." I let it go at that.

I looked for something to read from the limited Meadows library. I settled on a title by Eric Butterworth. Carla still wasn't satisfied and kept snooping around. About an hour later she poked her head out of the bedroom door. She had changed into her nightshirt.

"Is the car locked?" she said.

I nodded. "Why?"

"I left my purse in it."

"Do you want me to get it?"

"No. I don't need it. I'm going to bed." She studied me for a moment and said, "Someone was here. I looked in the drawers. Things were neater than before. The clothes were folded like a woman would fold them. Not my father. What could they have been looking for?"

It took a moment, then I remembered telling Captain Della about Charlie taking the money from Joe that Joe had taken from the fish militia. I told Carla.

She thought about that. "Good night, big mouth," she said and closed the door.

I continued to read for another hour or so. I reached up and turned off the lamp to rest my eyes for a minute. I sat peacefully in the dark listening to the crickets and promptly fell asleep fully dressed.

I don't know what woke me, the heat or Carla screaming.

It was no nightmare. I was covered in sweat, the room was filled with smoke. I saw flames. The house was on fire.

For the first time in my life I understood what was meant by a bloodcurdling scream when I heard Carla cry out, *"Harry!"*

THIRTY

THE SUFFOCATING HEAT took center stage like a sneak preview to eternal damnation. I was dry-mouthed and tasted ash. My clothes became an ill-fitting shroud for the guest of honor at a funeral pyre. I tried to get out of the chair and knew how it must feel to be strapped into the hot seat. My muscles were sluggish, slow to respond, as if sapped of all strength by a sweltering fever.

I stumbled to my feet and had staggered across the room before catching my balance. I was face to face with a fire crackling angrily in the kitchen. The shimmering flames greeted me with open arms, inviting me to join the procession of dancing debutante voodoo priestesses in some lewd arrangement of devil worship. I took two steps back and bumped into a piece of furniture. I could not see. I was blinded by a thick smoke darker than black magic that filled the room like the billowing midnight clouds of hell. I started to gag and went down on my hands and knees where the air was cleaner. I began to crawl, trying to discern shapes in the darkness, feeling my way toward Carla's room. This way, a few more feet. I banged into something harder than my head. Skin broke above an eyebrow, I felt warm blood trickling. Pain or smoke caused my eyes to water. I groped for my attacker. It was a table. I knew the bedroom was to the right.

The surface of the door was warm. The doorknob was hot. I grabbed the knob, twisted, and lunged into the room.

I was immediately engulfed in a rising tide of volcanic heat. An intake of breath became a lung full of smoke. At no time did the thought seriously occur to me that I was in any inherent danger of dying or that there would be an autopsy report that read: cause of death—smoke inhalation. If I had, it wouldn't have mattered. I was more afraid of having yet another someone I cared for die than I was of my own mortality. I could survive my death, but not Carla's.

There was a strange odor in the room, aromatic, almost a frankincense or a simmering perfume on a stove. It was a familiar smell that reminded me of a cellar in an old Roman chapel I had once visited. I could even see the pulpit illuminated by the flickering glow of torches. And then the realization there was no pulpit, no torches. The bed was on fire, the burning sacrificial altar of a black mass. Tendrils of flames taunted me like copulating pagan gods in flight.

I was too late. There was no other life in that room. Just me and the tail of Satan wrapping around my ankle, jerking me off my feet, pulling me toward the fiery depths of Lucifer's bed-and-breakfast.

I was being dragged across the floor out of the bedroom.

"Harry!" called a distant voice.

It was Carla. But where? I was too disoriented to tell what direction the muffled scream had come from. The bathroom, I thought. Maybe she had taken shelter in the bathroom.

I wasn't leaving without Carla. I kicked like a condemned man with unfinished business trying to break free of whoever was pulling me away from her. The grip tightened. It was strong, a man's hand. I reached out, searching for something to grab. I felt the blistering doorjamb and took hold, scorching my hand in final insult. Despite the pain, I held on and kicked furiously, shouting threats and bribes, bargaining for a stay of execution.

There was a tug on my ankle that broke my hold. As I was being dragged across no man's land, I clawed at the floor in a desperate attempt to reverse the momentum.

I didn't know if the gods were joking with me, but it felt as if the horrors of the underworld had begun to fade. The smoke vanished, the heat subsided. I was dazed, bleary-eyed, and the wound above my brow throbbed. I tasted dirt and felt the burst of sweet, precious air fill my lungs. I was outside. I made a feeble attempt to stand and gave it up, opting to lie there in wait for the next invasion of the body snatchers.

The tiny voice of an angel said, "Let me help."

A hand slipped under my arm and lifted.

It was an effort, but I got to my feet. I smelled of smoke. My face was sweaty, grimy, and bloody from the cut.

I looked at Carla. Her eyes were tearing, she was smiling. She told me I was lovely. She wrapped her arms around me and held on tightly as if protecting me.

"You?" I whispered.

She pulled back and looked at me. "What?"

"Was that you? You pulled me out of there?"

"No." She looked around. I followed her gaze. "He's gone."

"Who? Who was it?"

"The giant albino."

"The albino? Did he start the fire?"

Carla shook her head. "I don't know. I don't think so."

"You don't think so? There's no one else around. What was he doing here?"

"I don't know, Harry. But I do know that he saved you and he saved me."

Carla told me how she had been awakened by the sound of the bedroom window breaking. Immediately she smelled smoke and saw fire creeping out from the crack in the closet door.

"The next thing I know, the giant albino was climbing through the window. I was so scared I couldn't move. He wrapped me in a blanket and carried me out the window. When he put me down I realized what was happening—the house was burning. I cried out for you and started running for the door. The giant albino caught me and pulled me back and then he ran in the house after you. It doesn't make sense that he would start the fire and then risk his life to get us out.''

No, it didn't. Unless that was the workings of a brain-damaged man fascinated since childhood by fire.

The Angel's Cove patrol car roared into the yard, its running lights flashing. In the distance I could hear the wailing siren of a fire truck. Officer Wesley Butch got out of the car like Smokey the Bear emerging from hibernation.

"Everybody all right?" he said.

"Sort of," I said. "We're safe." Never mind that my hand was burnt and my head hurt.

"What happened?"

Carla and I told him what we knew.

He nodded. "We've already picked up Leonitus."

Making his nighttime rounds, Wesley Butch had spotted the glow of fire through the trees. He radioed the volunteer fire department and acting police chief Ray-Newton. On the way over Ray-Newton saw Leonitus running away from the scene and apprehended the giant albino. As we talked, Leonitus was on his way to jail in the chief's unmarked patrol car.

"That was quick," I said.

Wesley Butch shrugged. "Small town. Not much ground to cover."

THE FIRE destroyed everything in the house.

The alert response time of the pumper was not enough. The fire had spread too quickly. The truck arrived and the hose was unpacked and stretched and the nozzle turned on with a drill team precision. Still, all that was left to do was to keep the fire from spreading beyond the house. The rush of water streaming from the hose promptly doused the fire into a hissing fit of steam. The personal paradise of the late Charlie Meadows was up in smoke.

The cars had been spared. I still had the clothes I had fallen asleep in the chair wearing. Carla had her nightshirt. Call it divine interference or just dumb luck that Carla had left her purse in my car.

Wesley Butch was exhibiting all the classic symptoms of the I'm-in-Charge-and-You're-Not syndrome. Gut sucked in, chest pushed out, balls at attention, he insisted that Carla and I immediately go to the police station to fill out some forms. I told Officer Wesley Pooh it would have to wait until morning. He started to protest but Carla's we're-not-in-the-mood-for-this-shit glare convinced him otherwise.

My first concern was for Carla's safety. I wanted her out of Angel's Cove. She had her own agenda. She was worried about getting my wounds attended.

Carla and I drove that night to Port St. Joe. We took both cars. I followed her to make sure no one was following us.

Gillian Gable greeted us at her cottage door looking cool and distant as if we had rudely awakened her from a carnal dream costarring a smooth-tongued private detective. Like Carla, Gillian Gable was wearing a cotton nightshirt. Maybe I'm old-fashioned, but whatever happened to old-fashioned girls in black lace teddys and diaphanous negligees?

Standing in the door, we told Gillian Gable about the fire.

"Come inside." She yawned. "Carla can share my bed. Rice, there's a roll-away and sheets in the closet. Help yourself."

"Harry's been hurt," Carla said.

"Are you in pain?" Gable asked, flicking on a lamp.

"I laugh at pain," I grunted.

Gable and Carla exchanged knowing *men* looks.

After examining my hand and head wound, Gillian Gable told Carla to go on to bed.

"You," she said to me, "wait here. Let me put on some pants and I'll drive you to the emergency room."

"I don't think so."

Those simple words transformed my two lovely guardian angels into Leona Helmsley and Marge Schott with don't-give-us-any-lip expressions permanently etched in their hard-ened faces.

Gillian Gable and I got back to the cottage from the emer-gency room about an hour before the sun, my head sutured and my hand wrapped in gauze.

There's something to be said for an ambidextrous sex life.

THIRTY-ONE

"TAKE OFF YOUR SHORTS."

"Wh...what?" I muttered haltingly, somewhere between dreamland and consciousness.

"Take off your shorts."

My eyes fluttered open. Gillian Gable stood over me, my clothes bundled in her arms.

"Can I buy you a drink first?"

Gable suppressed a smile. "You're still dreaming, Rice. Cover yourself with the sheet and give me your shorts. I'm going to the laundromat. Your clothes smell like smoke. So do you. You need to shower, but keep your bandages dry. I'm also going to pick up some things for Carla and some toiletries for both of you. I should be back in about an hour or two."

"Where is Carla?"

"She's still in bed. Now strip."

ABOUT FIVE MINUTES after Gillian Gable left, Naked Man flew to the bathroom using the sheet for a cape. Without going into details, I did manage to wash the stench of smoke out of my hair and keep the gauzed hand and taped brow dry. Dressed in only the latest fashion from Cannon towels, I joined Carla in the kitchen. She'd made coffee and was sitting at the dinette.

She said, "Did you sleep?"

"No. You?"

She shook her head. "That was quite a scare last night."

"Yes."

"Someone tried to kill us."

"Yes."

"Are we going to the police station today?"

"I am. Carla, I want you to go home. I need you at the Sand Bar." Anticipating an argument, I added, "I'll stay here as long as it takes to find out what happened to your father."

She stared at me affectionately. "You're worried something might happen to me if I stay."

I nodded.

She said, "If I leave, then I'll be worried that something might happen to you."

"Carla, I do this for a living. Nothing is going to happen. I work better alone."

"I don't want to leave my father's ashes here."

"I'll get his ashes and bring them back to you."

"How will you get them?"

"I don't know, but I will. I promise. Okay?"

She thought about it for a moment and nodded. She reached across the table, squeezed my good hand.

I DECIDED to wait for my clothes before going to the police station.

IT WAS ABOUT eleven o'clock when Gillian Gable returned with toothbrushes, a razor, new clothes for Carla, clean clothes for me. The three of us had lunch together at a restaurant on Port St. Joe's main drag before going our separate ways— Carla headed south to home, Gillian Gable stayed to work on her story, and I drove to Angel's Cove.

A small bespectacled gray-haired man with a monogrammed shirt, orange suspenders, and a paisley bow tie sat on the visitor's bench in the police station waiting area reading a newspaper.

Acting chief Ray-Newton was bent over his desk eating a sandwich. He acknowledged my presence by gesturing for me to sit in the chair next to the desk. I sat and waited. He chewed like a camel with a mouthful of novocaine.

Ray-Newton leisurely finished his sandwich and rocked back in his chair.

I said, "I think I know who started the fire last night."

"You think you know? Now you see, that's why law enforcement is best left to the professionals. You think you know who started the fire? Well, I'm here to tell you I know damn well who started that fire. In fact he's in the lockup right this minute."

"Did he confess?"

"Not yet."

"Do you have witnesses?"

Ray-Newton's eyes narrowed. "You damned right I got witnesses. I got you and the Meadows girl."

I shook my head. "We didn't see him start it."

Ray-Newton leaned forward and slapped both hands loudly on the desk. "You know what your problem is, mister?"

"I don't have a problem."

"The hell you don't. I'm your problem. Did you not tell Officer Butch that you saw Leonitus there last night?"

"That's correct."

"Now you're telling me he wasn't there?"

"That's not what I said. I said we didn't see him actually start the fire."

"Really? Well, if he didn't do it, then who in hell did?"

"Royal Maddox." I explained why I thought Royal Maddox had started the fire. Maddox had experience playing with matches and burning boats in summer camp. Maddox had threatened me on two occasions. "Last night he tried to kill me."

"You're pissing on the wrong hydrant. Royal Maddox is no killer. That boy in there has already killed two people and he tried to kill two more last night."

"If he's a killer, why did he pull us out of the fire? Why didn't he just let us burn?"

Ray-Newton shrugged and pulled a cigar out of the desk

drawer. "Go figure. You're asking me to explain the mind of an imbecile."

"I can't think of anyone more qualified."

He gave me a stone-cold stare. The veins in his neck were like quivering worms. "You got anything else to say?"

"You must really want this job permanently, even if it's at the expense of possibly accusing the wrong person. Super cop Ray-Newton, solves murder cases in less than a day. What a guy."

He nodded slowly. "Is that all?"

"No, but it'll do."

"All right, my turn. There's all kinds of justice, different kinds for different problems. Right now the easiest way, not necessarily the best way, but the easiest way for you is to get out of here and don't come back." He pointed the cigar at me. "You keep pissing me off and you'll regret it for the rest of your scumbag life."

I was already on my feet. Under threat of police brutality, I walked out the door and down the steps. As a rule, I never get into a pissing contest with an elephant.

I was halfway to my car when I heard someone call, "Wait."

I turned. The small man with the orange suspenders who had been sitting on the bench in the police station was hurrying after me. He caught up to me and gasped, "Are you the man who was questioning Dr. Galen about Charlie Meadows?"

"Why?"

"Of course," he said. "Forgive my manners. I'm Winston Estrellita. Dr. Galen engaged me as counsel for Leonitus this morning."

"Good luck," I said and started walking away.

"You're wrong," he said. "It wasn't Royal Maddox."

I stopped and looked back at him. "Is that so?"

"Yes, sir, it is so."

"And how would you know that?"

"My client saw who it was running away from the house last night, and it wasn't Royal Maddox."

"Does your client know the name of the person he saw?"

"Indeed he does."

"Are you going to tell me?"

"Yes, sir, I am. It was one Jack Redgrave, a.k.a. Jack the Brit."

THIRTY-TWO

"DID YOU TELL THE POLICE?" I asked.

"No."

"Why not?"

Winston Estrellita wiped his brow and looked at me over the rim of his glasses. "Could we sit? River Park is a couple blocks over."

We walked in silence, me wondering if this was going to take long, and I imagined he was buying time to conjure an answer. It was one of those parks with an obstacle course of exercise stations. The park was empty, as though it had taken the day off. A pocket-sized breeze, studying to be a gusty wind, strained futilely to swirl leaves along the clay path. We sat on a bench shaded by an outstretched magnolia tree.

"You have a sense of the absurd, I hope," Estrellita said, sounding as if he was delivering an opening statement to the jury of a man without peer. He crossed his legs and glanced at me. "Leonitus does not speak to anyone except Dr. Galen. People who don't know him think Leonitus is mute. He won't even talk to me. I have to write down my questions and give them to Dr. Galen, who in turn talks to Leonitus. I can't even be in the same room with them."

"How do you know Leonitus can really talk then? Maybe Dr. Galen is lying to you."

"Dr. Galen is a fine man. He is not a liar."

"He falsified a death certificate."

Winston Estrellita cringed and nodded. "No matter. I've eavesdropped. Leonitus can talk. Now, can you imagine me going to Ray-Newton, without any supporting evidence, and telling him that my 'imbecile' client, who has a juvenile history of starting fires, has told me, through a memory-impaired interpreter, that Jack the Brit is the man the police truly want?"

"Sounds like you've got a problem."

"Yes, sir, I do indeed have a problem. Which is where you come in."

"Do I?"

"I have it on unimpeachable authority that you are an extraordinary and somewhat renowned investigator."

"Fertilizing the ego, are we?"

Winston Estrellita spread his hands. "Pardon my tactics. It's the nature of the legal beast lurking within me."

"No doubt. What's your unimpeachable source?"

"Rumors."

"I apologize for doubting you."

"So you'll help?"

"I don't know. What is it you want, a confession from Jack the Brit?"

The little man smiled. "I suppose that would suffice if that's the best you can do."

"How sure is Leonitus? I mean how well does he know Jack the Brit? Is there a chance he could be mistaken?"

"He's sure. They work together in the crematorium."

"At the Lighthouse?"

"There is no other. Will you help us?"

"What was Leonitus doing out there last night? That was the second time Carla has seen him around the house. Was he stalking her?"

"No, he wasn't stalking her. He was hiding from the police. He's been living on that sloop tied to Charlie's dock for two reasons. First, Charlie taught Leonitus how to sail on that boat, so the boy is comfortable there. Second, he stayed there because he was trying to summon the courage to apologize to Miss Meadows for cremating her father's body before it should have been. There's no doubt in my mind that Jack the

Brit deliberately set up Leonitus to cremate the body before its time. Leonitus told Dr. Galen it was just a mistake. That boy doesn't think ill of anyone. When Jack supposedly found out there had been a 'mistake,' he told Leonitus the police were angry. Jack told Leonitus to hide out for a while until he, Jack, could fix everything.''

"You think Jack had Leonitus cremate the body to cover up for a murder?"

"I believe so."

"Making Jack the Brit the killer?"

"I would argue that."

"Why would he kill Charlie Meadows and Joe Patti? Why would he try to kill Carla and me?"

"You were the one asking questions. As for Charlie and Joe, I don't know. That's what I'm asking you to find out. It's obvious that by telling Leonitus to hide out until he could fix everything, he made it look like Leonitus was running from the law. And he was. The boy was scared and he had no reason to be. He just did what he was told. Jack's also the one who told Dr. Galen to falsify the death certificate. He told Dr. Galen it was the only way they could save Leonitus' job. Jack the Brit was in the ideal situation to frame Leonitus. But I can't prove that.''

I sat there and thought it over. Winston Estrellita did not disturb me. He sat quietly staring at his shoes.

I said, "I'll want something."

"Dr. Galen has some money."

"No. I'll need information. I want a floor description of the mortuary. Can Leonitus do that?"

"I'm sure he can. It may take a while to get, depending on Dr. Galen. His state of awareness is catch-as-catch-can. Let me ask you under the cloak of attorney-client privilege, is it your plan to surreptitiously enter the Lighthouse and find the evidence I need?"

"That's the plan."

He pulled out his wallet and found a business card. "Be at my office tonight at nine o'clock. I should have what you want by then."

"Why so late?"

"As I said, it depends on Dr. Galen's state of mind and I've got midweek celebration at church this evening. Do you know where that address is? It's two doors down from Dr. Galen's office."

"I'll find it."

Winston Estrellita stood up. "I'll see you tonight."

"One more thing," I said. "I want to know exactly where they've stored the ashes of Charlie Meadows."

He looked at me curiously. "Why?"

"I'm going to steal them."

THIRTY-THREE

LEONITUS HAD PAID in full for my services when he pulled Carla and me from the fire.

Still, I wasn't thrilled about having to work the late shift. It was early afternoon and already I was suffering from an all-night disc jockey case of itchycoo park eyes from the lack of sleep. The choices were a nap, high-octane caffeine therapy, or keeping busy. I probably would have dozed off sitting on that slatted park bench had it not been for the wake-up call. It occurred to me that Jack the Brit must have been the mystery man who tailed Gillian Gable the other night after the tent show.

I'M THE WORST DRIVER I've ever ridden with. On the drive back to Port St. Joe my eyelids came down like the final curtain. The car went off the road onto a bumpy shoulder. I was jarred awake and jerked the car back on the highway. I was lucky the car hadn't veered to the left across the center stripe into the oncoming beer truck. The next trade-in will be for a used limo with driver.

GILLIAN GABLE opened the cottage door. She was wearing a silk kimono. Her hair was wet. She cocked her head, her eyes studied me for a long time. She smiled sympathetically and said softly, "You look tired, Rice."

"I don't think there's a word for what I am."

I followed her inside. The air conditioner was on. The room was cool and smelled of talc. We sat at the dinette. She had been working. On top of the table was an open laptop computer and an accordion file stuffed with loose notes.

I told her about Winston Estrellita and Jack the Brit. I asked her if the name Jack Redgrave meant anything to her.

"Redgrave," she repeated. "There's something familiar about that name. I should know it, shouldn't I? You said he worked at the Lighthouse?"

I nodded.

She started leafing through the accordion folder on the table. She shook her head. "It must be in the other file. I'll be right back."

Gillian Gable disappeared into the bedroom. I laid my head on the table to rest my eyes.

"I found it," she called. "Redgrave is an alias. His name is George Burton," she said, entering the kitchen. "Wake up, Rice." I sat up. She placed a file in front of me. She bent over the table and started flipping through the file. The kimono had fallen open at the neckline, exposing her nakedness beneath the silk. I wasn't hearing a word she said. I stared painfully at her glorious flesh, rediscovering territories I hadn't explored in a long time, wanting to lick the trickle between her scoop-sized breasts, to nuzzle her sweet fuzz and taste the drops of her vaginal dew on my tongue, to suck her toes. But with the fantasy, the torment returned. The sharp hurt was back, the depression that comes from a cancer that killed a special lady and ate away half my soul. I've always been amazed, and I think I always will be, at how soft women are. The sight of her skin was a heart-aching reminder of my empty life. I couldn't allow myself to think about the Gillian Gables. For so long I had systematically tried to forget about the past by seeking women I could never emotionally or spiritually connect with. It hadn't always been that way. But eventually it became a form of protection for me, a barrier from pain and misery. By consorting with mean-spirited, hard-hearted women, women who couldn't hurt me, I found there was no danger of risk or chance of loss. When those women dumped me I hadn't lost anything. Gillian Gable was not that type of woman. She was the kind of tender and affectionate woman I craved but avoided. That's the tragic flaw in my system. I can never win. I'll admit that to everyone but myself. If only there was a twelve-step program for recovering lost souls.

I felt her hand lay gingerly against my face. I looked up. Our eyes locked. "Carla tells me you're a good man," she said quietly. She reached out. "Give me your hand." I hesitated. She smiled. "Don't be nervous."

I gave her my hand. She led me into the bedroom. I stood there confused and rigid like a store mannequin. She unbuttoned my shirt and off it came.

She pushed gently on my chest. "Sit."

I sat on the edge of the bed. Gillian Gable knelt in front of me and took off my shoes and socks.

"Lie back," she said.

I did, my legs still over the edge of the bed.

She unfastened the belt, unsnapped the pants. "Lift your hips." She slid my pants and shorts off.

Gillian Gable looked at my friendless organ. She whispered playfully, "You really are tired." She winked. "Don't worry, I'll take care of that."

She picked up my legs and swung them around on the bed. She lifted my head and tucked a pillow under it. Next, she touched a finger to her lips and then touched my lips with the finger. "Relax. I'll only be a minute."

I watched her pick up her purse. She went to the bathroom and closed the door.

I sunk back into the pillow and closed my eyes. It felt so good I promptly feel asleep.

THE SMELL OF PIZZA roused me from the stupor of the ill-timed siesta. I stretched, rubbed my eyes, and looked around. The light was dim. I had been covered with a sheet. My clothes were folded next to me on the bed. I got dressed.

Gillian Gable was at the dinette. The laptop and files had

been replaced by a large pizza box and a beer can. She saw me and smiled.

"I hope you like pepperoni and onions."

I nodded. "What time is it?"

"A little after seven. There's beer in the refrigerator. Would you grab some paper towels, please?"

I glanced sheepishly back at the bedroom door and started foolishly groping for an excuse or an apology or whatever Hallmark epigram was appropriate under the circumstances.

She waved it off with a flick of her hand.

"Forget it," she said. "Two months from now you won't be looking back over your shoulder for a paternity suit."

Over pizza and beer Gillian Gable told me about Jack the Brit.

His real name was George Burton.

"How do you know that?" I said.

"I saw his passport."

About four months ago the Lighthouse had hosted a fifty-dollar all-day Saturday seminar for the independent sales contractors. The football coach from a parochial university of sports was brought in to give a motivational pep talk. During the breaks, Gillian Gable, ever the investigative reporter for a metropolitan newspaper, took advantage of the situation and snooped around.

On one of the breaks Gillian Gable wandered into the employee locker room. She found a British passport on the top shelf of one of the lockers.

"I just had time for a quick glance," she said. "I heard someone coming."

It was Jack the Brit. Same face as the picture in the passport, different name.

"He asked me what I was doing in there. I told him I was lost. I was looking for a ladies' room."

George Burton was a fugitive and an illegal immigrant.

I said, "Did you report him?"

"Not at the time. Actually I never followed up on it. I got sidetracked and forgot all about him."

"Did Charlie Meadows know?"

She nodded. "I told him about the passport, so he knew that Jack Redgrave was an alias. But he didn't know the other."

"What other?"

"I've been on the phone all afternoon while you were sleeping. About eight months ago George Burton was a purser on a cruise ship. He jumped ship at Dodge Island in Miami and absconded with nearly seventy thousand dollars from the ship casino. He nearly beat to death a casino teller. My editor is going to call INS."

I didn't say anything to Gillian Gable, but I had a suspicion that Charlie Meadows had just enough information to get himself killed and not enough information to save his life.

AT NINE O'CLOCK that night Winston Estrellita was waiting for me in his office.

He handed me a crudely drawn floor plan of the Lighthouse Mortuary and crematorium. "X marks the spot," he said, "for Charlie's ashes."

"Thanks. This is a big help."

"There's more." He held out a key. "Leonitus' employee key. It opens the back door with the blue check mark on the drawing."

I took the key.

"When are you going to go there?" Estrellita asked.

"Now."

THIRTY-FOUR

THE HEADLIGHT BEAMS penetrated the night like neon serpents with polio.

I drove slowly past the Lighthouse entrance, checking for any sign of activity. On the drive-by I didn't see any lights, cameras, or action. It appeared all was quiet on the funerary front. Almost a half mile up I turned off the highway and parked the car behind another deserted roadside attraction. Grabbing a Mini Maglite from the glove compartment, I got out of the car to circle back on foot to the Lighthouse. I crossed over the sand dunes. There was less chance of being seen on the desolate beach than there was walking alongside the highway. I listened for ghosts and heard only the haunting song of the breakers rolling in from the sea, serenading the forgotten lonely.

Tiny Tim would have been proud. I tiptoed through the sea oats and meandered through a palm grove, emerging at the rear service entrance to the mortuary. A van and a hearse were parked next to a loading dock with a steel bay door. The concrete-block rear of the mortuary was in sharp contrast to the delicately scrolled Victorian funeral home with the gingerbread eaves, beveled glass, and circular turrets that greeted the public in front.

Next to the loading dock were steps leading to a solid wood door. According to the drawing, that was the door the key should unlock. The key worked. I stepped inside and closed the door behind me. The place reeked of institutional disinfectant and was cave dark. I turned on the flashlight. The floor was a black-and-white linoleum checkerboard and the walls were hospital green.

I followed the penlight down a narrow hall. If the crudely drawn layout was right, there would be a storeroom right about here, where X marked the spot. The wrong spot. I shone the light in the room. It was like a little library with a couple of bookcases that had actual books. Technical books, I assumed, with titles like *No Better Living Than Death, The Joy of Embalming,* and other featured selections from the Undertakers Guild. I did not stop to browse.

I put the light on the drawing again and turned the map upside down to see if it worked better that way. This time I found the storeroom, which was no bigger than a typical linen closet. I ran the penlight across shelves of opaque jars, colored bottles, and there it was—a cardboard cube about seven inches high with a strip of masking tape that someone had printed meadows on with a felt marker. I slipped the Charlie-in-the-Box under my arm. It couldn't have weighed more than three or four pounds.

I started back down the hallway until I came to a double door that swung open. As I panned the flashlight around, I could see metal gleaming. I also saw that it was a windowless room. I found the wall switch and flicked on the rectangular overhead fluorescent lights.

For all the similarities, the room was decorated like either a physician's examination room or the Marquis de Sade's chamber of horrors. There was a stainless steel countertop and wall cabinets with glass doors crammed with an inventory of assorted fluid-filled jars, syringes, latex gloves, and an array of orifice-probing contraptions. One man's surgical equipment, another's toys of torture.

There was a sterile cleanliness to the room. Almost like a hospital kitchen. I nearly mistook the porcelain embalming table for a food-preparation counter. But I did not mistake the embalming machine for a blender or the trocars hanging in a rack for fondue spears.

I went through the drawers and cabinets without knowing

what I was looking for. I came up empty, except for the other door on the far side of the embalming room.

I opened the door and switched on the light. It smelled and looked like a locker room. If it looks like a duck and it walks like a duck... I counted a half-dozen lockers. Only one was locked.

The first locker was empty. The inside of the door on the second locker was beautified with cutout color magazine pictures of professional wrestlers sneering like angry dragons.

"He is not an albino. He bleaches his hair because he likes Ric Flair." So said Joe Patti about Leonitus.

The locker was filled with towels, long white coats, rubber shoes, and some other stuff. The top shelf of the locker was stocked with deodorants and shaving cream and disposable razors and a hair brush. I picked up the brush and plucked several long strands of bleached blond hair from the bristles.

"Found me out, have we?" said a voice with a distinctively British accent.

I was so startled I almost dropped the box of ashes on the floor. I turned around.

Jack the Brit had a gun. I had a little flashlight.

"I was looking for the men's room and got lost?" I said.

Jack the Brit was silent for a couple seconds. "She told you, did she?"

"Yes she did." We both knew who she was.

"You know who I am, then?"

"George Burton."

He nodded. "Quite right. I rather suspected her when I saw her at the Sister Star show. She was the one I caught in here. I was only out two minutes. Left the bloody locker unlocked for two minutes. She had to have seen the passport, I figured. I'd seen her with Charlie before. She had to have been the one to tell him."

"That's why you killed him, because he knew your name?"

"Bit of bad luck, I'd say. He was drunk, just a slip of the

tongue, I think. He called me Mr. Burton. No one else heard. Someone had rung the bar and Babycakes was talking on the telephone. I left the bar and waited for Charlie. When he came out I told him my battery was dead. Asked him for a jump, I did. When he opened his hood to attach the cables is when I did it. I slammed the hood down on his head. Knocked him cold. Dragged him to the sea wall and dumped him over.''

"Why Joe Patti?''

"I'm a cautious man, I am. Joe was the sort to figure it out. I couldn't chance that. He'd already begun to question things others took for fact. Ray-Newton is lovely, isn't he? Believes whatever I want him to. Joe was too smart. I happened upon him at the dock looking around. Odds were he would find me out. I've never been one to gamble. It was late. No one else around. I blindsided him with a crowbar.''

"Killing him.''

"Yes and I would have killed that woman had I not run out of petrol.''

A good thing Gillian Gable kept a full tank of gas.

"And last night,'' I said. "You tried to kill again.''

He shrugged. "I don't fancy you'd appreciate the cleverness in that.''

"Sure I do. It was part of your plot to frame Leonitus. Planting his hair to point the blame at him for Joe and Charlie. And even you were smart enough to realize that you couldn't just keep dumping bodies off the sea wall and expect people to think Leonitus was a loony serial killer. But knowing Leonitus' history, people might believe he set a house on fire killing the occupants, inadvertently or not.''

Jack the Brit smiled. "Got that, did you?''

"Yeah, I got that. But tell me, there's something I didn't get. How did you go from being a ship's purser to working in a crematorium without any experience?''

"Had experience,'' he said. "Learned the trade from me uncle. He was an undertaker in Liverpool. I worked part-time for him when I was a schoolboy. It's the perfect cover. Who would look for a purser in a mortuary?"

"That's true," I said. "It was good while it lasted. Now it's over. You're finished."

"I shouldn't think so. I'm the one with the gun." His finger moved on the trigger or it was an optical illusion born of fright. "I shot a prowler, that's the idea. Turns out you were the bloody prowler. Don't think anyone will be upset by that. You've been a bit of a nuisance, you have. Good riddance then. Jack the Brit is now Jack the Hero."

"You're forgetting something," I said, trying to think of something he forgot.

"The woman?"

That was good. "Yes. I'm not the only one she told."

He didn't like that. "Who else?"

"Her editor."

His jaw tightened. He was already realizing he was going to have to lighten his load and run. The last thing he needed was baggage, and right about then he was looking at me like a suitcase of dead weight. My time was about up.

All the while we were talking my thumb had been slowly prying loose the top on the box of ashes. I silently prayed that Carla would forgive me for what I was about to do. I threw the ashes into Jack the Brit's face and eyes, blinding him long enough to turn off the lights and haul ass out of there, thanking Charlie Meadows for coming to my aid.

I ran through the embalming room and switched off the lights before stepping into the cavernous black hole of a hall-way. Anything to slow down that ash-hole hunter in pursuit. I would have tried friendly persuasion if I thought reason would have worked. How many animals must die before men realize that hunting is not a cure for impotence? But I didn't suppose that was the time to stop and wax philosophical with a deranged Englishman.

So there I was, dancing in the dark, not knowing which way

to turn. I was so disoriented I had no idea which direction the exit was.

There were two options, left and right. I turned left and hoped it was right.

I sprinted down the dark hall when I should have been hurdling. I crashed into a chair and tumbled head over heels like a fool in love with a discount hooker. A shock of pain zigzagged through my leg. Shit. Charlie Meadows meet Charley Horse. I snuck a panicky glance back down the corridor. I saw the light flip on and seep from the cracks in the hall door to the embalming room. I stumbled gracefully to my feet and hobbled towards who knew where.

Suddenly the dark hall was goosed by a burst of bright light and the reverberating kaboom of fireworks on the Fourth. That was followed instantaneously by a clink overhead that sounded like a bullet ricocheting off a light fixture. That was no firecracker. The little turd was shooting at me. I crouched down and ducked through the nearest door.

The room was the size of a handball court. Before the door behind me swung shut, cutting off the light from the hall, I quickly scanned the room. In the middle of the opposite wall was a huge iron door with rollers protruding from its lip, as if it were a demon mask sticking out its tongue. Nearby was a gurney supporting a large flakeboard box the shape of a casket. There was no other choice. I slid back the top of the box, climbed in, and pulled the top back in place in one smooth motion.

Inside, the box was pitch black and lumpy. Something was sticking me in the eye. Using Braille, I groped around until I realized I was not alone. That thing poking me in the eye felt exactly the way I imagined a Post Mortem Restoration Bra would feel like. Not that I ever imagined. Granted, I do have my faults, but necrophilia is not among them.

I heard Jack the Brit storm into the room. I lay very still, trying to control the pounding of my telltale heart echoing in my ears. It was loud enough to wake my dead hostess.

I listened to footsteps walk across the room to the gurney. There was a tapping noise, like a raven at the door. An ensuing quiet followed. More footsteps, then a scraping sound. What the hell was he doing out there? And then he told me.

"Gotcha," he said.

Instinctively, I pushed on the top. It didn't move. He had secured it in place.

Jack the Brit said, "Welcome to me workshop. Time for a little improvisation."

I felt the gurney jerk. I was on the move. He was pushing the gurney across the floor.

"Comfy?" he said with an evil chuckle. "The retort is lined with fire bricks. Ever been in one?" He laughed. I assumed the retort was the oven or cremation chamber. "It will heat up to twenty-four hundred degrees. Makes me sweat just to say it, it does." He proceeded to tell me how in two to three hours me and Mrs. Norman, how do you do, would be reduced to bone fragments. An electromagnet would remove any metal mixed in with our human cremains, such as a belt buckle or the wire skeleton of a bra. What was left would be pulverized and placed in an urn, where Mrs. Norman and I would spend our deaths happily thereafter.

I may have had to take it lying down, but I was struggling to kick that top off. It was such a tight squeeze inside, I couldn't get any leverage. The more I pounded, the louder was his fiendish laugh.

"Up we go," he said, lifting the box onto the dowel rollers that led to the iron mouth of the oven. I heard the iron door squeak open. I could already feel the heat.

"Freeze!"

Freeze? Melt was more like it.

Voices, two of them.

"Get me out of here!" I yelled. Friend or foe, what did I have to lose?

Scuffling and a gunshot. I was moving again and then heard the iron door to the retort shut. Was I inside or outside the cremation chamber?

I saw light. They say when you die that's what happens. If I was in heaven I saw the face of God, and it looked just like the star of the Wesley Butch Show.

EPILOGUE

AFTER I HAD LEFT his office that night, Winston Estrellita had called Wesley Butch at the police station. Estrellita asked Butch if the officer was interested in proving acting police chief Ray-Newton wrong. Oh yes, Officer Butch was interested. Estrellita told Officer Butch what I was about to do. They agreed it was illegal. Even more so for the police to do such a thing without a warrant. However, Estrellita suggested, it might be a good idea if Officer Butch just happened to plan his routine rounds near the Lighthouse Mortuary in the next few minutes. In the event that Officer Butch should see or hear something suspicious, out of the ordinary, then he would have reasonable grounds for entering the building.

Wesley Butch considered a gunshot coming from inside a funeral home to be a bit out of the ordinary and entered the building.

Jack the Brit was shot and killed by Officer Butch in self-defense.

I found a whisk broom and swept up Charlie's ashes. Officer Butch didn't say a word when I carried the box of ashes out to the car.

Ray-Newton was not permanently appointed police chief of Angel's Cove. Nor was Jay-Newton, Wayne Newton, Fig Newton, nor Any Newton. Last I heard, Wesley Butch was still acting chief.

Carla gave her father's sloop to Leonitus when she learned her father had befriended the giant albino and had even taught him to sail on that very boat.

The money Charlie Meadows had sent to his daughter was returned to Angel's Cove. It would not be used to buy guns.

A trust fund was established to aid displaced fishermen getting started in clam farming or some other alternative to net fishing. Many turned to harvesting cannonball jellyfish. There was a strong Asian market for the jellyfish dehydrated and salted. It made for a crunchy food that took on the seasonings of other dishes. It was nearly a hundred percent protein.

Gillian Gable's exposé on the Lighthouse Mortuary was picked up by the wire services. It's too soon to tell if it will have any impact. So far it's been business as usually for Sister Star and company. Gillian did send a copy of her article to me at the Sand Bar. She'd clipped a note to it that said: "Rice, What did we do in your fantasy? I'll tell you mine if you tell me yours—G.G."

We never did find out who hung the kitten from the ceiling fan. It could have been Jack the Brit, but I didn't think it was his style. My guess was one of the bullies in the fish militia, namely Royal Maddox. I'm intent on blaming him for something.

THAT SECOND MORNING back home the ocean was as smooth as glass, the sky as clear as a gypsy fortune teller's crystal ball. Carla and I took Nick's Boston Whaler about a mile offshore, cut the engine, and drifted. I sat back quietly, leaving Carla with her memories. She reached over the side of the boat and swirled her hand in the cool saltwater. She pulled her hand in and picked up the box between her feet.

"Give Mom my love," she whispered. "Tell her I miss her." She poured the contents of the box into the deep blue sea and said, "I love you. Good-bye, Daddy."

MURDER AT THE MOVIES

CHARLENE WEIR
GEORGE BAXT
MAXINE O'CALLAGHAN

MURDER TAKE TWO
by Charlene Weir

Hollywood comes to Hampstead, Kansas, with the filming of a
new picture starring sexy actress Laura Edwards. But murder
steals the scene when a stunt double is impaled on a pitchfork.

THE HUMPHREY BOGART MURDER CASE
by George Baxt

Hollywood in its heyday is brought to life in this witty caper
featuring a surprise sleuth—Humphrey Bogart. While filming
The Maltese Falcon, he searches for a real-life treasure, dodging
a killer on a murder trail through Hollywood.

SOMEWHERE SOUTH OF MELROSE
by Maxine O'Callaghan

P.I. Delilah West is hired to search for an old high school
classmate. The path takes her through the underbelly of broken
dreams and into the caprices of fate, where secrets are born and
sometimes kept....

Available March 1999 at your favorite retail outlet.

Look us up on-line at: http://www.worldwidemystery.com   WMOM305